'You are a mystery,' Blase said hoarsely. 'You have spirit. Nothing can take that from you. Yet you hide yourself away like a recluse.'

He was perilously close. His gaze caressed her until every nerve-end pulsated, his proximity filling her senses. Although he made no move to touch her, a treacherous glow of expectancy spread through her body.

'I am content, sir.' Ruth was horrified at the breathlessness of her tone.

'Are you content to be but half a woman? The woman in the portrait I saw in the long gallery would not have been.'

His hands slid up her arms, and he drew her from the chair to stand at his side. How dared he taunt her so cruelly? She tried to whip her anger, but, irrationally, she wanted nothing more than to feel the strength of his arms round her and to surrender to the clamouring of her blood. He must never suspect her growing weakness. She twisted away, but his grip remained firm.

'Why do you torment me so?' she said brokenly.

To the 'Inspiration',
Chris.

CAVALIER'S MASQUE

Pauline Bentley

MILLS & BOON LIMITED
ETON HOUSE 18-24 PARADISE ROAD
RICHMOND SURREY TW9 1SR

*First published in Great Britain 1988
by Mills & Boon Limited*

© Pauline Bentley 1988

*Australian copyright 1988
Philippine copyright 1988
This edition 1988*

ISBN 0 263 76315 3

*Set in Times Roman 10 on 11 pt.
04-8901-82126 C*

Made and printed in Great Britain

CHAPTER ONE

'YOU SHOULD not ride alone, Mistress Ruth. It is too dangerous, especially now, if Cromwell's spy is in the district.' The meaty fist of the Melvilles' man-servant kept hold upon the bridle as he looked up at the tall slim figure astride the grey gelding. 'At least let me accompany you.'

Ruth Melville pulled the brim of her hat further over her face, and brushed some wisps of straw from the black doublet and breeches borrowed from her brother Adam's wardrobe. 'All the more reason why I must ride today, Sam,' she reasoned with this giant of a man who had served her family since before she was born. 'It must appear that Adam is still near by; he should have returned a week ago from escorting the king's men to the coast. If his absence should be noted by the Roundheads...' Her green eyes darkened with anguish. 'It is a risk we dare not take. There is too much at stake. Adam always rides alone, so the villagers will think it strange if you come with me.'

'That's as maybe, mistress,' Sam answered heavily, 'but this ruse has gone on for two years now. I never thought when we started that it would take so long for Charles II to win his father's crown.'

Ruth shifted her weight in the saddle, unable to explain a strange unease that had been with her since waking. She felt cold, her mind partially numb as though she were cast adrift and floating. With an effort she brought her concentration back to the servant, and smiled resignedly.

'At least the Scots have acknowledged Charles Stuart and crowned him at Scone. It cannot be long before a Royalist army is mustered in England. Until their victory, I am trapped by my various disguises.' She tossed back her shoulder-length autumn gold hair, her eyes sparkling with a fervent light. Sam knew better than to try to argue. 'But I regret nothing,' she went on. 'What is my small discomfort compared with the humiliation heaped upon our Sovereign? Adam says the Scottish Covenanters force the king to do long penances, and his army has been purged of many of his companions because their morals offended the high-minded Scots. I shall never desert his Majesty's cause, even though it means that I am now trapped in a role of semi-invalid and the only time I can escape it is by impersonating my brother.'

The servant released her bridle, wiping a large hand across the back of his thick neck as he did so. 'The danger surrounding those like us grows daily. Not all our friends have reached the coast in safety. Two more were found murdered this month, and not a mile from here.'

'They were betrayed, as were others before them.' Ruth's voice hardened with anger. 'Someone has turned traitor. He must be discovered and stopped.'

'That is for your brother to decide,' Sam warned. 'This is not women's work. You should be thinking of marriage and children, not...'

'I gave up such thoughts long ago,' Ruth reminded him sternly, but, seeing his worried expression, she relented. Sam loved her like a daughter. He and his wife Hettie were the only servants remaining at the Manor since the Melvilles' fortune had dwindled, and he was wholly committed to the cause they fought for. She sighed, but without self-pity or regret. 'At two and twenty, I am long past marriageable age. My heart and future died at Naseby with my betrothed. I am content enough, Sam.' Her green eyes flashed with devilment. 'If I find some of the restrictions I have placed upon my life wearisome, then each time we smuggle a Cavalier out of England, from under the noses of those sanctimonious Ironsides, I know it is all worth while.'

'Your poor mother would turn in her grave to see you thus!' Sam Rivers shook his balding pate. 'As for your father...'

'Father would have understood. He gave his life for his king. Adam and I continue to fight in the best way we can.'

So saying, Ruth touched her heels to the gelding's sides and the horse clattered over the cobbled courtyard. Once she left the drive and crossed the water-meadows, she felt uneasy for the first time upon such a venture. Sam was right: the danger was closing in. With Adam away, she must rely on her wits and trust no one—except Sam and Hettie. An icy shiver sped along her spine and with it a sense of foreboding. Where was Adam? Why had he not returned, or at least sent word? She strove to reassure herself. This was not the first time he had been away longer than planned, for secret information had often to be carried across country. It was likely that he had been forced into hiding, for he would never return to Saxfield with a troop of soldiers on his trail.

Throughout the late troubles, this part of Sussex had largely supported the Parliament. In the spring and summer of 1651 an increasing number of Royalists had used Saxfield Manor as a safe house, remaining hidden until a vessel could be found to take them to France. From the information they gave, she knew that the exiled King Charles was planning to reclaim his father's crown. Now it seemed that someone in one of the other safe houses along this part of the south coast had turned traitor, which could place all their lives in peril—especially if the other secret of Saxfield became known.

The weight of the sword at her hip was reassuring, as was a glance down at the pistol primed and ready in the saddle-holster. Ruth shuddered. Adam had taught her to use both skilfully, but could she truly take another's life, even if her own seemed in danger? The thought haunted her. She set her lips grimly. She was no squeamish milksop, and would do what had to be done. Nothing must endanger their cause. Charles Stuart was England's rightful monarch. She would not sit back and let Oliver Cromwell and his dour-faced parliamentarians steal his kingdom without doing all in her power to prevent it. There was always danger around them. She and Adam had known from the outset both the risks, and the penalty, for harbouring Royalist spies. It had not deterred them then, and neither would it now.

The wind caught at her tawny hair, whipping it back from her shoulders. Keeping an experienced eye on the landscape for any sign of danger, she pushed all thoughts of England's unrest from her mind. The sun warmed her cheeks as she gave her mount its head. It was weeks since she had been able to escape the role allotted her at the Manor. If it were not for her growing concern at her twin's absence, and the nagging feeling of fore-boding with which she had awoken this morning, she could have enjoyed this rare moment free from constraint.

Taking care to skirt the cluster of timber-framed houses and the church, she rode for some distance along the ridge of the sheep-dotted downs, where the big grey gelding could be clearly seen from the village. When she saw the Rector's wife walking along the track below, she raised her hat as Adam would have done, then galloped on down into one of the valleys that spread like out-stretched fingers through the gently swelling hills. Atop the next rise, the track turned inland to run parallel with the sun-spangled line of the River Adur. Slowing her pace, she shaded her eyes against the sun with her hand and looked across the valley. Her serenity was shattered at the sight of the broken, dejected ruins of Bramber Castle, which only a few years earlier had dominated the skyline before Cromwell's soldiers tore it down. The grim reminder of the terror of those years of civil war that had resulted in an uneasy Commonwealth, seething with distrust and suspicion, stripped the pleasure from her ride. From the edge of the coppice ahead a flash of light caught her eyes. Had the sunlight reflected off something metal? Her heart missed a beat when a troop of Cromwell's soldiers came cantering towards her.

She gathered up the reins, judging the distance between them, for they must come close enough to recognise Adam. All at once, her courage wavered. This was no ordinary troop; the distinctive white blaze on the lead horse's nose heralded the approach of Captain Henry Melville. Having no wish to encounter her cousin, who would certainly see through her disguise, Ruth cut across in full sight of the soldiers and veered the grey in the direction of Shoreham. With luck, Henry would think Adam was riding to the fishing village to visit an inn. A short distance further on she entered a wood, and once she was hidden by the trees, turned to ride back to Saxfield. If Henry Melville were in the vicinity, it was unlikely that he would miss an opportunity to come prying round the Manor, and she must return before he arrived. Ruth's hands tightened over the reins. That sly toad would give his right arm to prove that Adam was involved with the Royalists! Ever since her father had died, Henry Melville had coveted Saxfield Manor.

She slowed her pace as she approached the boundaries of the Saxfield estate, and a stab of fierce pride welled in her throat. Once it had been a modest fifteenth-century manor until it had been added to by her adventuring great-grandfather, who had turned from fisherman to buccaneering on the Spanish Main and returned with a fortune of gold to swell his grateful Sovereign's coffers, as well as his own. Lovingly her gaze travelled over the ivy-covered stone walls, scanning the tall windows of the ancient baron's hall and across the

centre gable with its great stone porch to the ruined west
wing.

Sorrow pierced her at a rush of painful memories, for
the scars left from the fire still remained—the fire which
had claimed her mother's life when the Roundheads had
come in search of her father. Her hatred of Cromwell's
men flared, and with it came the heartache of failure
and remorse. During the horror of that night she had
failed to bring her mother from the flames. Self-
consciously she rubbed her scarred forearm, yet from
the tragedy had also emerged the veiled figure of the
grey lady who had saved dozens of Cavaliers from death
as spies.

At a movement near by, Ruth pulled her thoughts up
short. She tensed, her hand going to the saddle-holster.
Behind an ancient oak on the edge of the lawn, a man
stood watching the house. Her throat tightened. Was it
the government spy Adam had warned her about? Who
else would be watching the Manor in such a way?
Tugging her hat-brim down to shadow her face, she eased
the pistol from its holster and laid it across her lap as
she urged the grey forward. The man's horse, tethered
a short distance away, whinnied at her approach, but
the stranger had already begun to turn, aware of another's presence.

She took care to advance with the sunlight behind her,
and before halting in front of the tall, broad-shouldered
figure, she had time to study him more closely. He looked
to be in his late twenties. His skin was bronzed, and a
narrow moustache above his full lips, together with the
straight black line of his brows, gave a dark, sardonic
set to his lean face.

'You trespass, sir!' She deepened her voice, and, as
was her custom when impersonating Adam, kept her
sentences terse. 'This is Melville land. Have you lost your
way?'

'The house is Saxfield Manor?' There was a steel edge to his voice which alerted Ruth to remain on her guard.

Beneath a battered deep-brimmed hat his thick black hair reached to his shoulders. His green leather jerkin, like the hat, had seen better days, but his black breeches were of fine linen and although the lace at the wrists of his white lawn shirt was beginning to fray, it was of a rich and exquisite quality. Obviously, once, he had been a man of wealth and position. Used to seeing such men, whose circumstances were now greatly reduced by exile or fines and taxation, Ruth wondered if he were seeking assistance on the king's business.

'That is so. Have you business there?' Natural caution warned her against speaking openly. There was something about his austere expression that set him apart from the others who had come seeking the safety of Saxfield.

The stranger showed no sign of awkwardness at being caught on Melville land. In fact his stance was challenging, causing her heart to beat uncomfortably fast as she noticed the poised balance of his long legs and the way his fingers rested negligently upon his sword-hilt. It was no use wishing that Sam Rivers were here to protect her: she must deal with the stranger on her own. Her gauntleted hand gripped the handle of the pistol, earning for herself a flicker of contempt in those penetrating black eyes.

'You must be Adam Melville.' The curt words were delivered as a statement, not a question.

'You have the advantage of me, sir.' Ruth's throat cramped with unease and the strain of appearing calm when any unguarded word could mean her arrest. He had not given the password revealing himself to be a king's man, yet he appeared to know something of her family and home.

He raised a mocking brow as he regarded the pistol in her lap. 'Unless you intend to try to use that weapon, and face the consequences, be done with it.' The controlled aggression in his tone sent a shiver of alarm through her. There was a forbidding quality about this man, and a tangible threat in every word and line of his body. He was clearly used to giving orders and to being obeyed, and had no doubt of his ability to disarm her.

'You have not told me your business on my land, sir!' She refused to back down, and, finding herself subjected to his piercing stare, her finger uncoiled from the trigger. She would learn nothing while continuing to threaten him.

The grim line of his lips slackened as he took a step back. Then, with almost insulting deliberation, he ignored her challenge and, turning his back on her, untethered his horse from the bush. Swinging himself gracefully into the saddle, he brought his mount alongside the grey. His movements held a leashed power, every inch of his lithe frame unconsciously asserting his dominance.

'Blase Drummond at your service, sir,' he rapped out brusquely.

She was careful to keep her head tilted, shadowing her features, but encountering his assessing stare, her gaze remained unwavering and as forthright as his. If he were indeed Cromwell's man, he would make a formidable enemy. Two frowning grooves appeared on the bridge of his Roman nose as he continued to regard her. She held her breath. Had he seen through her disguise?

'I expect we shall meet again, Melville.' His deep voice held a challenging ring. 'I am staying at the village inn. The King's Head, I believe it was once called.'

Ruth went cold at his barbed statement. He was testing her, she was certain. But without knowing his allegiance, she dared not risk arousing his suspicions. 'It is an old inn,' she answered smoothly. 'It has changed its name many times. What brings you to Sussex?'

'Property and horses. I was told you have some land you wish to sell.' He paused significantly, and Ruth's spine prickled with a sense of impending danger when he went on, 'Your father was a Royalist. Parliament has levied heavy taxes upon families such as yourself. If those taxes remain unpaid...'

'The taxes will be paid,' Ruth cut in harshly, unable to shake the feeling that he had far more sinister reasons for being in Sussex. And he knew far too much about her family for her comfort. However desperate their need of money, this man was far too dangerous to be allowed free access over Saxfield land and must be discouraged. 'I had hoped to raise the money without the sale of further land, sir.'

'The taxes are overdue. Do you not fear imprisonment?'

Was that a thinly-veiled threat? Did she imagine it, or had his face tautened with anger or, worse, suspicion?

'Perhaps your circumstances have changed,' he said tersely, his expression now guarded, 'and you have no need to sell land.'

Ruth stiffened at his bluntness. Just what was he implying, or was he trying to trick her into indiscretion? Anger sped through her. As a government spy, did he think their straitened circumstances would lead Adam or herself to betray their friends for gold? Her stinging retort died on her lips at the drumming hoofbeats from the road, and she anxiously glanced towards the sound. As she had feared, Captain Melville was about to visit the Manor. She had to reach the house unseen—and change before she could meet him. The house and stables were still hidden from the soldiers, but she dared not delay.

When she turned to face Blase Drummond, she found herself again being closely scrutinised. The wind ruffled his hair and she glimpsed a single gold earring, which, together with his swarthy complexion, gave him a roguish, devilish air. For all that she was on her guard, she could not help thinking that despite his stern expression, his lean rugged countenance was strikingly handsome and distinctly unsettling. But with Captain Melville only minutes from the Manor, she had no time to consider Blase Drummond's motives for being on her land. She had to get rid of him, quickly!

'The land could be for sale,' she admitted reluctantly.

'I shall call in a day or two to discuss the matter. It appears that you have guests.'

The steel was back in his voice, giving her the impression that any future meeting was likely to be a confrontation. Encountering his enigmatic stare, her throat dried with apprehension. His eyes glinted as coldly as black ice. He was a man who would show no mercy to his enemies. Did he regard her family among their number? Or had she somehow betrayed herself? Each thought speared her. All around her was danger, but fortunately he had not insisted on the meeting taking place at once. Was *he* the spy? She crushed the thought. With her cousin almost at the Manor, there was no time to pursue her suspicions now, but she could not dispel the feeling that she was being drawn into an invisible snare.

She replaced the pistol in its holster, saying curtly, 'Good-day, Mr Drummond. The figures and details of the land for sale are already drawn up.'

Without waiting for his reply, she touched her heels to the grey's side and galloped across the lawn towards the stables. Even fearing that Captain Melville would reach the house before her, she could not shake the image of Blase Drummond's commanding figure from her mind. There was an almost predatory stillness in the way he had watched her. Government spy or not, the stranger was not a man who could be easily duped.

Blase Drummond watched the rider, his attention reluctantly held at the way horse and man blended as one. Melville was a fine horseman, he would give him that.

An excited barking greeted Melville's wild dash across the lawn, and a huge black mastiff appeared from the direction of the stableyard to bound along at his master's side. Drummond's mouth thinned assessingly. There was something disconcerting about Adam Melville. Although his face had been partly hidden, his eyes had shone with defiance, yet there had been a softness about his mouth where he would have expected a more ruthless line. Even more noticeable had been the youthful smoothness of his chin. It was that effeminate softness of his mouth and jaw—a sign of weakness—which made Blase uneasy. Melville was hiding something, and his answers had been annoyingly obtuse.

He thoughtfully rubbed his hand across his moustache. Outwardly, Adam Melville in his black clothes and plain linen collar appeared to be simply another sober parliamentarian, and the biblical names of the family upheld this. But his father, for all his religious strictures, had been an ardent Royalist. Where did Adam Melville's loyalties lie? Blase frowned. Something was not right, but for the life of him he could not pin it down. There had been sharp intelligence in those cool green eyes. He had expected an inbred caution—that became second nature after the conflict which had split the country—but he had sensed there was something else behind that evasion. If his suspicions about Adam Melville proved correct, he would pay dearly for his treachery!

His attention turned upon the troop of soldiers. At the sight of their buff jackets, steel breastplates and helmets, his eyes narrowed. When he recognised their leader, his hand closed over his sword-hilt. Captain Henry Melville—damn his misbegotten hide! He had a long overdue score to settle with that murdering dog!

Blase smothered his scalding hatred. Until now he had not connected Henry Melville with this family. Were they related? It would seem likely, if the Captain was visiting Saxfield. The need for vengeance that had driven him since Marston Moor burned deeper. Henry Melville had changed sides more than once during the years of conflict between king and Parliament, uncaring who he betrayed so long as his own worthless skin was safe. Treachery came second nature to him. Did that trait run throughout the family? Deliberately he rode out of the trees across the path of the Roundheads. At some time during his stay at the inn, his papers would be inspected, and better now, when surprise would give him the advantage over Captain Melville.

Ruth arrived breathless in her bedchamber. 'Hettie!' she called, as she shrugged off her doublet. 'Quickly, I must change. Captain Melville is riding up the drive!'

The maid bustled forward, shaking her head. 'Another narrow escape! You take too much upon yourself, Mistress Ruth.'

'You and Sam worry too much.' She smiled fondly at the thin woman, who nervously wrung her hands before helping her off with her boots and breeches. 'I do what must be done,' Ruth added, pulling the shirt over her head and reaching for the full-sleeved chemise and petticoats.

'No good will come of it!' Hettie remonstrated in an all too familiar vein as she laced the back of Ruth's grey gown. 'Parading as that twin of yours one moment, then swathing yourself in these hideous veils and hiding yourself away like a recluse for weeks on end! It is unnatural, and a sin.'

'It serves its purpose. The villagers think I was badly burned in the fire. They do not question the occasional carriage-rides of a heavily veiled figure from the Manor. It has proved too valuable a disguise to get our friends safely out of England for me to cast it aside now.'

'You are a young and beautiful woman—too independent for your own good. You need a strong-willed man to tame your wildness!'

'I am content enough. Marriage is not the answer to my dreams.'

Ruth moved across to the window, puzzled that the riders had not yet ridden into the courtyard. The reason for their delay was alarmingly obvious. Blase Drummond, sitting his horse relaxed and at ease, was speaking with her cousin. Her stomach lurched when she saw him reach into his jerkin and hand something to Captain Melville.

'Do you want your cousin arriving and you not ready?' Hettie cried. 'You cannot meet him with your hair loose. Sit down, mistress, so that I can pin it up for you.'

Tempted to watch what was happening outside, Ruth dared not. Time was short if, dressed as a woman, she were to greet her cousin. Picking up a white velvet mask, she seated herself before her looking-glass, fretting impatiently while Hettie pinned her hair. The last pin in place, she positioned the mask over her upper face and stood up, her unease growing as she saw her cousin and his troop continuing towards the house. From the centre of the drive where they had left him, Blase Drummond watched the soldiers for a long moment before he turned his horse and set it trotting towards the village. From the courtyard below the bedroom window, Captain Melville's shrill voice commanded Sam to take the horses. Ruth felt Hettie start, her hands trembling as she drew the concealing veil over Ruth's masked face, distorting her vision of the drive.

'You are not a woman who can live without love, Mistress Ruth. If I can find happiness after what those Roundheads did to me, you will, too.'

Ruth reached out to take her fluttering hands. Hettie had good reason to hate the Roundheads, since she had been dragged outside and raped by two of them on an occasion when Ruth and her mother were being questioned by one of Cromwell's captains. Although the brutal attack had left Hettie nervous ever since, she had married Sam six months later.

'Sam is a good man,' Ruth said. 'His love has given you the strength to overcome your ordeal. You hate the Roundheads as much as I do, so surely you understand why we must continue the fight?'

'I would see you happy, mistress. As I have found happiness.'

'I had my chance to love, and was denied it, when Tom was killed with Father at Naseby,' Ruth said resignedly. 'In recent years I have had to act and think like a man too often to be a suitably submissive wife.'

Hettie, unconvinced, shook her head and paused in pinning the heavy grey veil into place. 'Pretending to be a man to stop those cursed Roundheads prying into Master Adam's whereabouts is one thing, but to deny your womanhood is quite another! It is six years since the battle at Naseby—you were scarce more than a child when your betrothed was killed, for all you believed yourself in love with Thomas Penbury. I pray that one day, Mistress Ruth, you will meet a man who will capture your heart.'

Ruth laughed mirthlessly. 'You are a hopeless romantic, Hettie. I have no wish to marry.' She plucked irritably at the veil covering her hair, her voice filled with longing as she stood up. 'When the time comes and I can escape from this ruse, I want freedom, Hettie. Freedom to be myself! I will be no man's chattel.'

Ruth could already hear her cousin's boots resounding over the floorboards as he paced the parlour at the foot of the stairs. Picking up an ivory-handled walking-cane, she leaned heavily upon it and adopted the slow limp which completed her disguise. On the landing, she paused briefly to pat the mastiff who had settled himself on guard outside her door. 'Come, Spartan. We have guests.'

Hettie hurried on ahead, and when Ruth entered the panelled room, she was pulling the curtains across the windows to shut out the bright sunlight.

A low growl rose to Spartan's throat as they entered the parlour. Even when he was a puppy, the dog had never liked her cousin.

'Good-day to you, Henry,' Ruth said, seating herself in the recess in the darkest corner of the room. The maid started at the sound of gruff voices coming from the kitchen, and, knowing Hettie's unease in the company of Roundheads, Ruth signalled for her to take Spartan with her for protection.

With a scowl Captain Melville waited until Hettie and the dog left the parlour, then with a terse movement flung back the curtains, allowing the sunlight to stream in. 'There is no need to hide yourself in darkness on my account, cousin. Saxfield is too beautiful to be shrouded in gloom.'

Ruth rested both hands on the carved handle of her cane, her knuckles whitening as she mastered her temper at his rudeness. 'I fear Adam is not at home. I do not expect him back for some hours.'

'I saw him on the road.' Melville's voice was heavy with antagonism. 'He did not trouble to stop.'

'Adam was late for a meeting,' Ruth countered, her disparaging gaze noting the flamboyance of her cousin's scarlet velvet jacket trimmed with gold braid. Although his pale blond hair was worn shorter than he had once affected, he still retained his small beard, which stood out whitely against his ruddy complexion. An inch under six foot and stockily built, he was an imposing figure and the only member of her family, since their great-grandfather, to bear the striking flaxen colouring of a distant Viking ancestor. 'If you knew Adam was not here, what brings you to Saxfield, Henry?'

'Concern for your welfare, my dear,' he declared arrogantly. 'I have long suspected your brother to be a Royalist spy, but I have found no proof—yet.'

'Nor will you,' Ruth said with more confidence than she felt, controlling an inward shiver, uncomfortably aware that he was trying to discern her scars beneath her veil. The fairness of his brows and lashes gave his round face a bland appearance, but despite his foppish jewels and velvet, he was a fiend who cared for nothing but his own self-interest. 'Adam and I live simply here,' she told him. 'What grounds have you for so unjust an accusation?'

At the way he looked round the room with a proprietary air, Ruth's temper flared. When he picked up a gilded Venetian glass bowl and examined it, assessing its value, she bit back a tart rebuke. He was being deliberately provoking, and she refused to give him the satisfaction of responding to his petty taunts.

'There are disturbing tales concerning this Manor,' he contended roughly. 'The villagers grow wary of passing the estate at night. Strange noises have come from the grounds. It is said to be haunted.'

A frisson of fear sped down Ruth's spine. His strange blue eyes glinted sinisterly. One iris had a brown cast that gave him a shifty air which, considering the ease with which he had changed allegiance during the recent troubles, well suited his selfish ways. This was no social call. What exactly did Henry suspect? She conquered her moment of alarm. It could be speculation—nothing more! If he had guessed the truth, he would not have hesitated to arrest Adam or herself.

'The villagers are superstitious and ignorant,' she answered smoothly. 'They have probably seen me walking in the grounds at dusk. I rarely go out during the day.'

'A convenient ruse, if the need arose.'

Ruth stood up, her veil trembling in the wake of her indignation. 'Just what do you mean by that? My life was destroyed by the men you now serve!' She shook her cane, whipping her anger to cover her growing fear. 'You dare call this a ruse! May the good Lord forgive you, Henry Melville!'

'Still a hell-cat!' Henry stroked his beard reflectively. 'Your spirit certainly was not tempered by the fire. I have often wondered just how badly you were burned that night.'

He made to touch her veil, but, fearful as to his intentions, she slapped his hand away. 'How dare you! You are a guest in my home.'

His coarse laugh chilled her blood and he jerked her roughly towards him. When she held herself rigidly away, his voice unexpectedly gentled. 'You misjudge me, my dear. Your brother is a fool if he involves himself with Charles Stuart. You must have heard that the bodies of two Royalist spies were found not a mile from here. There is talk in the village that one of them was seen on your land.'

'Would you heed the malicious gossip of ignorant fools?' Ruth flung back, as she tried vainly to free her arm.

Henry's fingers bruised her flesh as her struggles continued. 'Be still, woman!' he snarled, his grip pushing back the loose sleeve of her gown to her elbow. 'I mean you no harm. On the contrary...' His voice trailed off as he stared down at the ridge of flesh beneath his fingers.

Ruth stiffened. His thin lips twisted with revulsion as he removed his hand and saw the dagger-shaped scar that disfigured her forearm. He released her abruptly.

Pulling down her sleeve, Ruth took a step back. 'You had better leave, Captain Melville,' she said coldly.

'One day, cousin, I will learn the truth behind those veils. Now that I am posted in the district we shall see more of each other. If Adam is involved with the

Royalists, it is but a matter of time before he is caught,' Henry pronounced gruffly. 'But you should not suffer as a result of his misguided loyalty. Would you see Saxfield Manor sequestered by the government and fall into the hands of strangers? It was once my home, too.'

'That will not happen,' Ruth responded hotly, but her stomach quaked at what her cousin implied. After Adam's safety, it was what she dreaded most. They had lost so much during the troubles. The silver and jewels had gone years ago to raise money for arms for the king. It was bad enough having to sell the land to strangers, but the house, never!

'Will it not?' His tone was too confident for her peace of mind. 'Adam has been lucky, so far, but there are reports that Charles Stuart is planning to ride south into England. There will be no mercy for his followers. Marry me, and I shall ensure that Saxfield Manor is safeguarded.'

Ruth controlled the impulse to fling her contempt in his face. So that was his ploy! Yet it did not come as a complete shock: ever since the death of her father she had suspected that Henry Melville saw himself as master here. If he could not find evidence to condemn Adam, he meant to win Saxfield by whatever means he could. He was not interested in her welfare. It was Saxfield he wanted, and he would even wed a scarred cripple to gain his ends. She drew a long steadying breath, knowing that if she antagonised him, he would persecute Adam even harder.

'Your offer is generous, but it is you who are misguided.' She strove to keep her disgust from her voice, yet for all Henry's threat was no idle one, she knew her wits could outmatch his. Not so the danger she had sensed from Blase Drummond earlier, when the memory of that meeting returned to destroy her composure. Was Blase Drummond in league with her cousin? 'Adam is no traitor!' She dragged her mind back to the matter in

hand, again defiant. 'And, for myself, I have resolved
never to marry.'

The side of his mouth twitched with suppressed anger.
'Noble words, but Saxfield Manor is already in danger.
The taxes are overdue. Can you meet them?'

'They will be paid.' It was a vow. She would see
Saxfield razed to the ground before she allowed Henry
Melville to get his greedy hands on it!

'Perhaps they will, this time, but at what cost to the
estate?' He moved to the door. 'I shall leave you to dwell
upon my proposal. It is too important to be considered
lightly, as you may yet discover.'

He paused with his hand on the doorknob, turning to
face her as though a thought had just come to him. 'Did
you hear that a fishing-vessel from Shoreham known to
be carrying Royalist spies was sunk in the River Severn
just off Bristol last night? There were no survivors.'

She fought against a wave of dizziness and fear; her
legs seeming to have no strength. Glad now for the
support of the cane, she drew a deep breath, aware of
her cousin studying her reaction. 'God have mercy on
the families of those fishermen,' she managed to force
out.

The door slammed behind him, and Ruth crumpled
on to the chair. The sensation of floating and coldness,
which had been with her since waking, returned. Dear
God, let it not be true! Let it just be Henry's cruel jest
to torture her. Pain lanced through her breast, robbing
her of breath. She knew why Adam had not returned.
He had been on that ship! And there had been no
survivors.

From the courtyard, the rough voices of soldiers
drifted to her. She straightened her back. No—Adam
was not dead! She would feel it more acutely if he were.
He was her twin, a part of her.

Her sense of foreboding intensified. If Adam had been
injured, it could be some days before he returned to the

Manor. And, with Henry already suspicious, that could place them both in danger. She would have to continue to impersonate Adam until his return. But Henry was not the only danger. A spasm of alarm clutched at her throat. There was also the stranger to contend with. How would she deal with Blase Drummond?

CHAPTER TWO

TWO DAYS later, after a night of heavy rain, Ruth was in the long gallery inspecting a patch of damp that had penetrated the temporary wall which blocked off the ruined wing. As she leaned closer to touch the stained plaster, her veil fell forward over her face, impeding her view. Impatiently sweeping it back, she frowned across at Sam Rivers.

'The outer wall damaged by the fire needs further rendering. Every time it rains, the water seeps through.'

Sam rubbed his neck worriedly, his gaze falling on the fireplace at the centre. 'Ay, but I don't like the thought of having workmen here just now.'

He touched a horse's head carved into the surround of a wooden reredos depicting St Francis, which had been rescued from the village church some years earlier before Cromwell's men could smash it as a symbol of idolatry. A concealed door swung open in the linenfold panelling by his shoulder, and, holding a horn lantern aloft, he stepped into the dark hole. Ruth wrinkled her nose at the musty smell coming from the secret chamber, the yellow light revealing a narrow oblong room with no space for anything but a truckle bed.

Sam nodded, apparently satisfied. 'No water has penetrated this far, and a fire lit up here will dry out the dampness within the chamber.' His expression was drawn as he looked at Ruth. 'As to the end wall... With Master Adam away, I dare not bring builders in. Especially with the high reward offered for any information leading to the capture of Royalist spies.'

'Then the work must wait,' Ruth replied. 'Adam is convinced that the king will raise his standard in England soon. We have been through too much to lose it all now. Since Cromwell defeated his Majesty's forces last year at Dunbar, treachery is everywhere.' She shuddered with remembrance. 'I still cannot believe our gallant Marquis of Montrose is dead...and betrayed by his own countrymen.' Her voice cracked as she recalled the fate of a traitor's death awarded to the king's most loyal and faithful commander. Wiping a single tear from the corner of her eye, she continued firmly, 'We must trust no one. Especially with the government spy in the district.'

Apprehension stabbed through her as she recalled Blase Drummond's impending visit. It was not land he had been interested in when she had caught him watching the Manor. His presence in the district was a threat to those such as themselves. And what was his connection, if any, with Captain Melville? She pressed a hand to her brow, taking a grip upon her fears. She had no proof that Drummond was a government spy, but his conduct had been suspicious, and she had lived with danger too long to let her guard slip now. Yet it was more than what she believed him to be that troubled her: she could not shake from her mind the image of his self-assured figure. It was always there, like a dark shadow behind her unguarded moments.

At the sound of a footstep on the stairs, Sam quickly closed the panel while Ruth adjusted her mask and flicked her veil over her face. Her precautions had been unnecessary when it proved to be Hettie.

'Mistress, Mr Fowkes is awaiting you in the parlour.'

With a smile of pleasure, Ruth untied the large white apron she wore over her grey gown and handed it to the maid. 'I shall see him now. Have a fire lit in this grate, Hettie. If this rain keeps up, I shall take what exercise I can up here.'

Gripping her cane firmly, she walked back along the gallery past the row of portraits. Half-way along, she paused to gaze at Adam's image. He was dressed in half armour, a scarlet cloak about his shoulders over his deep lace collar. How handsome he looked, so young and carefree, despite his military attire. A knot of emotion rose in her throat, for there was still no word from him. She swallowed against the constriction. She had not again experienced the eerie floating sensation, but at times she felt decidedly strange, and there was not exactly a pain encasing her ribs, but a persistent pressure. Closing her eyes, she concentrated, willing herself to sense her brother's presence, or thoughts, as she had sometimes done in the past. It was a game they had played as children that needed no words to communicate what the other was thinking. This time there was nothing; just the certainty that Adam was alive. She opened her eyes to see her own portrait next to her brother's. The paintings had been commissioned by their mother to comme-morate the twins' eighteenth birthday. Had she also ever been so young and carefree? The veil seemed to hang about her face, smothering her life's breath. Would she ever be free of the restraints her disguise imposed upon her? She suppressed her restlessness, for her role here, although confining, was important.

A low whimper accompanied a moist nose thrust into her palm. She looked down at Spartan and absently ruffled his ears, her fingers lingering upon the scarred ridges across his neck and sleek back. For the first time she noticed the greying hairs about his wide muzzle; Spartan was getting old. They had been through so much together in the last twelve years. It was he who had dragged her unconscious form from the burning room. His scars came from the same blazing rafter that had showered Ruth with burning splinters, leaving the scars on her own shoulder, arm and temple. The faithful dog rarely left her side, but although she was a prisoner in the house, he did not have to be one also.

'Sam, will you see that Spartan gets some exercise? I have a yearning for rabbit pie.'

As the servant and dog left the long gallery, Ruth envied them their hunting. Daily the veils became more smothering, but she checked her restless thoughts. Worry over Adam was making her discontented. Daniel Fowkes would cheer her and take her mind from Blase Drummond's impending visit.

When she stepped into the parlour, she sensed that something was wrong. There was a tautness about Daniel's slender frame as he stood by the window, slapping his leather gauntlets against his thigh.

'Daniel, this is a pleasure,' she said brightly, hiding her unease. 'It has been too long since you last visited us.'

'My dear Ruth! My business in London took longer than expected.' He took her hand and pressed it to his lips, but his welcoming smile was strained. There was a tightness to his voice she had not heard before, and his slightly pock-marked skin, the only imperfection in his handsome classical features, was unusually pale. 'Where's Adam?'

'He's away from home.' She evaded his question without quite knowing why. Adam and Daniel had been friends since childhood. They had joined the king's army together, fighting side by side throughout the war, and now continued to support Charles II in whatever way they could. They even shared the same women in good-hearted rivalry. There were no secrets between them, and she quashed her momentary doubts. Adam's absence was making her edgy. If she could trust anyone, surely it was Daniel? The veil stifled her, and since Daniel was party to her secret, she tossed it back over her head. 'Adam has been gone more than a week,' she said raggedly. 'There has been no word. And a Shoreham fishing-craft has supposedly been sunk near Bristol...' Her voice broke.

Daniel turned even paler, and raked his hand through his wavy brown hair. 'Dear God! Was Adam on that ship?'

'I don't know, but I fear so,' she forced out. 'I am certain he is alive, but I can feel he is in danger.'

'You must not put yourself to such torment.' Daniel tossed his gauntlets on a table beside his plumed hat, adding fiercely, 'Adam can take care of himself. I saw him the afternoon the ship sailed, but he did not mention travelling in it. There is word that King Charles is preparing to ride into England, so Adam is probably spreading the news for our people to be ready.'

'And, no doubt, toasting the success of such a venture with enthusiasm!' Ruth attempted to overcome her fears. Daniel placed his arm comfortingly about her shoulder, giving her the strength to go on. 'The past days have been a nightmare. Henry Melville is back in the district, nosing around, and I never know when he will visit. I would tell him to go dance with the devil, but I fear that if I antagonise him, he will persecute Adam even more.'

'You should not be alone in this house.' His hand slid down to her waist, turning her to face him. 'Come and stay at the Grange until Adam returns. My mother and sisters will welcome your company.'

She shook her head. 'Your offer is tempting, but impractical. Your family know nothing of my secret and I would be a prisoner in my veils. Besides, my place is here. Cousin Henry must suspect nothing. I doubt he will harm me, for the moment.' She laughed mirthlessly. 'He has other plans. The knave had the audacity to propose marriage!'

'A plague on his insolence!' Daniel growled, his face working with fury. 'Should that cur lay a hand on you, he will die!'

The pressure of his fingers biting into her flesh shook her. With some misgivings, she suspected that Daniel's words were driven by something deeper than friendship. 'Captain Melville did not harm me. You are a good friend, Daniel.'

He dropped his hands to his sides, looking more drawn than ever as he strode to the window, his voice gruff. 'I would be more than a friend to you, dearest Ruth.'

'You are as dear to me as Adam,' she parried. 'And you are contracted to wed Mistress Frith in the spring.'

'A marriage arranged by my father,' he replied tersely, 'because her dowry will save the Grange. I do not love her.'

A heavy silence stretched between them, her sharp eyes noting the fine quality of his blue worsted jacket and the richness of the lace about his wrists and at his throat. With a smile to ease the tension between them, she flicked the silver studs decorating a new leather sword-belt slung across his chest. 'That is a fine baldric you're wearing. Have you come into a fortune, Daniel?'

He drew back from her with a forced laugh. 'The landlord of the London inn where I stayed did not hold with the new gaming laws. Lady Luck smiled on me.'

His attitude surprised and hurt her. Did he think she would condemn him for such frivolity? Since the death of his father last year, Daniel had changed, growing more serious by the month. Part of his estate, like Saxfield, had been sold to meet the taxes and, with a mother and three unmarried sisters to support, his responsibilities must weigh heavily. She looked searchingly at him, concerned by the worried furrows creasing his brow and the lack of vitality in his smoke-blue eyes.

'I do not regard gambling as a sin, and am glad at your good fortune.' She plucked at her grey gown, the frayed hem of which had been mended more times than she cared to remember. 'Although I cannot come to the Grange, I would welcome your company when I ride abroad dressed as my brother. No one must suspect that Adam is away from Saxfield. There is a government spy in our midst.'

Daniel dropped his hands to his sides, his expression hardening. 'Do you know who it is?'

'I believe so. When I returned from my ride two days ago, Saxfield was being watched. I questioned the man, but he made some excuse that he was interested in buying land. I am expecting him to call today. His name is Blase Drummond.'

'Drummond!' Daniel repeated with a start.

'You know him?'

He stared at her incredulously, then gave a bitter laugh, his lashes shielding his eyes. 'I know of him. He is dedicated to his duty and shows no mercy to his enemies. A deadly adversary. They would send such a man...' His voice trailed off and he recovered himself with a start to look worriedly at her. 'Take care, Ruth. If Drummond is in Sussex it is for a purpose, and I warrant it is not to buy land.'

Then hoofs clattered in the cobbled courtyard and Daniel swung round to peer out of the window, declaring, 'From the look of it, that's Drummond now. Much as I hate to leave you alone, it's best that I am not seen here. Some weeks back I had a near run in with him when I was helping a king's man to escape Cromwell's patrols at Arundel. He might recognise me. My presence would place Saxfield under greater suspicion.'

'Go quickly through the old hall and out by way of the kitchens,' Ruth urged. 'Hettie is too experienced to bring him in here. She will show him into the long gallery to wait. Take care, though; the windows up there overlook the stables.'

They fell silent, and could just make out a man's deep voice in the entrance porch and Hettie's softer reply.

There was the ring of spurs across wooden floorboards, which faded into the distance.

'Make haste,' Ruth persisted, pushing Daniel towards the door. 'Do not fear for me. Sam will not be far away.'

Daniel paused to press a light kiss against her cheek. 'Promise me you will do nothing rash while Adam is away.'

'I cannot shirk my duty.' Ruth tipped her chin defiantly. 'Saxfield has never turned a Royalist from its door.'

'You loyalty is not in doubt.' Daniel's eyes darkened with anguish. 'But Cromwell's troops are everywhere. And now there is Drummond to contend with. However courageous you may be, you are but a woman.'

From beneath the white mask, Ruth's eyes flashed with affronted pride. 'I shall do what must be done. I am no craven!'

He had the grace to blush at her scorn, his face taking on an odd expression. 'That was not what I meant, Ruth. You are adept enough with a sword, but you could be no match for Drummond—especially as a woman! He is an unprincipled scoundrel who will stop at nothing to gain his own ends.'

The vehemence of Daniel's tone shocked her. She had sensed the danger and ruthlessness in Blase Drummond, but at the same time she had been aware of the pride of his stance. He had struck her as a man of honour.

'So you agree that Drummond is the government spy?' she asked, puzzled. 'I have never seen you so incensed against any man. Even your views of Cromwell are pale by comparison!'

A haunted look came into his eyes. 'It is you I fear for.'

She relaxed. It was affection that made him speak so harshly. 'Nothing will happen to me. Drummond is but a man—and no man is invincible or infallible. I shall be on my guard against him. Now he has been cooling his heels long enough.'

Daniel opened the door just as Hettie was about to knock and enter.

'Mr Drummond is here,' the maid announced. 'I thought it best to put him in the long gallery. Will you be wanting refreshments?'

'Just some ale and honey-cakes,' Ruth replied. 'But, first, see that the coast is clear for Mr Fowkes to leave the house unobserved.'

With growing trepidation Ruth pulled the grey veil over her face and mounted the stairs to the long gallery. Her words had been brave enough to Daniel, but the prospect of facing Blase Drummond's inscrutable stare caused her stomach to twist uncomfortably. On the landing she hesitated. There was no sound within the gallery; her heartbeat quickened in alarm. Drummond had been left alone for some minutes. Was he prying about the house? If so, had he discovered the secret chamber?

Her hand tightened about the ivory handle of her cane and, her soft leather shoes silent upon the polished floor, she took care to make no sound as she approached. At the open doorway to the gallery her step faltered. Blase Drummond stood motionless, the corner of his full lips curving upward in appreciation as he studied her portrait, unaware of her approach. A ray of sunlight through the window enriched the sheen on his long dark hair beneath his hat. His sharp profile with that proud Roman nose, which was a little too long to be perfect, the square chin and lean cheeks too angular to be classically handsome, were nevertheless more compelling because of their ruggedness, and a whisper of anticipation fanned Ruth's body in a warming heat. Her heart fluttered. Did he think her beautiful? Instantly she suppressed the thought, irritated that this knave had pricked her vanity. Yet, despite her resolve to be unruffled by his presence, she did not lean as heavily as usual upon the cane when she walked towards him.

He swung round at the thud of her stick on the oak boards. Momentarily his dark eyes widened at seeing her veils, then his lashes quickly shuttered their expression from her. There was an intensity about that brief glance that shattered her composure: it missed nothing. After studying the portrait, had he already seen through her disguise of impersonating Adam? She held her breath to calm her scudding heartbeat. She was allowing Daniel's warning about Drummond's ruthlessness to make her nervous. Although she had no intention of underestimating him, it would have taken a necromancer to see through her disguise at a single meeting. She had played the role too often to give herself away so easily.

Even as her apprehensions sped through her mind, she saw that his gaze, although guarded, remained upon her, showing none of the discomfort or pity the first sight of her veiled figure usually evoked from strangers. With an elegance to equal that of any courtier, he swept his battered hat from his head and bowed low.

'I am Ruth Melville,' she said crisply, as he straightened. 'I regret my brother has unavoidably been called away.' His full lips tightened, though whether from annoyance or suspicion she could not tell. 'Adam told me you were interested in the land on the northern boundary of the estate. Do you have any objection to dealing with a woman?'

A smile lifted his lips, transforming the stern face into softer and disturbingly sensual lines. 'My happiest memories are of my dealings with women, Miss Melville.'

The boldness of his words startled her. She could feel his stare burn through her veils and audaciously travel over her figure, lingering upon the narrowness of her waist and then the fullness of her breasts. Again his mouth tilted provocatively in appreciation, but instead

of outrage at his insolence, her pulse quickened. With
a start she checked herself. The man was a reprobate,
and her enemy! He showed none of the antagonism she
had witnessed previously, but appeared relaxed and self-
assured, and far too worldly for her peace of mind. She
raised her guard. What manner of libertine was prepared to pay court to an apparent cripple? Blase
Drummond was all Daniel had warned her against—and
very likely more.

'The papers are in the library,' she continued stiffly,
indicating a door on her right. 'In my brother's absence,
I can answer any queries you may have concerning the
land.'

With a lightness of step surprising in so large a man,
he was before her, lifting the latch to open the door,
then standing back for her to pass into the adjoining
room. She crossed to the desk, opened a drawer and
lifted out the appropriate documents. Unrolling a map
of the estate, she put a weight at each end, then handed
him a scroll stating the precise boundaries and details
of the land in question. Finding his nearness in the close
confines of the small chamber unaccountably disturbing, she moved aside while he read.

He scanned the parchment quickly, shooting her a
narrowed look as he lowered it. 'There is no mention of
water rights.'

'As you will see from the map, the land borders this
spring-fed pond.' She pointed to the area in question.
'For an additional yearly rent, you may purchase the
right to draw water from it.'

He leaned forward studying the map and their arms
brushed, the contact sizzling through her body like
droplets of water on a hot cooking-spit. Instinctively she
moved away, but, to her dismay, discovered the toe of
his boot trapping the hem of her skirt. Catching her
movement, he looked sidelong at her. They were so close
that, even through the grey-misted screen of her veil, she

could see the fine texture of his bronzed skin and the
faint dark smudge along his jaw of his beard, though
he had obviously shaved that morning. The force of his
attraction hit her like a blow from a pikestaff. A slow
smile parted his lips to reveal white teeth, one slightly
chipped one adding to his roguish air as he lifted his foot
to free her skirt. Feeling it would now be an act of cow-
ardice to draw back, she stayed where she was, tense and
on her guard against his next move.

'What price had your brother in mind for the land?'
He disconcerted her by returning to the matter in hand.
The figure she stated made him raise a questioning brow.
'I would have thought half that amount.'

'Then you have sadly misjudged the worth of the
land!' Her temper flared. However desperate their need
to pay the taxes, she would not let land that had been
in the Melville family for generations go for a pittance.
Quickly she began to gather up the papers. 'If that is
your opinion, we have nothing more to discuss, Mr
Drummond.'

Amusement brightening his eyes, he took her arm,
staying its movement. 'Oh, but I think we have, Miss
Melville.'

Her green eyes flashing indignantly, she met his bold
gaze. His face was no more than a handsbreadth from
hers, his breath wafting the edges of her veil. At this
closeness, it would hide little from such intense scrutiny.
Her breathing slowed. He showed no sign of revulsion,
but instead, his stare fixed on her lips and with difficulty
she stopped herself running her tongue across their
sudden dryness. Did he look at all women that way, as
though considering what it would be like to make love
to them? She pulled her thoughts up short, frightened
at seeing his gaze moving over the smooth skin un-
hidden by the mask and on down to her throat. Belatedly she recalled the danger of his discovering that
her mask was a ruse, and she stiffened.

He released her arm. 'Would you deny me the pleasure of bargaining with a charming and intelligent woman?' he taunted. 'I would be a poor businessman to accept your price without a quibble.'

'Pray state your offer.' Ruth began to mellow, for he was treating her not with condescension but as an equal.

For several minutes they jousted in verbal combat over the price, and when she refused to consider any amount lower than the true value of the land, a gleam of admiration, and something far more precious to her, respect, turned his eyes to black velvet.

'You protect your brother's interests well, but you have an unfair advantage over me.' The seductive deepness of his tone brought a blush to her cheeks, something that had not happened to her for years. It drained as suddenly at the importuning of his next words. 'How can I assess my bargaining power when your veil conceals your mood? Will the mask not suffice? From your portrait, your eyes are too beautiful to be hidden.'

Blase hardened himself against her gasp of outrage. He had no wish to cause her pain, but how could he judge whether she was telling the truth while she remained hidden behind those cursed veils? His curiosity was pricked. He had seen the resemblance at once to Adam Melville in the two portraits, but it was the woman who had held him fascinated. There was an arresting quality in her beauty, her full lips hinting at sensuality, but it had been the vibrancy and life in the emerald eyes staring down at him, which the artist had captured so successfully, that intrigued him. He did not want to believe she was a party to treachery. That same vibrancy had struck him the moment she walked into the room; even those damned veils could not conceal it. He had heard of the fire which had reputedly left Ruth Melville horribly scarred. Was it a tragedy, or merely a clever ruse? Those veils could hide many secrets.

'You are impertinent, sir,' she chided. 'Perhaps you would prefer to wait until my brother returns, to negotiate with him.' At seeing her hands clench, he reluctantly admired her courage. The portrait had not lied. Scarred or not, she had spirit and pride. Here was the strength of character he had found lacking in her brother. If only he could see her eyes more clearly, he would know whether she were a traitor.

'I have other property to see in the district. I would prefer land with its own water.' He changed tactics, and gently probed, 'What about the acres to the east of the house? They have their own water supply fed by the river. For them, I would give you double what you are asking for the land to the north.'

Ruth shivered despite the warmth of the sunlight streaming through the traceried window. What had made him suggest that particular part of the estate? It was the main route they used for taking the Cavaliers to the coast. She forced a laugh. 'That land is not for sale. It is too close to the house. The beauty of Saxfield Manor is its seclusion.'

'Away from prying eyes!' he countered with the speed of a striking hawk.

Behind her veil, Ruth flinched. How deftly he had led her into a trap. She tossed back her head, the veil quivering as she drew herself to her full height, and was relieved that her voice showed no sign of her inner quaking. 'Far away from prying eyes, sir!' she blazed. 'Do you think I do not know that I have become a creature of ridicule and superstition amongst the villagers?'

A spasm of anger, for she could not believe a spy of Cromwell capable of compassion, darted across his rugged face. 'Your pardon, Miss Melville,' he said tautly. 'I meant no offence.'

'Did you not, sir? Then to what could your impertinent remarks refer?'

At her challenge, he looked freezingly at her. For a long nerve-juddering moment their gazes held, both unflinching, their eyes flashing with suspicion and antagonism. The tension in the room crackled like the air before an impending storm. Clearly, he did not like, or expect, to be questioned so bluntly by a woman. The hollows of his chiselled cheeks deepened as he fought to control his anger.

Unaccountably, she was gripped by a hollow sinking sensation. From the outset of their meeting he had manipulated the conversation to a point where she would betray herself. How could she have been so gullible as to lower her guard? Against her will she had enjoyed their verbal sparring, drawn by his easy, treacherous charm. Even as she glared her hatred at him, her heart tugged painfully. Why was he so disturbingly attractive, so in command of himself? Or was it the leashed power of a primeval hunter she sensed in him that held her fascinated? His was the strength she needed to draw upon while Adam was away, but disastrously, that iron will and sharp wit were in opposition to all she believed to be right. She dared not prolong any contact with this man who was here to destroy her—let alone trust him.

Fortunately at that moment a knock upon the door broke the strained silence, and Hettie, carrying a tray of cakes and a pitcher of sack, entered the library.

'If you please, Mistress Ruth, affairs in the kitchen need your attention.'

A sliver of alarm sped down Ruth's spine. Only one thing would make Hettie call her away. A sharper glance at the pinched whiteness of the maid's face confirmed her fear. Of all the times for it to happen, there was a Cavalier in the kitchen seeking shelter!

'I shall come directly,' Ruth answered, turning to Blase. In these circumstances alone, she was prepared to ease the friction between them. There was no point in arousing his suspicions further. 'Forgive my earlier rudeness. Being shut away and so rarely seeing visitors has made me forget my manners. I must attend to the matter in the kitchen. It should take but a few moments. Would you care for some sack while you continue to look over the papers?'

'With your permission, I shall ride over to inspect the land,' he replied smoothly, but there was an unsettling hardness to his expression as he followed her to the door. 'I shall return later to inform you of my decision.'

His words were innocent enough, but the clippedness of his tone sent a chill through Ruth. In silence he followed her down the stairs to the entrance hall. Turning to him, she controlled the nervousness in her voice. 'Ride where you will, sir.' She leaned heavily upon her stick. 'But I see few visitors, and our meeting has overtaxed my strength. Pray call on the morrow with your decision, when my brother will receive you.'

They had paused at the foot of the stairs, and to Ruth's distress she saw several spots of blood on the light oak floorboards. The Cavalier seeking their help must be seriously wounded if he had been brought through the front of the house. Aware that Drummond's sharp stare missed nothing, she sought to allay his suspicions and prayed that the maid would back her up. 'Hettie, there's blood on the floor. Is Sam hurt? Why did you not say!'

Hettie looked flustered. 'You know Sam doesn't like a fuss. It's his hand. He cut it on the scythe.'

Ruth found herself subjected to a narrowed assessing stare from Drummond. 'You have matters to attend to, and I have taken up too much of your time already. I shall call upon your brother tomorrow, as you suggest. Good-day, Miss Melville. You have been most helpful.'

He bowed. When he straightened, the bleakness in his eyes warned her. He knew. Dear God, he knew! At any moment expecting him to thrust himself into the kitchen and discover the Royalist, she gripped her cane. It was a feeble weapon, but she would use any means in her power to prevent him.

To her astonishment, he spun on his heel and marched to the door, his spurs resounding sinisterly through the panelled corridor. She could not believe he had so readily accepted that Sam was injured. Or had he? Did he go to inform the authorities? Somehow she did not think that was his way. What was he up to? The questions ran through her mind, giving her no peace. Each encounter with Blase Drummond left her perplexed and indecisive.

She watched as he stooped to pass under the low wide arch of the portal, momentarily shutting out the light with his tall frame before he disappeared from sight. At the sound of his horse's hoofs clattering across the courtyard, Ruth whirled and hurried towards the kitchen. She had been given a reprieve, but only temporarily... A man such as Blase Drummond did not wage war on women. It was Adam he was after.

Her resolve strengthened. There was not a moment to lose. She must get the Cavalier out of the house at first dark. She dared not risk Drummond returning while a Royalist lay hidden here.

CHAPTER THREE

'IS THE man seriously hurt?' Ruth asked, as Hettie followed her to the back of the house.

'One of them is, and I fear he cannot be moved. I'd not have troubled you, not with Mr Drummond in attendance, if the matter were not grave.'

'How many of them are there?' Ruth asked worriedly.

'Three.'

Ruth sighed. 'In the last two weeks we have had more Cavaliers in the house than during the whole twelve months since the king landed in Scotland. At last, events must be moving. The good Lord grant his Majesty victory.'

She fell silent as she entered the spacious kitchen, her glance falling upon the wounded man slumped on the wooden settle by the fire. The pale unconscious face looked heart-rendingly young; he could be no more than eighteen. But Adam had been seventeen when he received his first bullet-wound, such were the times they lived in. His companions had removed the man's jacket, revealing his shirt crimsoned with blood at the shoulder. Ruth lifted the wadding that had been placed against the gaping bullet-hole, and hardened though she was to such sights, she was sickened to discover he had been shot in the back. Fortunately the roundshot had passed straight through the top of his shoulder and she could tend him herself, for the village physician was an ardent supporter of Cromwell. The greatest danger lay with infection if soiled cloth from his jacket had remained in the wound.

After gently examining the angry, festering wound, she gravely faced his companions. One was dressed inconspiciously enough; the other, the shorter of the two, wore a profusion of lace about his throat and wrists and his haughty bearing was unmistakably that of a nobleman. He was probably no more than a year older than herself, but her blood boiled as he looked through her, rather than at her. Dabbing a lace kerchief to his nose, he glanced disdainfully around the kitchen, declaring, 'Where is Mr Melville? Have him brought to me at once.'

Ruth stiffened at his rudeness. It was the arrogance of men like him which had brought England to this sorry pass. Nobleman or not, she would not be treated disrespectfully in her own home. 'My brother is absent,' she replied curtly.

At his answering scowl, she ignored him, turning instead to his companion, who was several years his senior, his long hair shot through with grey. He was bent worriedly over the wounded man and, from their likeness, she assumed them to be brothers. Belatedly she recognised him as Sir Robert Barcombe, who had commanded her father's troop and whose land, before Parliament had sequestered it, had been on the other side of Steyning. These were no ordinary Royalists. Sir Robert had lost everything during the war and now lived in poverty and exile in Holland. Yet from Adam's tales he was a frequent visitor to England, working for the king's cause. There was a reward of £200 on his head, and another £100 for the capture of his brother Godfrey.

She curtsied politely. 'We are honoured, Sir Robert, that you have chosen our house. I fear your brother's fever is mounting and that he will die if he is moved. It could be a week before he is strong enough to travel,' she said heavily. 'He must stay, of course, but I cannot guarantee the safety of both you and your companion. The house is being watched. There is but one hiding-place here. Your companion must leave at once for another house.'

A disparaging grunt sounded behind her. 'We passed several troops of Roundheads on the road. It is too dangerous to leave. You told me, Barcombe, this house was loyal to our cause. Yet all I find is a crippled woman left in charge.'

Ruth spun round to face him, her temper flaring. 'No Royalist has ever been turned from our door! But to safeguard this escape route, I must ask you to take shelter at another house. It is but a mile distant. You will probably find the grandeur of Fowkes Grange more to your liking.'

'I'll have no woman telling me what to do!'

'Enough, Colbourne,' Sir Robert said with quiet authority. 'Our lives are in Miss Melville's hands.'

'If your lordship will condescend to adopt a disguise,' Ruth continued, unimpressed by Lord Colbourne's haughty glare, 'you will be conveyed to the Grange, safe from any soldiers' prying eyes, I assure you.'

'The devil I will!' Lord Colbourne exploded.

'You will do as Miss Melville suggests, Colbourne,' Sir Robert warned sharply. 'These good people risk their lives to help us.'

The defiance died from Lord Colbourne's eyes as he regarded Sir Robert wearily. 'As always, you are right.' He turned to address Ruth, his tone more gracious. 'We were forced to land at Littlehampton yesterday because of a Parliament ship patrolling the Channel. Then later we were almost captured by a troop from the garrison at Arundel. That was when young Barcombe was shot. I make no bones that I would be happier if your brother were here to guide us, Miss Melville. Each of us has a reward upon his head—enough to keep a poor man in luxury for the rest of his days.'

'No man, or woman, is poor while they have their honour, my lord,' she replied coldly.

'For shame on you, Colbourne!' Sir Robert remonstrated. 'Miss Melville's father served under me. A more

honest and honourable man it would be hard to find.'
He smiled warmly at Ruth, soothing her ruffled pride.
'What disguise would you have my Lord Colbourne
adopt?'

'He will leave here dressed in my veils and travel in a
closed carriage attended by my maid. I often visit my
parents' grave in the ruins of the old priory. It is a secluded place on the border of Mr Fowkes's land. Word
will be sent by pigeon, and Mr Fowkes's manservant will
be waiting to take you safely to the house.'

'I'll not dress as a woman!' Lord Colbourne snapped.

'My friend, if you value your hide, that is just what
you will do!' Sir Robert held up a silencing hand, his
voice threaded with amusement. 'It is time you learnt a
little humility.'

Ruth ignored the arrogant nobleman and continued
to address Sir Robert. 'What of your horses, or did you
arrive on foot?' She grew serious, fearful that Blase
Drummond might discover their mounts tethered close
by.

'An innkeeper sympathetic to our cause provided us
with horses. Your man-servant took charge of them.'

Ruth breathed more easily. Sam would have taken the
horses to the wood behind the house where the old ice-
house, cut into the side of the hill, had been extended
to hide Royalist horses throughout the day. The immediate worry of discovery lessened, she continued
frankly, 'I had hoped that you would be able to leave
tonight. It is too dangerous for you to stay. A man pro-
fessing to be interested in buying land was here when
you arrived, and I believe he is a government spy. There
was fresh blood in the hall, and although he appeared
to accept my story of a servant being injured, he will be
back to see my brother tomorrow.'

'We had no choice but to enter by the front,' Sir Robert
said apologetically. 'We heard someone moving in the
shrubbery near the kitchen. Your man-servant had left

with the horses, and, fearing discovery, we squeezed through an open window. It was then that my brother lost consciousness. Fortunately your maid heard the noise and brought us to the kitchen.'

'You heard Daniel Fowkes leaving. He probably hid in the shrubbery, thinking that you had accompanied my visitor and were inquisitive. He thought it wise for us not to be seen together by Cromwell's man.'

'Fowkes left you to deal with the man alone?' Sir Robert said, astounded. 'And you would place our lives in the custody of such a man?'

'You wrong Daniel!' She defended her friend. 'It is because Saxfield is being watched that he left. We dare not risk both the safe houses in this area falling under suspicion.'

Lord Colbourne shot a fierce look at Sir Robert, who nodded resignedly and drew a large watch from his jacket. 'It wants an hour until noon, Miss Melville cannot be placed in unnecessary danger. Lord Colbourne will leave at once for Fowkes Grange. We shall meet at dusk to continue our journey, for in three days I must be in London. My brother must be got safely back to Holland when he is fit enough to be moved. Can that be arranged?'

Despite his politeness, Ruth saw in his eyes his doubt of her ability. Although the knowledge rankled, she kept her voice smooth, answering without hesitation, 'My brother should return before dark. If Lord Colbourne is at the priory at dusk, Adam will show you both the safest route out of the county. In the meantime, if you would carry your brother upstairs, he will be cared for and a ship procured to take him out of the country.'

'You are most kind.' Sir Robert took his brother's arm and heaved him over his shoulder. 'Lead on.'

Half an hour later, Ruth watched anxiously from the long gallery window as Sam drove the closed coach away from the house with Lord Colbourne and Hettie inside.

The midday sun, obscured by gathering rain-clouds, added to her worry, for even in summer a hard downpour could turn the downland tracks into a quagmire. Moving from the window she looked through the open panel of the secret room at the unconscious Cavalier. Godfrey Barcombe's cheeks were flushed with fever, his breathing shallow after losing so much blood. Sir Robert had assured her that the wound had been cleaned, but, worried by the extent of the infection, she had applied a poultice to draw out the poison. Her gaze moved from the wounded man to his brother crouched at his side. Sir Robert looked grey with exhaustion.

'I'll tend Godfrey, while you take some rest, sir. My brother's room is the last door on the right. Sleep the day through; you will need your strength tonight.'

He stood up, easing the stiffness from his shoulders. 'We are indebted to you, Miss Melville.'

She shook her head. 'Let there be no talk of debts. We each do our duty to our Sovereign.'

Sir Robert bowed, his eyes brightening with respect as he gazed at her veiled figure. 'You are a brave woman. Your father would have been proud of you.'

The unexpectedness of his compliment sent a sharp pain through her. Even after so long she missed the father she had idolised. A deeply religious man, the same adventuring blood ran in his veins as in his buccaneering grandfather's and, because of it, he had spent hours closeted in the library reading his Bible. His faith had given him the strength to harness his wildness, channelling his energy into breeding one of the finest dairy herds in the south of England—until Cromwell's soldiers had stolen them during a raid on the estate. Ruth knew how difficult it was to conquer the inclinations of a free-roaming spirit. It was the image of her father, his head bent over his Bible as he prayed for guidance, that gave her the strength to continue in her self-inflicted role of a semi-invalid. Sir Robert's words were the highest accolade anyone could pay her.

Through the long afternoon she sat at Godfrey's side listening to the soft patter of rain upon the tiny windowpane. As she placed another cool compress on his burning brow, she could not help wondering if Adam were lying somewhere wounded like this. She thrust the thought aside. She could not afford to be distracted by fear for her brother; three men's lives were in her custody this night. Until Godfrey Barcombe regained consciousness, a constant watch would have to be kept upon him, his presence heightening the danger closing round her.

The day passed with her nerves strung out. Hettie had returned over an hour later than expected because Daniel Fowkes's servant had not come to the meeting-place. When Sam had walked over to the Grange to investigate, he had seen several army mounts waiting by the main entrance. Such random searches used to be infrequent, but of late they had increased. Meanwhile the disgruntled Lord Colbourne had been forced to spend the day hidden in the priory undercroft, and Ruth fervently prayed that the troop would not also visit Saxfield.

Fortune was with them. By dusk no soldiers had arrived at the Manor but, just as she began to hope all would be well, the outer kitchen door flew open, bringing with it a cold blast of air as Sam burst in, his rain-glistening face ashen. 'Mistress, 'tis word, by pigeon, from Mr Fowkes. He can give us no aid this night. Soldiers are billeted at the Grange! He warns you to make the king's men fend for themselves.'

Ruth looked blankly at Sam. Was Daniel under house arrest? She rubbed a hand across her temple, thinking rapidly. 'Then we shall act without Mr Fowkes. It changes nothing.'

'Master Adam will have my hide, and rightly so, if he learned that I allowed you to continue with this madness.

Tell the king's men the truth. They will not expect a woman to face such danger.'

'That is why nothing will be said,' Ruth returned sharply. 'It is our cause we fail if I abandon Sir Robert now. Soon his Majesty will ride into England. All those who would follow his banner must be alerted. Our duty is clear.'

'Your father would be proud to hear you say such words.' Sam's huge frame sagged with defeat. 'But I fear that this night the devil will be riding at our shoulder, and laughing.'

The creak upon the floorboards above warned Ruth that Sir Robert had risen from his bed. 'I doubt we shall be visited by soldiers this night,' she told Hettie, her voice almost lost against the sound of the rain. 'But, if we are, you are to say that Master Adam is dining with friends in Shoreham and that I have taken to my bed, too ill to see anyone.'

'Sam, bring the horses from the wood,' she ordered, hurrying from the kitchen to change before joining Sir Robert in the parlour. 'Sir Robert and I will meet you at the edge of the clearing.'

She was just jamming her brother's hat on her head when a firm tread sounded outside the door. Quickly adjusting the cumbersome weight of the sword against her hips, she pulled on the leather gauntlets as Sir Robert entered the parlour.

Touching the brim of her hat, she bowed to the knight, her voice deepening. 'It is an honour to serve you, sir. I regret your stay must of necessity be brief. We ride at once, for soldiers are billeted at the Grange. Lord Colbourne has been forced to spend the day hiding at the priory.'

'I would pay my respects to Miss Melville before I leave,' Sir Robert insisted.

Discomfited, Ruth cleared her throat. 'My sister is indisposed. Her scars—you understand—the rain and cold bites into them. Now, if you are ready, Sir Robert, we must leave at once.'

From his hiding-place in the wood Blase Drummond saw the light in the Manor kitchen extinguished, and waited expectantly. The blackness around the door deepened. Then two cloaked figures, their heads bowed against the rain, emerged, and hugging the shadows, they sped across the lawn to where he knew Sam Rivers waited with the horses. But why only two men? Blase frowned. He had learned that three Cavaliers, one believed wounded—which confirmed the blood he had seen in the hall—were in the district. Had he been wrong not to follow Ruth Melville and her maid when they took a carriage-ride earlier? His need to confront Adam Melville on his return had been greater. But when he had glimpsed Melville's face at a window in the long gallery, he had checked his desire to question him immediately. It puzzled him that he had not seen Melville return to the Manor, although he could have missed him while he himself had been doubling back to Saxfield. His unease grew. He had no proof as yet that Melville was a traitor, but all was not as it seemed, and experience had long taught him to follow his hunches.

What devious game were brother and sister playing? His suspicions deepened, reluctantly drawing Ruth Melville into their web—she had been hiding something. He had been struck by her courage and dignity—all he knew of human nature told him she was no traitor, but the evidence of his eyes belied that.

He strained his eyes against the darkness as the two figures disappeared from sight and, moments later, he heard the sound of muffled hoofs moving through the wood. Untethering his own horse, he leaped into the saddle, the sound of its hoofs also muffled by sackcloth as he followed. He wondered briefly what was happening at the Manor. Obviously the wounded man was too ill to move, yet the fact that only two men had appeared troubled him.

Blase cursed beneath his breath when his horse stumbled into a hole. They had travelled no more than half a mile, keeping away from the usual tracks, when he heard the horses ahead halt. Following suit, he absently ran his hand over his mount's neck as he listened. The moonlight barely penetrated the clouds, but he knew from the direction they had ridden that they were close to the ruins of a priory. He tensed. It was quiet—too quiet. Not even a rabbit scurried in the undergrowth. His stomach twisted with rage and suspicion. There was treachery afoot—he could smell it in the air.

Ruth glanced anxiously across at Sam. Her spine prickled. Something was wrong. She scanned the pale outline of the flintstone ruins. Why did Lord Colbourne not show himself? All at once the moonlight broke through the clouds and the scene was lit with the yellow flashes and crack of discharging pistols. A shot whistled past her head. Then, like demons rising from the depths of hell, their snorting horses leaping over a broken wall, a troop of Roundheads sprung out of the ruins where they had lain in ambush.

'Follow me!' Ruth shouted, wheeling her mount towards the lower slopes of the downs. At the same moment her horse veered sharply, and her gaze fell upon the object that the mare had avoided. Her blood chilled, nausea rising in her throat. The figure flashed before her eyes, the brightening moonlight showing her a deep lace collar and above that a pale face with wide staring eyes. Lord Colbourne was dead! The priory must have been searched, and he had been routed out and murdered by the soldiers now giving them chase.

A bitter oath from behind told her that Sir Robert had seen the body, but it was the drum of hoofs closing on them that alarmed her most. Out in the open they would

stand little chance of escape. They must make for the
trees and try to shake off their pursuers so that they
could gain the next valley and hide in the outbuildings
of a farm.

'Stay close to me,' Ruth commanded, as they entered
the wood. She hunched her shoulders against a fresh
shower of rain, but with it came the chance of escape
as the clouds again obscured the moon. On the crest of
a hill, the trees thinned. Taking her bearings from the
tiny dots of dim rushlights showing through the cracks
in the cottage shutters, she ignored the nearest buildings
and headed for a distant light, to the right of which was
a crumbling barn.

She glanced over her shoulder. The darkness was
almost total, but she could hear her companions close
on her mount's heels. When she pulled her mare to a
slithering halt behind the barn, it was too dark to make
out Sir Robert's and Sam's faces, their silhouettes darker
outlines against the flintstone wall. Moments later, a
dozen horses pounded past, their hoofbeats gradually
fading. Just as she thought they were safe, an angry cry
went up, and to her horror she heard the horses
returning.

'Stay here!' Sam ordered. 'I'll draw them away.'

Before Ruth could protest, he galloped off across the
fields. Risking a glance round the side of the barn, she
saw the soldiers giving chase. When Sam was halfway
across the field, she led Sir Robert in the opposite
direction along a little-used farm track. Within moments, her spine notched with returning dread. They were
not alone on the track. Someone was following them!

Giving her horse her head, she was dismayed when
Sir Robert's mount began to lag behind. Although the
rain had stopped, the stiffening wind was dispersing the
clouds and an occasional star was visible. Ahead lay thick
woods, but first they had to cross two open fields. Ruth
urged her flagging mount on, but with each passing

second the sky was brightening, disastrously. They were only halfway across the last field when the moon burst through to spread its treacherous light across the valley. Ruth looked fearfully behind her. Sir Robert was further back than she had realised and, directly behind him, rapidly closing the gap, was their pursuer.

'Faster, Sir Robert!'

The warning shout was whipped away by the wind. Horrified, she saw Sir Robert's horse lurch, then crash to the ground, and he was hurled over his mount's head. The Cavalier lay unmoving, and the horse, after raising its head and giving a shrill whinny, fell back, warning her that its leg was probably broken. But what of Sir Robert? Fear churning her stomach, she swung round to ride back to him. He lay where he had fallen. Dear God, let his neck not be broken! But, even if he were unconscious, how could she save him? Their pursuer was almost upon him!

Slowing her pace, she drew the pistol, her hands shaking as she aimed it at the man bearing down upon Sir Robert. When her horse brought her into range, the rider's face was raised in her direction. It was Blase Drummond! Her finger froze upon the trigger, her instincts to fire momentarily betrayed by the tug of attraction she had felt towards him. Angrily she quashed her weakness. Blase Drummond was her enemy! Too late she steadied her aim. Drummond was already on the ground, his horse forming a shield between them as he heaved Sir Robert's unconscious figure over his saddle. Then he moved to one side, his sword drawn in readiness to fight.

'The game is up, Melville,' he sneered, moving closer.

The wind lifted his cloak, and she aimed just to the right of the white of his shirt visible beneath his jerkin. But as her finger squeezed the trigger, something within her, and beyond her control, moved her hand and the shot went high, tipping his hat back on his head as it passed through its wide brim.

She urged her horse forward. Even at the risk of her own life she had to save Sir Robert. Both he and Lord Colbourne had trusted her to get them to safety. Colbourne was already dead, and she must not fail Sir Robert. As she replaced the spent pistol and drew her sword, everything seemed to be played out with a slow nightmarish clarity. Drummond's sword came up on guard, his eyes glittering with a brittle fury that held no mercy. She had but to cry out that she was a woman and she knew instinctively he would not fight her, but pride sealed her lips. Unwittingly, she had been the cause of Lord Colbourne's death and the capture of Sir Robert. Honour demanded that she fight to regain the Cavalier's freedom.

'Devil's spawn!' she spat at him. 'I knew you had no interest in the land.'

Her sword slashed downwards, jarring against Drummond's blade. Then his fingers clamped like an iron manacle about her wrist and, before she could react, she was hauled bodily from the saddle, the ground rushing towards her as she was propelled through the air. Biting back a cry at the pain shooting through her shoulder as it slammed into the ground, she rolled upon impact as Adam had taught her, and, still clutching the sword, rose dazedly to her feet. Her whole body juddered as she parried Drummond's flashing blade with her sword. She staggered back, needing every ounce of her slim frame to deflect Drummond's lightning attack. Within moments she was tiring, her arms leaden from absorbing the force of those vicious blows. By some providence, she had not been wounded.

Then, with humiliating certainty, she knew he was just toying with her. Her temper flared, and forgetful of all Adam's teachings to remain cool-headed, she lunged wildly, straight at her opponent's heart. She never even saw his sword countering her attack, so swiftly did he strike. Her hand was on fire as his blade locked with the basket-weave sword-hilt and, with a flick of his wrist, he wrenched the weapon from her bruised fingers. It fell to the ground several feet away. Refusing to admit defeat, she made a dive towards it. As her fingers closed over the hilt, a booted foot came down on the blade.

'On your feet, Melville!' Drummond snarled. 'Do not force me to run you through like the snivelling cur you are.'

The insult smarting her pride, Ruth straightened, shakily, to face Drummond's towering form. She had lost her hat in the tumble and the wind blew her hair into her eyes and mouth. Tossing back her head, her hair blowing back from the jutting line of her jaw, she defiantly held his gaze. His lean handsome face was hardened with contempt, and as she drew a steadying breath, she knew it was likely to be her last.

CHAPTER FOUR

BLASE WAS unprepared for the shock of seeing Adam Melville's face clearly for the first time. The resemblance to the portrait of his twin sister was remarkable. The difference was in their characters. The soft curve of Melville's lips and the roundness of his high cheekbones betrayed him for the weakling he was, confirming Blase's suspicions of his treachery. Although Melville had ridden back to Barcombe's side, had that been to help the Cavalier, or to run him through before he could talk?

Blase brought up his sword, pressing it against his opponent's throat. If Melville was a traitor, he deserved to die. Sir Robert was in his keeping, but Godfrey Barcombe was still at Saxfield Manor.

'You misguided fool, Melville,' he ground out in disgust. 'Did you really think you could play the traitor and keep your life?'

He increased the pressure of his sword against Melville's throat and curbed his hatred of what this cur stood for. Melville swallowed convulsively, but did not cringe as he had expected. Unaccountably, the memory of Ruth Melville's fierce pride stopped him from dealing with her brother as he deserved.

'It is your kind who are the traitors, Drummond!' Melville flung back scathingly, only the higher pitch of his voice showing his effeminacy.

Expecting him to beg for mercy, Blase was surprised at the anger flashing from the younger man's almond-shaped eyes. So Melville did have some redeeming qualities! Blase stepped back. Dead, Melville was just another traitor brought to justice. But, alive, he might prove useful. He doubted Melville was in this alone, and he might unwittingly lead him to others whose loyalty had wavered. Besides, there was more than one mystery surrounding Saxfield Manor—Ruth Melville intrigued him. He had no intention of letting her off his hook just yet.

A groan warned him that Barcombe was stirring. He had to get him away.

'Tonight I spare your life,' he rapped out, lowering his guard, 'but you will pay for your treachery. I swear it!'

'It is your kind who will eventually pay,' Melville retorted, his youthful face twisted with loathing. 'You are thieves and murderers—all of you!'

Unable to control his anger, Blase lashed out, and was startled by the frailty of Melville's body as his fist crashed into the young man's face. Like corn beneath the scythe, Melville lay flattened on the ground. Gritting his teeth, Blase checked himself from giving him the thrashing he deserved. He could kill him as easily as snapping a twig in two. As he glared at the pale face, noting the trickle of blood running down his cheek and the slanted eyes glittering with hatred, the moonlight played tricks upon his mind. He turned away, disgusted by his weakness. It was as though he had struck Ruth Melville, not her lily-livered brother!

'Do not think this is an end to the matter, Melville!' he declared, swinging up behind Sir Robert's unconscious form slumped over the saddle.

Seeing Melville's horse a few feet away cropping the grass, Blase snatched off his hat and slapped it down hard on the beast's rump. With a whinny of surprise, the mare started forward and disappeared from sight as she headed back towards her stable. Looking down at her owner, who had stood up and was scrambling back to pick up his sword, Blase grinned mockingly.

'The five-mile walk back to Saxfield will give you time
to reflect upon your treachery. Next time, I shall not be
so lenient.' He rode away without a backward glance.

'Curse you, Drummond!' Melville shouted after him.
''Tis the devil's work you do this night.'

The first pink streaks of dawn were lightening the sky
as Ruth leaned wearily against the wall of the dovecote.
'Curse you, Blase Drummond!' she repeated for the
hundredth time, having reviled him each time she
wrenched her ankle or was forced to battle through waist-
high bracken. The knave had disarmed her with the ease
of taking sweetmeats from a child, and that rankled.
She was a competent swordswoman, for although her
strength was no match against her brother when they
practised, she was quicker and lighter on her feet, often
slipping under his guard with a potentially lethal thrust.
Throughout the cold wet night, anger had kept her blood
boiling. She hated Blase Drummond! She refused to
consider that he could have killed her, but instead had
spared her life. For what purpose? Did he think her so
weak-witted that she would lead him to others loyal to
their cause? That was just how his devious mind would
work! Fury stung her blood. She knew him now for what
he was! If Blase Drummond were unwise enough to
return to Saxfield, she would be ready for him! If she
could not match his strength, she would be more than
a match against his one apparent weakness. Too tired
for further consideration of her plans for revenge, she
staggered into the kitchen and was almost knocked over
by the enthusiasm of Spartan's greeting.

'Praise be, you're safe!' Hettie dropped the wood she
was stacking by the fire and threw her arms round Ruth.
Then, recalling her position, she drew back. 'Forgive
me, mistress, but I've been that worried.'

Ruth smiled tiredly. 'You are more friend than servant,
Hettie.' She rested a hand on the maid's shoulder,

drawing comfort from her loyalty. 'It has been a night I shall not forget. At one time I thought I would never see Saxfield again.'

'Hush ... You are safe now,' Hettie soothed, her eyes mirroring her concern. 'Sam returned hours ago, as did your mare. We feared you had been captured. What happened? Oh, just look at your poor face!'

Ruth touched her bruised cheek and ordered Spartan to sit, before answering with bitterness and remorse, 'It is nothing. Sir Robert was captured. Drummond has him.'

'Did Drummond recognise you?' Hettie asked.

'He recognised whom he thought to be Adam Melville.'

'And he let you go?' The surprise was evident in the maid's voice.

'Only because he thinks I will lead him to higher game.' Ruth threw off her wet cloak and moved closer to the heat of the fire. 'Drummond's arrogance will be his downfall.'

'And lung-fever will be yours!' Hettie tutted at the steam rising from Ruth's doublet and breeches. 'Up to your room and off with those wet clothes. Sam will bring up hot water for your bath, and I shall heat some good strong broth. Then you are to take to your bed for the rest of the day.'

The offer was too tempting to refuse. After stooping to kiss Hettie on the cheek in gratitude, Ruth dragged herself up to her room, her muscles already stiffening after her night's exertions.

A low growl from Spartan brought her awake. All drowsiness vanished at the sound of heavy boots stamping up the stairs. She drew back the bed-hangings, reaching instinctively for her mask, and bit back a gasp of pain at the stiffness contracting the muscles in her arms and legs. The footsteps were closer, and did not belong to Sam or Hettie. A brief hope flared and died.

Spartan would never growl if Adam had returned. Positioning the mask over her face, she searched for her robe, which had fallen to the floor, Drummond's parting threat echoing through her mind. Sir Robert was his prisoner. Had he now come to arrest Godfrey Barcombe?

She smothered the impulse to leap from the bed and confront him, her role as an invalid forcing her to stay where she was. If Drummond suspected the truth behind her disguise—she shuddered fearfully—all at Saxfield would hang. The door to her bedchamber was flung open, and Spartan's growls deepened.

'Who's there?' she demanded, shrinking back into the shadows of the hangings, unwilling to show herself without her veil.

A deprecating snort from the intruder greeted her query. His heeled boots resounding across the floorboards, he strode across the room and opened the shutters. Even as Ruth fumed at this outrage, she drew the bedclothes over her breasts, her thin silk nightgown adding to the vulnerability of her position. The hangings were flung wide and the intruder glowered down at her. Spartan growled, his hackles raised as he stood stiff-legged, placing his large body between his mistress and Captain Melville.

'Call that hell-hound off!' Henry paled, taking a step back, his hand on his sword. 'Or I'll run the mangy cur through.'

'Down, Spartan!' Ruth ordered, knowing that the dog would protect her if her cousin tried anything untoward. The mastiff sank to the floor, his growls subsiding to a warning rumble. 'Devil take you, Henry!' she began, but remembered just in time to curb her fury. She was supposed to be weak with pain. 'What do you mean by bursting into my sick-room like this?'

'Where's Adam?'

'I have no idea.' She fought to stay calm and hide her dislike for this blustering coxcomb.

At that moment Sam, panting from a hard run, burst into the chamber. 'I was in the stables when Captain Melville arrived. He pushed past Hettie when she told him you were indisposed.'

'It is all right, Sam. You can escort Captain Melville out in a moment. My cousin's manners were never endearing, even as a child.' She regarded Henry disdainfully. 'For the last two days I have been in my sick-bed. I have not seen Adam since he came to wish me goodnight last evening.'

'You'll be telling me next you know nothing of the Royalist—Lord Colbourne, no less—found hiding in the priory,' Henry Melville persisted savagely.

'A Royalist hiding in our priory?'

The image of Lord Colbourne's murdered body lying on the grass smote her, and she strove to control the shaking in her voice. Seeing Sam edge forward to confront her cousin, she put up a hand to stay him. A slight stiffening of the giant's frame showed his disapproval, but he paused.

'If what you say is true, it is serious indeed,' Ruth countered smoothly. 'But, as you see, I have only Sam and Hettie as servants. There is no gamekeeper to patrol the estate. If you knew the amount of game lost to poachers, it would not surprise you that the ruins are used by Royalists, or even smugglers.'

'They shall be used no more.' The ruddy colour deepened in his face. 'I have ordered the walls to be razed to the ground and the undercroft filled in with rubble.'

'No!' She could not stop herself protesting.

'So you admit it is used as a hiding-place for spies?' Captain Melville seized upon her words.

'I admit nothing of the sort! Have you forgotten that my parents' graves are within the ruins, and those of your grandparents? They are a place of peace and beauty. It is barbaric to tear the walls down.'

'I have heard that you visit the place often. If they are so important to you, it could be arranged that they are not touched.' He stroked his blond beard haughtily. 'Colbourne did not travel alone. He was with two other companions. Tell me where they are, and your precious ruins will remain undisturbed.'

Her hatred for her cousin rose up, almost choking her. Nothing was sacred in his eyes. The ruins were one of her favourite places on the estate, but she would not play the traitor to her king to save them. As she fought to overcome the remorse searing through her at the proposed desecration of her parents' resting-place, the full import of her cousin's words became clear. He still thought Sir Robert was at large. Blase Drummond would have reported his capture. Or was this a trick of Henry's to make her reveal all she knew?

'I am flattered that you believe me capable of so ingenious a plot to protect Royalist spies. You have such a low opinion of women, usually.'

'I know your hoydenish ways of old, cousin. You were always into scrapes.'

'That was a long time ago, before . . .' She paused, her lower lip trembling as she played her part with practised ease. 'Before the fire left me as I am today. My life is quiet enough now. I rarely leave the Manor. The villagers look on me with superstition and shun me. We have few visitors. Have you not put Lord Colbourne to the question? He will surely know where his companions lie hidden.'

'Colbourne is dead, as if you did not know!' Henry took a step closer to the bed. When Spartan sprang up, fangs barred, with a scowl he froze, his voice hardening. 'You're lying! On the evidence I have, I could have you taken to Headquarters for questioning. But I would spare you that, if . . .' His gaze travelled insultingly over her figure.

Ruth attempted to draw her knees up to her chin to hide the outline of her body visible beneath the thin summer coverlet, and the stiffness in her joints reminded her that she was supposedly an invalid. She gasped dramatically as she lowered her legs.

'Can you not see that my mistress is in pain?' Sam commented acidly.

'I think you had better leave, Henry,' Ruth said, fearing that Sam would antagonise him. When angry, Henry was unpredictable. She did not believe he would harm her—not while he saw her as his future bride and the means to win Saxfield—but she would not put it past him to drag Sam away to face torture. 'I do not know how long I can control Spartan. We have suffered enough at Saxfield because of the conflict with the last king and Parliament. Even now, Adam is selling more land to pay the taxes. We wish only to live quietly here.'

'You always did have a way of twisting words!' Captain Melville glowered at her, the brown cast in his blue eyes giving him the sinister air of a Grand Inquisitor. 'It is strange that Adam is never at home when I call. Don't play me for a fool, Ruth. For all your pretence of innocence, you are hiding something, and I intend to discover what it is!' His gaze rested upon her neck. 'I see no scars upon your body, and your mask in itself is provocatively mysterious. I shall enjoy taming you to my will, sweet cousin.'

Sam sprang forward, fists clenched. 'You will not speak to my mistress like that!'

'Get out, Henry!' Ruth shouted above Spartan's snapping and snarling. 'You disgust me. I would sell myself on the streets and see Saxfield a burnt-out ruin before you become master here.'

'That can easily be arranged,' Henry proclaimed, as Sam propelled him towards the door. 'Neither you or Saxfield will escape me.'

An hour later, as she helped Hettie in the buttery, Ruth was still fuming at the insolence of her cousin's treatment. His threat, although not an idle one, was not the most immediate danger she had to contend with. Henry was a pompous braggart. He had no proof against Adam—yet—and without it he could do nothing. She still had some rights on her side. Even as she made light of Captain Melville's bluster, an uncomfortable feeling lodged within her breast. Who would take her side against her cousin? Henry was now a man of some standing in the district, and his temper was such that few people would risk crossing him. She shuddered. There were also Sam and Hettie to consider. Her cousin would strike when they were most vulnerable, as he had proved by bursting into her bedchamber—no doubt hoping to catch her unmasked. From this moment, she would keep a loaded pistol by her bed.

If only she had someone she could turn to and trust. There was Daniel Fowkes, but he had worries enough of his own. The proximity of the priory to his land would also place him under suspicion of hiding Royalists. Adam's last words tolled through her brain: 'Trust no one while I am away. No one!' It was sound advice. She was capable of dealing with most emergencies, but with danger pressing ever closer, she could not help wishing there was some broad shoulder she could lean on.

'Oh, Adam, where are you?' she voiced her thoughts aloud, the cool buttery growing unaccountably warm. Her skin felt on fire, and there was a fever raging in her mind. Swaying, she gripped the scrubbed table for support, and the ladle she was using to skim the cream from the milk clattered to the tiled floor.

'What ails you, mistress? You look so strange.'

'It's Adam. He's alive, but only just. He's burning with fever.' She rubbed her side, where each breath stabbed razor sharp.

Hettie paled, her voice quavering with fear. 'Now you stop that! 'Tis the devil's tricks that makes you see and feel as your brother does. Is there not enough danger here without your being suspected of witchcraft?'

Ruth inhaled deeply. The pain in her side and the feverishness vanished, leaving her pale and shaken. 'Adam is in danger,' she said, distraught. 'And I am trapped here, unable to help him.'

'Master Adam can take care of himself!' Hettie patted her shoulder comfortingly. 'You have been cooped up in the house all day. Why not walk awhile in the garden before it starts raining again? I'll finish the work here.'

The offer was tempting, but Ruth shook her head. 'You have too much work as it is, Hettie. Even with half the house shut up you could do with another two women to help.'

'And where would you get the money from to pay their wages, apart from the danger of their tattle-tongues? Honest work never hurt anyone, and you do far more than any mistress of the house should. Off with you and enjoy your walk.'

'I walked enough last night to last me for a month, but I shall stroll through the garden and pick some roses for the parlour after I have fed the chickens and ducks.'

Ruth pulled off her large white apron and drew the veil down over her face. By the door, she picked up her walking-cane before crossing the yard to the out-buildings to collect the grain. Outside the house she never knew if she was being spied on. Even in the privacy of the outbuildings she dared not leave off her disguise in case someone should come to the house unexpectedly. And today the mask had the added advantage of hiding the bruise below her eye where Drummond had struck her.

She frowned as she measured out the grain into a wicker basket, pushing aside Spartan's inquisitive nose when he came bounding over from the stables. The

memory of last night's events were bitter and frus-
trating. She blamed herself for Lord Colbourne's death—
she should never have turned him from the house. And
what of Sir Robert? Certainly her cousin had known
nothing of the Cavalier's capture. What fate had he suffered at Blase Drummond's hands?

Commanding Spartan to stay back so as not to frighten
the chickens, she scattered the seed and then moved on
towards the duck-pond. Here Spartan bounded ahead
of her, his muscles rippling as he took off after a heron
that rose out of the corner reeds. The herons flying inland
from the river constantly stole the trout, but fortunately
there were fish to spare, and as Ruth watched the bird
fly majestically upwards, she could not resist pushing
back her veil to see more clearly its grace and beauty.

'At last the swan emerges from her covering reeds.'
The deep voice close behind startled her. Hastily replacing her veil, she turned to face Blase Drummond,
her heart hammering with the knowledge that he did not
refer to the fowl swimming on the pond.

'Is it your habit to steal over another's land like a
thief in the night?' she retaliated. Her breath caught in
her throat. He tipped back his hat in a mocking salute.
His swarthy complexion emphasised by the whiteness of
his shirt, he stood, arms folded, leaning against a tree.
How long had he been spying on her? She smothered
her anger and hatred after all he had subjected her to.
She had vowed to even the score between them, and her
only weapons were her sharp wits and femininity.

A warning of something being out of place prickled
her skin. Why had Spartan not growled to announce the
intruder's presence? To her amazement, he edged
forward, his stumpy tail wagging. The image through
her veil was slightly distorted. Her incensed gaze noted
with unease the pistol stuck into Drummond's belt and
the sword prominent at his hip. When he reached down
to stroke the mastiff's scarred head, her temper erupted.

Apart from herself, Spartan allowed no one, not even Adam, to fondle him.

'What devilry have you performed upon my dog?'

'He knows I mean him no harm,' Drummond said softly. 'Or you!'

Exasperated, she called Spartan to her side, and although he obeyed her command, her apprehension increased, feeling she had been betrayed by her closest friend. Spartan had never showed such bad judgcment of character before, and her resentment added to the humiliation she had suffered last night. She longed to challenge Drummond about Sir Robert, but aware she was still responsible for the safety of Godfrey Barcombe hidden in the house, she curbed her retort. How much did he know? Better to play the innocent and pretend she knew nothing.

'Have you come about the land?' she asked, in what she hoped was a natural tone. 'I fear that again you find my brother away from home.'

Drummond thrust himself forward from the tree, his long strides catlike and predatory as he untethered his horse from a nearby branch and led it down to her. 'I shall enjoy negotiating with you, Miss Melville.' His expression revealed nothing of his thoughts. 'Your brother is fortunate to have in you such an able steward. He seems to take little interest in the affairs of his estate, or, perhaps, he misunderstood me. I thought I had made it clear that our business was unfinished when we met last evening.'

Ruth quailed, feeling that shrewd black stare penetrating the thickness of her veil, leaving her stripped and bare of all pretence. 'Adam mentioned no such meeting,' she parried. She longed to order the knave from the estate, but could not risk his returning with troopers. Later Sam would find some excuse to send Drummond on his way.

'Did he not? Strange. We had a long conversation last evening.'

'I have not seen Adam today.' She leaned heavily on her cane as they moved back to the house. Each painful step reminded her of her vow to even the account with Blase Drummond.

At that moment Sam appeared, a pitchfork balanced in his hands. One word from her, and he would throw the intruder off her land. Drummond rested his hands casually on his hips, but there was a stillness about his pose, the alertness of a trained soldier ready to counter any attack. Against such a man, she suspected that even Sam's giant strength would be no great advantage. Besides, a show of force would solve nothing.

'Sam, take Mr Drummond's mount to the stables.' She decided to play a more subtle game with this government spy in order to bring him down. 'And then ask Hettie to bring wine and brandy to the winter parlour.'

For a heart-jolting moment she thought Sam meant to challenge Drummond, but after he cast a puzzled look at Spartan sitting calmly between the two figures, he silently took the reins and led the horse away.

Their approach to the house took them through the sunken garden, where a dozen curved stone steps led up to the side terrace. Pausing to gather up her skirts in her free hand, Ruth started as Drummond boldly slipped his arm through hers.

'Your servant, dear lady. You are in pain. Permit me to help you.'

How solicitous he sounded! Ruth fumed, as she forced herself to suffer his hold. Where his fingers touched, her flesh flamed with indignation. He lost no opportunity to play the gallant to Ruth Melville, when, only hours earlier, he had threatened to destroy her brother. It was upon that very gallantry that she meant to prey.

'You are very kind, sir. Most men are repelled by my affliction.'

'Kindness has nothing to do with it, Miss Melville. And I consider such men to be fools.'

There was an odd catch to his voice, and aware of the strength of his muscles beneath her hand, a tingle of foreboding shot up her arm. Whatever this man's susceptibility to women, it was no weakness, as she had at first suspected.

The sky had darkened considerably, and they quickened their pace to avoid the first drops of rain. Upon entering the house, he relinquished his hold upon her arm, but instead of relief, she felt strangely cast adrift.

'The fire is set in the winter parlour.' Ruth covered her confusion by trivialities. 'I shall fetch a taper from the kitchen; it will not take a moment. Please be seated, Mr Drummond.'

In the kitchen, Ruth found Hettie wide-eyed with fear. 'What is Drummond doing here? We shall be undone, mistress!'

'He was prowling in the gardens, and claimed to have an appointment with Adam. We both know the lie of that. If I sent him away, it would only add to his suspicions. I shall entertain him in the parlour and hope to divert him from any idea he may have concerning young Barcombe being here.'

'I'm worried about Barcombe.' Hettie sighed. 'His fever is mounting. The wound must be infected. You will have to look at it, mistress.'

'I shall do what I can, later.' She raised her voice above the drone of the rain and picked up a lighted taper. 'Now I must return to the parlour. Will you bring us wine and brandy? We must hope the rain eases quickly, or I shall be forced to ask Mr Drummond to stay for dinner.'

On her return to the parlour, Blase Drummond uncoiled his long form from the chair where he was sitting and took the taper from her hand. Their hands touched, the brief contact like a spark falling from the lighted brand to scorch her fingers. She pulled her hand away, too quickly for the gesture to be natural, and felt his stare sharpen, the light from the taper reflected like a tiny golden sun in his dark eyes. Flustered, she sat down on the cushioned settle opposite the chair he had vacated. Secure behind the protection of her mask and veil, she watched him touch the flame to the kindling. Spartan padded in and with a contented sigh flopped down before the fire, his nose resting on the toe of Drummond's cuffed boots. For some moments Drummond crouched, hands on knees, as he satisfied himself that the fire would not die. Without rising, he turned a searching, sidelong glance upon Ruth, the expression in his eyes shadowed by his straight black brows. Her throat cramped with sudden trepidation. His full lips had set into a grim line, the dark slash of his moustache making his handsome face stark and severe.

'It is time, Mistress Melville, that you and I had a serious talk.'

CHAPTER FIVE

'I WELCOME the opportunity to talk, sir.' Ruth forced a lightness into her voice, while icy fingers kneaded her chest at his words. 'We have so few guests.'

Removing his hat, Drummond placed it with his gauntlets on the floor at his side. The fire bathed him in an orange glow lighting the hollows of his angular face, and his shoulder-length hair, speckled with raindrops, shone with the rich colour of brandy. For an instant his black eyes flashed as he regarded her sternly. Her bravado cracked. He was a man like any other, but she strove to combat the erratic thumping of her heart.

He rose languidly, his tall form dominating the low plaster-ceilinged room. 'This must have been an exceptional week for you.' The double-edged thrust was delivered in a brusque undertone that intensified her feeling of intimidation.

Although the veil concealed her emotions, she cursed the barrier which prevented her from seeing his features clearly. How much did he know? He sat down opposite her, stretching his legs before the fire in a manner that was far too proprietary for her peace of mind.

'A busy week indeed, Mr Drummond,' she countered, determined to maintain a role of innocence. 'This is the second time you have honoured us with a visit.'

'And each time your brother happens to be absent.' He changed tactics with a speed that disconcerted her. 'If I were a suspicious man, I would believe he was avoiding me. He does not seem to take his responsibilities seriously.'

'It is those responsibilities which take him so often from home,' Ruth flared, the humiliation she had suffered at this man's conduct returning.

'And what would those responsibilities be?'

Ruth could feel the jaws of the trap closing about her. She must conquer her antagonism towards Blase Drummond or her temper would make her incautious. Verbal combat against him was as deadly as crossing swords. 'Unless we are to lose our land altogether, or be imprisoned for non-payment of taxes, the estate must become more profitable.'

'How vexing these matters of finance can be! Yet there are fortunes to be made.' He paused, running his forefinger reflectively along his dark moustache, while his gaze seared through her veil. 'There are many rewards offered for information laid against criminals and the like.'

Ruth ran her tongue over drying lips. It was not criminals he spoke of, but betraying Royalists! Her pride rose to conquer her apprehension. 'Only a knave would inform against his fellow man for gold!'

'Proud words, Mistress Melville, but what if you knew a traitor was in your midst? Is it not your duty to inform the authorities? What harm when, duty done, you receive a reward for your loyalty?'

'How would you define a traitor, sir?' she fenced, her temper surging. He was trying to ensnare her, while revealing nothing of his own convictions, and somehow she had to draw him out. She, too, could resort to innuendo to probe for the truth. 'Shall we take the case of the Marquis of Montrose?' she went on smoothly. 'He was Charles Stuart's most able commander and supporter, but suffered a traitor's death for a cause many still believe just. To some, Montrose is revered as a hero and martyr; others saw him as an insurrectionist and traitor. How would you judge him, Mr Drummond?'

'Any man who does not falter in his loyalty has my respect. Whether such loyalty was misguided or not.'

She felt a glow of satisfaction as he crossed his legs and sat more stiffly in the chair, but she had not expected him to be so evasive. Surely, in the eyes of any man loyal to Cromwell, the support Montrose had given Charles Stuart made him the greatest traitor of all?

'You have not answered my question, Mr Drummond,' she persisted, knowing that his answer would bring their differences out into the open, and even give her an excuse to order him from the house. 'In your eyes, was Montrose a traitor who deserved to die?' The subject of Montrose's death caused violent emotions in most people's breasts. Adam, who had idolised the Scottish leader, had locked himself in his room and stayed drunk for three days when he heard the news.

He stared for some moments into the fire before answering, an almost imperceptible drawing together of his dark brows showing his anger at her question. Then he turned to her, the corner of his mouth lifting in a provocative grin. 'Such a morbid subject for conversation,' he drawled. 'There are more pleasant subjects for a man and woman to discuss. Love is a more fitting topic than war.'

Ruth bit back an acid comment, wondering why he refused to give her a direct answer. Did he think to trick her, to use his charm to flatter and cajole her into speaking indiscreetly?

'You are right, sir. We digress.' Her tone sharpened at his forwardness. 'Our purpose was to discuss the price of the land.'

Spartan sat up, sensing the friction between them. He put his large head on Ruth's lap, reassuring her. He would be a formidable protector, should the need arise.

Hettie appeared with a tray just as the room was illuminated by a blue-white flash and a loud boom of thunder directly overhead made speech impossible. Her hand shook so violently that the wine slopped over the sides of the pewter goblets and on to Ruth's gown.

'Forgive me, mistress. How could I be so clumsy?' Hettie apologised, her glance darting meaningfully to the door, warning Ruth that her agitation was not because of the storm. 'Come quickly, and I shall rinse the skirt before it is stained.'

Ruth pushed Spartan aside and rose to her feet. Whatever had caused Hettie to take such drastic action must be serious. 'Your pardon at having to leave you unattended, Mr Drummond,' she said, moving to the door. 'I fear I have no choice but to change.'

He stood up, a lock of hair falling forward over his temple, softening the stern line of his brow, and giving him a devil-may-care appearance. How different he looked from the cold-blooded hunter of the night before! Had she not been playing this dual role, it would be all too easy to be deceived by the magnetism of his darkly sensual looks.

'I would not have your gown ruined on my account.' His easy charm, never far from the surface in the company of women, momentarily disconcerted her. 'Clearly your brother will not return in this weather.' He paused, as another crash of thunder drowned his voice, then went on, 'I shall take my leave.'

She glanced at the window being lashed by wind and rain. 'You cannot ride out in this.' The words were out before she realised it. But, the laws of hospitality aside, she could scarcely turn him away in such weather. Besides, she had yet to discover what had happened to Sir Robert. If he were in prison, there might be a way to effect a rescue. 'You have not drunk your wine; there is brandy if you prefer? Of course you will stay for dinner. We eat in an hour.'

He bowed, the sparkle in his eyes rekindling her antagonism. Had he ridden here, knowing that the storm was imminent, and was awaiting a chance to search the house? Panic raced through her. The storm could last for hours! With Godfrey Barcombe hidden upstairs, she should have ordered him to leave. Every moment Blase Drummond spent in the house was filled with danger. What on earth had made her insist on his staying?

The answer lay in the tingling awareness of his masculinity. And, more than that, in the way he was regarding her. Accomplished gallant that he was, he was looking at her as though the veil did not exist and she was a beautiful and desirable woman. Not since the fire had any man looked at her in that way, making her feel vibrantly alive. She hardened herself against the strange breathlessness his gaze evoked. Was not his apparent fascination to women, all women, the very weakness she meant to play upon and use to her advantage? The sharp sting of anticipation shot through her as a cautious voice whispered in her mind: Would any woman gain the advantage over Blase Drummond? Danger, now a part of her life, added spice to her secluded existence. He was flirting with the image in the portrait, not the scarred figure she had become. Devil take the rogue, he would look at a wizened grandmother as though she were queen of his heart, if he thought it would gain his own ends! The challenge of outwitting this government spy set her pulse racing. What harm could a little light flirtation bring?

'Your servant, mistress,' he answered with a broad smile. 'The pleasure of dining with such a charming companion is one I cannot refuse.'

Only then did Ruth realise that to sit at the same table and dine with him would mean she would have to remove her veil. She would order Hettie to keep the candlelight to a minimum so that her masked face would remain in shadow. Uncomfortably she already felt that the situation was slipping from her grasp.

'Spartan will keep you company while I change,' she said lightly, following Hettie from the parlour. The dog would stop Drummond from searching the house while she was absent.

Once away from Blase Drummond's commanding presence, it was easy to convince herself that all would be well. He had shown no sign of suspecting that Hettie's clumsiness was a ploy to spirit her mistress away.

'Your poor gown,' Hettie groaned as they walked up the stairs. 'I hope it's not ruined. I was at a loss what to do. Now I've made matters worse—you had no choice but to ask him to dine.'

'The weather was the cause of that, Hettie, not you,' Ruth reassured her. 'My gown is not important. What's amiss?'

'It's Mr Barcombe.' Hettie quickened her pace as they rounded the stairwell and could no longer be seen from the hall below. 'He's delirious. I heard his voice from the landing—shouting out in fever, he was. I managed to calm him, but if he starts raving again... What with Mr Drummond downstairs, we should all be undone!'

'I shall see him before I change my gown,' Ruth said, entering the long gallery. 'If he is as bad as you say, I must ensure that Mr Drummond remains distracted throughout dinner. Put out my ivory silk. I shall wear that.'

'Mistress! To entertain a man alone is scandalous enough, but in that gown it is... brazen! Have your wits addled? That was your betrothal gown. You've not worn it for years.'

'What difference does that make?' Ruth declared. Her mind made up: she was in no mood to by swayed. 'Apart from these sober greys and black, which I grow daily more weary of, I have nothing else. Do as I say.'

The maid's sniff of disapproval was cut short as a muffled voice carried to them from the secret chamber.

'Dear Lord, let his mind not start wandering again,' Hettie prayed, her face growing tense as she pressed the horse's head at the side of the reredos and the panel silently opened. 'I hope you know what you are doing, mistress. You dance with the devil by tempting Drummond, parliamentarian or not. He's no sober-sides. There'll be a trail of broken hearts left in that handsome rogue's wake, unless I miss my guess.'

'My heart remains intact. I know him for what he is!'

Ruth stopped short as she entered the small chamber, her breath catching at the odour of sweat, damp and candlewax. The pungent smell of infection churned her stomach with dread. Throwing back her veil, she moved the lighted candle closer to the bed and peeled back Barcombe's linen shirt. The bandage she had changed that morning was streaked with yellow and brown—a bad sign. Gently lifting the corner of it to examine the extent of the infection, she checked at his low groan. Her heart sank. She knew enough about such wounds to know that if Barcombe were not tended to shortly, he would die.

'The wound must be bathed and cleaned,' she said over her shoulder to Hettie. 'Whoever tended this poor man made a poor job of it. The roundshot passing through the shoulder must have forced some material from his jacket or shirt into the flesh. If it is not re-moved, he will die of blood poisoning.'

At the sound of her voice Barcombe's eyes opened, their expression glazed and unseeing, and he began to mutter incoherently. Ruth chewed her lip, her mind racing. The air in the tiny chamber was foul. Barcombe should be moved to her brother's chamber to speed his recovery, but how was that to be accomplished without alerting Drummond that a wounded Royalist was in the house?

'I shall do what I can to make Barcombe more com-fortable for now,' she stated, her mind set upon a course, despite the dangers it presented. 'First lay out my gown, Hettie. I dare not stay long from Mr Drummond. Then summon Sam here. After that, prepare a posset mixed

with betany and rue, which will lessen the fever and make
Barcombe sleep more peacefully. Make haste, there is
little time to lose.'

A draught wafted over Ruth as the door opened and
closed behind Hettie, and she shivered. Alone with the
wounded man, her confidence wavered. Upon her
shoulders, for the next hour or two, lay the balance of
life and death. Barcombe would die if he were left in
this foul airless room, which had been built to hide
someone for a few hours, not for days. Yet to move him
jeopardised not only the lives of everyone in the
household, but the function of the house itself, to give
aid to hunted Royalists.

The mutterings from the pallet grew louder, and
thrusting the defeatist thoughts from her mind, Ruth
soothed the wounded man. Just because Drummond's
strength had bested her in a sword-fight did not mean
that he could outwit her! Over the years she had played
cat and mouse with Cromwell's Ironsides during their
sudden raids upon the house. She would not fail him as
she had failed Sir Robert. For several minutes she concentrated on calming Godfrey Barcombe. She placed a
cool cloth on his hot brow and spoke softly to him,
urging him to silence. Nothing she said made any difference. His voice was rising, and her own flesh was
flushing first hot then cold as she feared he would be
heard outside the room. At any moment she expected
the door to open and Drummond stride in, his deep voice
loud and triumphant, announcing their arrest.

When a loud cannonade overhead shook the rafters,
she flinched, shakily acknowledging that such a storm
coming in from the sea sometimes faded but usually returned to last for several hours. Drummond could be
stuck here all night! Yet, having placed her in this
dangerous situation, the storm was now her saviour. The
constant rolls of thunder drowned out Barcombe's voice

and her fear changed as she saw the stain spreading across his bandage.

'Rest easy, sir. You're among friends,' she said more sharply, praying that her tone would penetrate his fever. 'You're safe now, but Cromwell's spy is close by. Hush, man, before you betray us all!'

Something of her urgency must have registered, and he lay still. Beneath the three-day stubble of reddish beard his face looked sunken and skull-like. Then his mouth began to move, his voice cracked and barely audible. Fearing his ranting would begin again, Ruth took his hand to place it beneath the covers. It was gripped with surprising strength.

'Get message to...' His voice broke, droplets of sweat breaking out on his brow as he struggled to speak.

'You must rest, sir,' Ruth implored.

Her hand was gripped tighter. 'Warn...Major...' His words were drowned by a crash of thunder, and she leaned forward, straining to catch the occasional word. '...escape...Drummond...must warn...trust him...'

'Trust whom?' She fastened on the words, cursing the constant thunder that was making conversation so difficult.

The effort to talk coherently above the storm was weakening Barcombe. After several attempts, Ruth became worried that he would exhaust himself when he needed all his strength to fight the infection.

'I understand,' she told him, piecing together his garbled words as best she could. Did they not confirm her own suspicions? 'We know the danger and will guard against it. Now rest. You will need all your strength if we are to get you safely to France.'

The hand holding hers fell back on the coverlet, and Godfrey Barcombe closed his eyes, his breathing shallow but regular.

Ruth took the compress from his hot brow and soaked it in cold water before replacing it, her anxiety in-

creasing at seeing the lines of pain carved around the
young man's mouth. Once the wound had been
thoroughly cleaned, she was certain he was young and
strong enough to recover from the infection. It was
Drummond's presence which was the threat. The sudden
rush of air from the door opening behind her sent a chill
down her spine. She froze, fully expecting Drummond
to announce her arrest.

'Go about your business, mistress,' Sam said,
squeezing past to sit on the far side of the pallet. He
held the posset to Barcombe's lips. 'I shall do what must
be done.'

Ruth backed towards the door, her gaze on
Barcombe's now still figure. 'Save him, Sam. I have
failed so miserably in this escapade. I could not bear it
if another died because of my carelessness.'

'You are not to blame for what happened yesterday.
It was ill fortune that Lord Colbourne was discovered.
And you could do nothing against Drummond capturing Sir Robert.' Sam's expression hardened with
regret. 'That man's a devil! He's downstairs devouring
Master Adam's best brandy and pacing the room with
no little impatience. And now it seems that you must
entertain him alone. You take care, mistress. Beneath
the lion there lurks a wolf.'

CHAPTER SIX

HOW ACCURATELY Sam's words summed up her own sentiments regarding Blase Drummond, Ruth thought bitterly as she hurried to her room to change her gown, but however predatory Drummond's intentions might be, she had no intention of becoming his prey.

She inhaled sharply as Hettie finished lacing her ivory silk gown. The bodice was constricting by its tightness and as she ran her fingers over the gold lace edging its neckline, she was appalled at the fullness of her breasts swelling above the glittering lace. She had been willow slim when the gown was made for her betrothal to Thomas. How long ago that all seemed! Instead of the familiar ache memories of Thomas always brought, she felt only emptiness and, to her dismay, she could no longer recall his features clearly.

'You'll not be going downstairs in that!' Hettie cried aghast, cutting through her troubled thoughts.

'I have no time to change.' Ruth suppressed her own misgivings. 'Where's the lace collar, the one that falls to my waist? I shall wear that over the gown.'

She bore the maid's disapproving silence as Hettie tied the strings of the collar. Its points falling demurely to her waist brought a return of her confidence. Hettie put a final pin in the coil of hair high on the back of Ruth's head and secured a white scalloped-edged veil in position over the ringlets hanging over her ears. With a last sniff of disapproval, she handed Ruth a white silk mask, shaking her head as it covered her eyes and nose, but leaving the the lower part of her face exposed. The maid's eyes filled with tears.

''Tis the devil's work you do this night! No good will come of it. Yet I have never seen you look more lovely. If you must continue this madness, you will at least put Drummond in his place by looking the gentlewoman you are. Any man must be made of stone to resist you. The mask does not hide, but rather adds mystery to your beauty.'

'What nonsense you speak, Hettie!' Ruth laughed, but she was uneasily reminded that her cousin had said much the same.

She turned to regard her reflection in the glass and found herself staring at the image of a stranger. The blood ran faster in her veins. A bolt of lightning lit the room, making her appear tall and ethereal. The creamy white veil thrown back off her face emphasised the golden lightness of her hair, and beneath the mask her almond-shaped eyes sparkled like emeralds. For the first time in years she felt truly a woman, and with the feeling came the thrill of combat at meeting Drummond with the advantage for once in her favour.

'I know that look!' Hettie warned, drawing the veil down over Ruth's face. 'Take care that the mischief in your eyes is not your downfall.'

Ruth stared past Hettie to her image in the glass. The gossamer delicacy of the veil blurred rather than hid the oval face beneath.

'You will not be covered by the veil when you eat,' Hettie proclaimed darkly. 'Oh, mistress, this whole scheme is madness! Let me make your apologies to Mr Drummond. I shall tell him you are indisposed.'

'He will already be suspicious at the length of my absence. Would you have the man arrive tomorrow with a troop of Roundheads to have the house searched? Let us trust that his conceit will be appeased when it appears I have taken such pains with my toilette on his account. Have you made sure that the candlelight at the table is subdued, since my face will be protected only by the mask?'

'Ay, there's just the single candelabrum at one end of the table. Though what advantage Drummond will take of that, I shudder to think. Your poor mother would turn in her grave if she knew you were entertaining a man, other than your husband, in so intimate a manner. It's asking for trouble.'

'Nothing will happen.'

'In some matters you are as innocent as a babe in arms. Just you make sure to keep the handbell close to your side! Sam will not be far away, if you need him.'

'Sam will be occupied with Mr Barcombe for some time.' Ruth brushed aside the maid's warning and, picking up her cane, moved to the door. 'It is to divert Drummond from poking into our affairs that I must play this role in the masque which dictates our present lives.'

As Ruth walked down the stairs she heard the measured tread of Drummond pacing the floor. At the same time, the French clock in the parlour struck, and her throat locked in alarm. She had been away more than three-quarters of an hour; longer than she realised. The sound of the footsteps halted, the silence more oppressive than the impatient pacing. She had no way of gauging his mood, but after her long delay it was unlikely to be favourable.

Drawing herself up proudly, she scarcely placed any weight upon the stick as she entered the parlour. It was a dangerous risk and an unnecessary vanity, but suddenly she could not bear the thought of this man pitying her. To her surprise, Spartan was fast asleep by the fire, unconcerned by the presence of the stranger. Drummond was standing by the window, watching the storm which had passed over into the distance.

'Your pardon, Mr Drummond. I have been an unforgivably long time.'

He spun round, the fierce line of his straight brows shooting up first in surprise, then in pleasure at her appearance. 'Is it not a woman's prerogative to keep a man waiting? I am honoured that, having been forced to offer me hospitality, you treat my visit with such consideration.' Placing his hand over his heart, he bowed gracefully, his eyes dancing with merriment as he straightened.

'You mock me, sir!' she returned stiffly. 'In my father's day, Saxfield was renowned for its hospitality, but we seldom now have the pleasure of entertaining. I would be ashamed if a guest left with the impression that he had not been made suitably welcome.'

'Then I am indeed honoured.' His bold gaze swept appreciatively over her figure. He looked relaxed, the informality of his sleeveless leather jerkin and full sleeves accentuating both his masculinity and the intimacy of their surroundings. 'What a dullard you must think me! It was a compliment I intended, not mockery. You are a vision of loveliness.'

He placed his hand on his slim hip. The firelight caught the gold hooped earring, completing his buccaneering image. The surface gallantry was just that, Ruth reminded herself. Everything else proclaimed him a man used to living by his wits, quite capable of taking what he wanted by force if need be.

'Remember well that it is just a vision, sir—a façade. What lies beneath this mask would make you turn from me in disgust,' she countered quickly. The disarming effect of his smile was causing her heart to pound wildly, and she felt in danger of losing the initiative. 'Shall we go through to the dining-room, where Hettie has served dinner? I regret our fare is simple. Hettie has many duties, and there was no time to bring extra staff in from the village.'

'You should not have gone to so much trouble on my account.'

He offered to escort her, and when she placed her fingers lightly upon his arm, her whole body was startlingly aware of the sensuality emanating from him. Her breath caught in her throat as she again encountered his black eyes. The fierceness and suspicion had left them, replaced by admiration that made them gleam like polished ebony as he pierced the fragile barrier of her veil.

'You should not shun the world because of an accident of fate,' he said with unexpected warmth.

'You are impertinent, sir!'

'Beauty comes from within,' he continued unabashed. His hand clamped over hers as she lifted it from his arm. 'What are you afraid of? You have wit, intelligence and grace, accomplishments many women would envy and men admire and respect.'

The sincerity in his voice moved her. It was not idle flattery. He was a man of principle. His loyalty was as fierce as hers or Adam's. In any other circumstances, she would admire such traits. As they walked through into the dining-room, she looked sideways at him, and bit back a bitter laugh. The gallantry he showed to her now was starkly different from that of the Blase Drummond, bent upon revenge, she had encountered the night before. She must never forget he was her sworn enemy. This was an act to trap her, however much she was acting to dupe him.

She was about to call Spartan to follow, but as the dining-room door would remain open, it seemed unnecessarily discourteous to make a show of the mastiff's presence as a protection against a guest in the house, so she let him stay by the fire. The three candles burning at one end of the table created a more intimate atmosphere than she would have wished, but she dared not risk a brighter light.

If Drummond was surprised, he gave no indication. Showing the consideration which was fast undermining her antagonism, he led her to the shadowed place-setting

at the end of the oak table and held out the chair for
her to be seated. As Hettie was not in attendance, he
filled both their goblets from the wine flagon before
taking his place at the far end. Although the table could
comfortably seat five people along its length, it seemed
to Ruth's strained nerves that Drummond would be uncomfortably close when she must remove her veil.

'Please help yourself, Mr Drummond.' Ruth indicated the platters laden with cold sliced chicken, the hare
pie she had herself made earlier, and various other
savouries. Selecting the choicest slices of chicken, he cut
a thin wedge of the pie and presented the plate to her.
She took it graciously, waiting for him to sit before
raising her veil.

She toyed with the food on her plate for some moments, conscious that he must be staring at her. When
she did not look up, he began to ask her questions about
the history of the house. Without realising it, she was
chatting to him naturally and, when their glances met,
he showed no sign of curiosity about her mask or the
scars which supposedly were hidden beneath. He laughed
easily at her anecdotes and, no longer feeling self-
conscious, she began to enjoy his company. She felt
stimulated in a way she had not been for years and it
was becoming harder to maintain her guard against his
accomplished charm. She must not forget he was still
her enemy, the most dangerous of the men who would
destroy all that she and Adam worked for.

'More wine, Miss Melville?' he interrupted her flow
of speech. The meat dishes had long since been pushed
aside and they had eaten a generous portion of Hettie's
rich fruit cake topped with walnuts. With a start, she
realised that he had skilfully manoeuvred the conversation so that she did all the talking and she had learned
nothing about himself.

He stood up and held the wine flagon over her goblet,
awaiting her answer. She nodded, uncomfortably aware

of his nearness, of the intense masculinity of the fine hairs upon the back of his elegant hands as he held her goblet out. Their glances held. The air crackled with a tension that had nothing to do with the storm which had returned to rage overhead. She felt light-headed. How could she have forgotten—even for a moment—that this man was her enemy! Yet she had, and, worse, the way he was looking at her gave her a sense of wonderment.

Beneath that piercing stare, her cheeks burned, and she pulled the veil down over her face. A deeper fear pitted her. They had been eating for some considerable time, yet not once had Hettie put in an appearance. That could only mean that she was with Sam. Was Godfrey Barcombe's condition worsening? Did she imagine it, or was that a hoarse cry muffled by the wind and rain driving against the windowpanes?

A shadow passed across Drummond's face as he sat down on the bench beside her. Had he, too, heard the cry?

'You hide behind that veil and mask like an eastern princess, yet a man could drown in the depths of your emerald gaze.'

The persuasive gentleness of his tone crumbled her defences. If he had not heard the shout, what subtle trickery was this? She studied him warily, but his nearness was destroying her composure.

'Will not the mask alone suffice for this night?' He lifted the corner of the veil reverently, his expression deep and unfathomable as he raised it over her head.

When she would have pulled back, a light blazed in his eyes, staying her movement. She gazed at him, uncertain of his mood. What was happening to her? She no longer had the power to think rationally, and the touch of his hand where it had grazed her cheek left a trail of fire. She dragged her eyes from his spellbinding gaze and drew back, but did not lower the veil.

'You are a mystery,' he said hoarsely. 'You have spirit. Nothing can take that from you. Yet you hide yourself away like a recluse.'

He was perilously close. His gaze caressed her until every nerve-end pulsated, his proximity filling her senses. Although he made no further move to touch her, a treacherous glow of expectancy spread through her body.

'I am content, sir.' She was horrified at the breathlessness of her tone.

'Are you content to be but half a woman? The woman in the portrait I saw in the long gallery would not have been.'

His hands slid up her arms, and he drew her from the chair to stand at his side. How dared he taunt her so cruelly? She tried to whip her anger, but, irrationally, she wanted nothing more than to feel the strength of his arms round her and to surrender to the clamouring of her blood. He must never suspect her growing weakness. She twisted away, but his grip remained firm.

'Why do you torment me so?' she said brokenly. 'It is the mask that intrigues you. Are you like the others, forever curious? I know what they say. They do not trouble to lower their voices even in church: She was pretty once... must be a fearful sight now... enough to turn the stomach of Old Nick himself. A fire can twist a face into...'

'Stop it!' He gave her a gentle shake. 'I have no such morbid curiosity. I know well what scars a fire can leave. I have dragged human torches from buildings being razed by the enemy. So you have a scar or two. That does not change what you are inside.'

Suddenly she was frightened. She could not understand his motives, but his touch was destroying her self-control. She had to stop the spell he was weaving about her. Had he begun to suspect she was living out a lie? He, of all people, must never guess the truth. She snatched her arm away and, pushing back the lace of her sleeve, thrust the scarred arm out, expecting him, despite his denials, to turn away with revulsion as her cousin had done.

'If you think I want your—or anyone's—pity, sir, you are mistaken!'

Instead of revulsion, his eyes shadowed, guarding his thoughts from her as he took her hand. Before she could guess his intent, he bent his head and brushed his lips against the disfigured skin. The light contact caused her heart to beat tumultuously. 'I have the greatest respect for your bravery and courage,' he said, raising his eyes. 'I have heard how you were burned trying to save your mother.'

There was a soft whine from the doorway, and Ruth glanced across at Spartan, who, alerted by their raised voices, was standing braced and ready for her command.

'Down, Spartan! I am in no danger.'

'You are in danger, sweet lady—in danger of forgetting you are a woman.' Drummond's voice was a velvet caress, his hand sliding up her arm to draw her closer.

'I will hear no more of such talk,' she began, pushing against his hard chest, while against all reason her head tilted, unconsciously offering her lips to him. His mouth claimed hers, the touch of his moustache briefly tickling, then adding to the sensual experience as his lips moved with expert thoroughness over hers. Her fists clenched in preparation for pushing him away when, most shockingly, he parted her lips with his tongue and she tasted the sweetness of his breath. For an endless moment she was enslaved by the urgent mastery of his lips. Her betrothed's kisses had been hot and impetuous, and too often his roving hands had roused her anger, not desire, when they demanded more than she had been prepared to give. A sharp word had brought Thomas to his senses, and she had always been in control. But Thomas had never kissed her like this! The blood pounded in her ears, and her hands fluttered against his chest, no longer pushing but spreading out across his leather jerkin and feeling the vigorous beat of his heart. Her senses swirled, her thoughts chaotic. Would his kiss never end? Oh, let its sweetness, more potent than the breath of life, go on and on. Light-headed, she clung to him as his lips left her mouth to nuzzle against her ear.

'Do not waste your life, sweet Ruth. Never forget that you are a woman.'

A shocked gasp behind them made Ruth jump guiltily away, but the smile tugging at the corner of Blase Drummond's full lips showed that he felt no similar pangs of conscience. Giving her usual loud sniff of disapproval, Hettie began to collect the dishes. 'Is there anything else you will be wanting, mistress?'

'No, that will be all, Hettie.'

Too embarrassed to look her maid in the eye, Ruth walked through to the parlour. The wind and rain hammering upon the panes of glass echoed the violent disruption of her emotions. Summoning what she hoped was a cool voice, she glanced sideways at Blase Drummond.

'The storm shows no sign of abating. If you will take a seat by the fire, I shall have the guest-room prepared for you. You cannot journey tonight.'

'You are angry with me.' Drummond was at her elbow, his breath a soft caress upon her cheek. 'I make no apologies for abusing the rules of hospitality. You are a desirable woman.'

Her blood ran cold as he held out her walking-stick. She had completely forgotten her role as cripple when she swept from the dining-room. No wonder he was looking at her so intently! 'I am glad you did not act out of charity, sir.' She covered her confusion with sarcasm. 'The incident is best forgotten. It will not be repeated. My brother is away from home...and I have the protection only of a man-servant and my dog.

Nevertheless I shall not turn you out into the storm, but, if it is a doxy you want, your interest will be best served at the inn.'

'You belittle yourself and your charms,' he responded stiffly. 'I'll not force myself upon you, if that is what you fear. I have no quarrel with you, Ruth Melville.'

'I am glad to hear it, sir! But you have vowed to be avenged upon my brother. Did you think a kiss or two would sweeten my lips into betraying him?'

'Then you admit that he has something to hide?'

Eyes smarting, she jutted her chin as she glared back at him. Like a fool, she had succumbed to his expert seduction. How could she have been so gullible as to allow herself to believe he desired her? It had been nothing to him but a ploy to trick her into betraying her brother.

'If one of us has not been open with the other, it is you, sir.' She seated herself by the fire and motioned him to sit opposite. When he remained standing, her gaze remained unflinching upon his guarded expression, her tone hardening. 'For an hour or more you have subtly been questioning me about my life here, yet you have told me nothing of your own. You say you have come to Sussex to purchase land, but you do not look like a farmer.'

The firelight played over the strong planes of his face as he lowered himself into the carved chair she indicated. Despite her qualms, a shiver of expectancy shot through her. Even relaxed, there was a latent power emanating from him. She sensed she had touched a raw nerve by questioning him, yet there was no sign of wariness in his expression, simply that insufferable unruffled calm that betrayed nothing.

'I should have known that your woman's curiosity could not be curbed all evening.' He smiled with calculated measure, but this time she was determined not to be swayed by the devastating effect it had upon her senses. Though her face muscles strained at the rigidity she was forcing upon them, she remained unsmiling, waiting for him to continue. 'Apart from breeding horses, I have interests in the sea. My brother and I are partners in a merchant ship. He is at present trading in the South Seas.'

'And your home port, where is that?' she fired at him.

'My brother trades from La Rochelle.'

Ruth's heart leapt. Could she have been mistaken? He was studying her closely, awaiting her obvious question. 'Your home is not in England, then?'

'The Puritan yoke is not for me,' he quipped, his eyes again guarded as he qualified his statement. 'As a younger son, I had need to make my own way in the world. I had a mind to travel, and have spent several years abroad seeking my fortune.'

'And you succeeded, if you are part owner of a ship.'

'Luck smiled on me.'

She frowned, exasperated by his reticence. She was clinging to each word, wanting to trust him, yet he was deliberately holding back. Her stare forthright, she persisted, 'Modesty is a virtue, Mr Drummond. It is also infuriatingly evasive, and a powerful weapon if one seeks to hide the truth.'

'Would you make of me a braggart, Ruth?' he mocked. 'I saw a young boy fall into the river. Together with two of my companions, I dived in to save him, and just happened to reach him first. The boy's father was a French Count, and immensely wealthy. He rewarded an impoverished Englishman with an extravagance that far outweighed my simple act. It was from that money I purchased the ship.'

At the way he so lightly dismissed his bravery, Ruth's antagonism melted. Their gazes held, his black eyes transmitting a silent, sultry, promise that robbed Ruth of coherent thought. Inexorably they moved closer, his hand raised to touch her face. Her breathing slowed. If he spoke the truth, she had badly misjudged him. Was he telling her that he was a Royalist living in exile? It was what her mind and soul cried out to hear.

His mouth brushed hers, softly and sensuously, her questions scattering as her lips parted in answer. Her fingers curled through his long hair, drawing him closer as an uncontrollable tremor of longing craved appeasement.

Abruptly the spell was shattered. A wild shouting filled the air, setting the hairs at the back of her neck on end. It was Barcombe! Her gaze flew to the stairs, but before she could move or speak, Drummond was out through the door and bounding up the stairs two at a time. Her blood turned to ice. Blase had tricked her! How many times had he used that story to win a woman over, or indeed to allay the suspicions of Royalist sympathisers? It was all carefully rehearsed lies. In his eagerness to apprehend a suspected Royalist spy, Blase had betrayed that he was Cromwell's agent!

CHAPTER SEVEN

'SPARTAN!' RUTH commanded, desperate to stop Blase from discovering Godfrey Barcombe. 'Go, boy! On guard!'

The dog leapt forward, his great paws slithering on the polished floor as he took off after him. Lifting her skirts high above her ankles, Ruth followed. But Blase, with a keen ear for direction and, in the darkness of the upper floors of the house, the devil's own intuition, was already running along the upper corridor in the direction of Adam's bedchamber.

Dear God! All was lost. Her soul rebelled at the way he had undermined her guard. How was she to stop him? At the sound of Spartan's fierce growls, her heart raced with renewed hope. Would there be time to reach the loaded pistol by her bed?

'Take care, mistress,' Hettie cautioned shakily from the stairs behind her.

'Bring some light!' Ruth called, trying to pierce the darkness of the corridor and see where Blase was.

From the direction of Adam's door, the dog's growls carried to her, and as she began to move forward, a flash of lightning snaked across the oriel window at the far end, its brightness showing her that two of the bedroom doors had been flung wide, her own included. Her glance swivelled to the centre of the landing where Blase stood frozen, kept at bay from entering Adam's room by Spartan's bared fangs. Then, to her horror, she saw in his hand a dagger-blade glinting in a lightning flash. Ruth strained her eyes, her heart thudding a wild tattoo as she saw the tall, black silhouette moving across the lighter background of the window. Blase was half-crouched, his weight balanced ready to strike as he waited for the mastiff to spring, while all the time he was speaking to him in a low sonorous voice. She had seen no fear on his face, and when Spartan attacked, it would be a bitter fight. Darting into her own room, she pushed from her mind the injuries those massive jaws could inflict. Blase had lied to wheedle his way into the house, as he had continued to lie and ply her with false compliments all evening. To her shame, he had almost won her over and, traitorously, her lips still throbbed from the imprint of his mouth. It was the humiliation of the false promise behind that kiss that spurred her anger. If he discovered the truth, he must never leave Saxfield alive.

Her fingers were shaking as they closed round the pistol. Could she—would she—be able to shoot—to kill a man in cold blood? Dear Lord in heaven, she prayed, give me the strength and guidance to do what is right. Her fingers tightened over the pistol-butt, the embossed design familiar and reassuring. By the light of the bedroom fire she checked that the weapon was primed and ready and, satisfied, she ran back into the corridor. It had taken only seconds to get the weapon and return to confront Blase, but the tone of the mastiff's growls had deepened, warning her he was about to attack.

'Down, Spartan!' she ordered, bringing up the pistol. 'Mr Drummond, drop your dagger and unbuckle your sword. My pistol is aimed at your chest.'

'Where's Barcombe?' he snapped, ignoring her order.

A pale yellow light from behind Ruth moved over the pannelling as Hettie, breathing heavily from her exertions, held a candle aloft to illuminate the landing.

In the shadows thrown up by the flickering light the hard planes of Blase's face were taut and satanic. Menace sparked in the air between them like flying cinders scorching Ruth's skin, while Spartan continued to growl, adding to the mounting tension. Silencing the dog, Ruth

set her lips grimly, her fear succeeding to anger at the
way he had tricked her.

'There is no one of that name in this house. You have
abused every law of hospitality. Storm or not, I order
you to leave.' When he made no move to put aside his
weapons, her eyes narrowed. Had he really thought a
woman was so easy to dupe? Steadying the pistol in both
hands, she drew back the firing-hammer with her thumbs
in readiness to shoot. 'Get out, and do not come back!'
she declared coldly, gesturing with a jerk of her head
that he should move towards the stairs. 'No tricks! I
know how to use this. And, at this distance, I could not
miss!'

He sheathed his dagger but, instead of removing his
sword-belt and obeying her instructions, he placed his
hands on his hips in arrogant defiance.

'Barcombe's here. And he's wounded,' he proclaimed, the black line of his moustache emphasising
the ruthless set of his lips.

'So say you!' she bristled. 'Are you willing to gamble
your life upon such an assumption?'

'I said I had no quarrel with *you*.' His voice was softer,
coercing. She hardened herself against the glint of admiration in his eyes as his gaze swept over her. 'You
have proved your worth.'

When he took a step towards her, Ruth's finger
quivered on the trigger. He was doing it again, using his
persuasive charm to trick her. The candlelight flickered
over the walls as Hettie, holding an iron poker in her
other hand, moved to Ruth's side, her voice low with
warning.

'Don't listen to him, mistress. Remember Master
Adam's last words to you. Trust no one!'

'That's sound advice,' Blase parried, weighing up the
possibilities of overpowering her. It would be all too easy
to disarm her by force. Only the shallowness of her
breathing betrayed her fear, but there was no hesitation

in the hard gleam of her green eyes. A false move from
him, and she would shoot; not that fear of the conse-
quence would normally stop him attacking an adversary, but it was something more complex even than
his natural reluctance to fight a woman that checked him
now.

'You have no choice but to trust me, Miss Melville.'

'And if I choose not to, sir?'

A pang of regret tore through Blase at what must be
done, its intensity surprising him. He had never allowed
emotion to cloud his judgement or impede his duty, but
he was now subjected to such open scorn from those
slanted eyes, and the lips that had parted so invitingly
beneath his, now clamped tight with hostility, stabbed
at his conscience. What a tigress she was! A woman of
remarkable spirit. He knew Barcombe was here. And
this woman was prepared to give her life to protect a
Royalist from being taken. Not so her false-hearted
brother!

He took another step forward. The woman had to
know something of his mission in Sussex, and instinct
told him he could trust her—but only up to a point. He
mastered a stab of anger, unable to rid himself of the
suspicion concerning Adam Melville's loyalty. Lord
Colbourne had been betrayed. He had been murdered
on Melville land by this woman's cousin. If she was innocent of treachery, her brother was as guilty as hell.
Why was he not here? Had he already gone to Captain
Henry Melville—this time to betray Barcombe?

'Stay back, sir!' The hard edge to her voice halted
him. 'You have proved your treachery. You never had
any interest in buying Saxfield land.'

'Treachery is a dangerous word, Miss Melville. It is
all around us. I had my reasons for not making my intentions obvious to you from the start. I say again—I
have no fight with *you*.'

'Mistress, you must not listen to him!' Hettie wailed.

Ruth hardened herself against the subtle persuasion of his voice. That was not respect she saw in his eyes. It was the devil's own deception he practised, and she was not about to fall prey to his charm a second time.

'Do not take me for a fool, sir,' she responded fiercely, for although her heart gave an involuntary twist of regret, her hand upon the trigger did not waver. 'I know what happened last night. You threatened my brother's life.'

'Is that why he is not here now? Has he fled at the first sign of danger?'

'Adam is no craven. He would never run away. It's not his fault that his...' She bit back the words, shocked that she had almost said too much. The reminder of her brother's plight cut her like a knife. She had to keep faith. Adam was alive. How could she continue this fight if he were not at her side. For Adam, she must be brave— she must safeguard his inheritance. Devil take Drummond! He was clever. Too clever. 'The storm has detained Adam,' she added coldly.

'Your loyalty to your family is commendable.' The hated mockery was back in his voice; obviously he thought Adam unworthy of such loyalty. 'I am not con- cerned about Melville tonight. It is Godfrey Barcombe I seek.'

Her mind raced. Sir Robert was this man's prisoner, but he would never betray his own brother. This knave insulted her intelligence. Until he had proof, he could do nothing. Frantically she sought a solution without having to kill Blase. Before she could speak, a shout from the depths of Adam's chamber chilled Ruth's blood. Barcombe was again raving in delirium.

'Heaven help us!' Hettie moaned, as Blase leapt across the floor, his hand lifting the door-latch.

'Stay where you are, sir!' Ruth demanded. 'You will not have him.'

Before she could pull the trigger, Spartan attacked, his jaws closing round Blase's arm as the door swung open. Terrified of wounding the dog, Ruth held her fire.

'Call the dog off!' Blase ground out through clenched teeth as he staggered back against the doorpost. As yet, Spartan's hold was firm but restrained. If the man tried to move into the room, though, the jaws would close and break his arm.

The shouts from the inner room continued, and she heard Sam's voice vainly trying to quieten Barcombe. The wounded man had betrayed them all. Blase Drummond knew too much!

'I gave you fair warning, sir. I do not make idle threats. You took Sir Robert, but you will not have his brother.'

Sam's appearance in the bedchamber doorway momentarily distracted her. 'The lad's in a bad way, mistress,' he said worriedly, 'He needs urgent care.'

Her heart lurched sickeningly. What was she to do?

''Odsblood, woman!' Blase raged, undaunted by Spartan's dangerous hold. 'I would help you. We are on the same side.'

'Devil's lackey!' she flared. 'Keep silent. I have heard enough of your lies.'

She did not believe his words. How could she, after the way he had acted last night—capturing Sir Robert and threatening Adam's life?

'Easy, Spartan,' she ordered. 'Back slowly from the door, Mr Drummond, and Spartan will release you.'

Keeping her gaze level with his, she gave orders to the servants. 'Hettie, bring fresh bandages and hot water. You, Sam, take the pistol... You know what must be done to those who spy for Cromwell.'

A look of astonishment crossed Blase's face as she handed the pistol to Sam. Calling off Spartan, Ruth patted the dog's scarred head as he padded to her side. Her duty was done—she had saved Barcombe from arrest. Why, then, did her victory over Blase taste so bitter? No longer able to meet his flashing eyes, which were uncowed by pain or defeat, she moved towards the inner room to tend the fugitive.

'Your servant, Miss Melville.' The deep voice, no longer mocking, halted her. 'But you are mistaken. My allegiance is not to Noll Cromwell, or to any other crop-headed parliamentarian. I serve his Majesty. As Barcombe.'

Ruth swung round to outface him. 'You expect me to trust you when you captured Sir Robert from my brother last night? Where is Sir Robert? Mouldering in a prison somewhere? Now you seek the same fate for his brother. I despise you for what you are! Because of your spying, Lord Colbourne is dead.'

She turned aside, disgusted with herself that Blase's proud figure could still arouse remorse at what must be done.

'I had nothing to do with Colbourne's death.' Ice dripped from each syllable he spoke. 'As for Sir Robert, he should be in London by now, and, God willing, still a free man. Yes, I was watching this house. That was why I was sent here—to ensure that no more Royalists fell prey to Cromwell's men. In Colbourne's case, I failed lamentably.'

Ruth grappled with his explanation. How plausible it sounded, but was that not his way—to charm and cajole? She desperately wanted to believe him, but dared not just yet. There was too much at stake.

'Those are fine words, Mr Drummond,' Sam said heavily. 'Why, then, did you fight Master Adam, if it was not to take Sir Robert prisoner?'

'It is *Major* Drummond of the king's own lifeguards, to be precise. My only concern was to save Sir Robert.' His lips curled disdainfully. 'There was no time for questions. I acted as I saw fit. With Colbourne dead, I could not take chances. Besides...' his voice hardened as he stared at Ruth, 'was not Colbourne murdered on your land? It was your betrothed's troop who was lying in ambush for Sir Robert!'

'Whose troop?' Ruth gasped, surprise quashing her mistrust.

'Captain Henry Melville's!'

'That conceited popinjay is not my betrothed,' Ruth blazed. 'Nor is he ever likely to be!'

'Then you are not aware of his boast last evening in the taproom of the inn, declaring that he would be master of Saxfield by harvest time?'

'That's a lie!' Ruth countered, convinced that this was another trick. The man would say anything to confuse her and gain time to win his escape. The tender words he had spoken earlier taunted her. They had sounded so sincere, but were used only to deceive her while he bided his time to set his trap. 'Everything you have said this evening is a lie. Everything!'

'He speaks the truth about your cousin,' Hettie said from the corridor. She edged past Sam, the soft linen for bandages draped over her arm, and a bowl and pitcher of water gripped tightly in her hands. She looked from Ruth to Blase. 'I heard it from Goody Ticehurst when I met her gathering kindling in Fox's Wood this morning. I said nothing because I thought you had worries enough, mistress.'

Ruth linked her fingers together, desperately trying to make sense of the turmoil crowding her brain. So Henry was paving the way to become master here without arousing the villagers' suspicions? Yet even married to her, Henry could never possess Saxfield while Adam lived. What evil was her cousin planning? His bragging of their impending marriage was not without reason. Did Henry think to force her into the match? She would see him in hell first!

If Blase had not lied about cousin Henry's boasting, had he then spoken the truth in all matters? Was he the king's man? The garbled warning Godfrey Barcombe had spoken in his delirium had mentioned a Major. Was Blase that man? Her gaze swept over his tall, self-possessed figure, and she felt a traitorous tug at her heart. His lean countenance looked like a sculpture from marble, the chiselled planes noble and proud as a thirteenth-century warlord. She did not want to believe he was a spy. Throughout her assessing silence, Blase held her stare. Absently he massaged his arm, every inch of his six-foot frame defiant, despite the pistol trained upon him. She wavered. It would be like an answer to her prayers to have him on their side, and not against them... But dared she trust him?

A frenzied shout from the bedchamber cut short her deliberations. Godfrey Barcombe needed her. When Blase stiffened and looked anxiously towards the inner chamber, she drew a long steadying breath, her voice grating like a blunt woodsaw. 'A sick man needs my attention. I have no reason to trust you, Major Drummond, but I would not condemn a man without a hearing. If he tries to leave the house, Sam, shoot him.'

It was a compromise. Not a very satisfactory one, but what choice did she have. With Hettie at her side, Ruth entered the bedchamber, where it was worse than she had feared. The stench of infection hung heavily. Unmindful of the finery of her gown, she pushed back the fall of lace over her scarred forearm and bent to examine the wounded Cavalier. He was deathly pale, his face awash with perspiration, and when she touched his brow it was like thrusting her hand across a candle-flame. His fever was high—dangerously so. She would have to work quickly, if she was to probe the wound successfully to remove all trace of the cloth that was causing the infection, there must be no risk of a sudden movement making the knife slip.

Her hesitation was brief. 'Sam, I need your help. He must be tied down.' She looked directly at Blase, who had come into the room with the servant. 'I must ask for your word that you will not try to escape or over-power us. If my servant does not hold Barcombe still, the young man will die.'

'You have my word.'

Turning away, Ruth snatched off her veil when it fell over her face. Very gently she removed the soiled bandage and forced herself to ignore the queasy churning of her stomach as the pulpy mess was revealed. After Sam had tied the man's uninjured arm to the bedpost and moved round behind her to grip the wounded arm and press it firmly down on to the bedcovers, she took up the knife Hettie had brought.

'That is not woman's work,' Blase said fiercely, striding to the foot of the bed. 'Permit me to tend the wound.'

'And afford you the chance to plunge the dagger into Barcombe's heart, and then turn it upon us?' Ruth scoffed. 'You have given us no reason to trust you, Major. I know what must be done.'

He folded his arms across his chest, his expression forbidding. He was not used to having his authority questioned. And this chit of a woman flouted him at every turn. Even now, with Ruth and the servants oc-cupied, the dog squatted alert and on guard by the door.

As he smothered his impatience, his professional eye showed him that although very pale, Ruth Melville was dealing with the wound with an expertise he had not expected. Most women would have swooned at the stench and gory sight, but not she. But every encounter had proved to him that she was no ordinary woman. She certainly deserved better than marriage to Captain Henry Melville. A bitter taste rose to his throat at the thought of Ruth in Melville's clutches, and his hand curled over his sword-hilt. He had asked for this mission upon learning that Captain Melville had been given command of a troop in this district. He had his own score to settle with that turncoat. Melville would curse the day he saved his own skin by handing a sixteen-year-old boy over to Cromwell's henchmen to be tortured and hanged! Blase closed his eyes briefly—after seven years the pain of his younger brother's death still cut deep.

When he opened them, he allowed his gaze to slide appreciatively over the curves of Ruth Melville's trim figure, moving up to linger upon the pale, smooth cheek just below the mask. Inexplicably he felt the need to protect her, to save her from the danger her weak and selfish brother would bring upon her. Yet any run-in he had with Adam Melville would earn the enmity of this woman. Why in the name of Hades should that trouble him? Yet it did.

For the first time he found his duty distasteful, as he studied the scene before him. A strange tightness formed in his chest at witnessing the tender care Ruth was lavishing upon the unconscious man. She was all womanly softness, speaking low while she worked, as she would comfort a child, for all Barcombe could not hear her, yet beneath the spell of that sultry voice he grew quieter despite his pain. To his surprise, Ruth was adept with the knife, working quickly. Barcombe screamed once, and her face was drained of all colour as she worked on, ordering Hettie to hold the candle higher. Seconds later, she produced a small, bloody and shot-blackened piece of linen.

'It is over, Godfrey.' Her voice was shaky as she continued to soothe the restless man while she pressed a cooling poultice against his shoulder to draw out the last of the infection. 'The pain will ease now. You are safe with friends, and must rest.'

Blase felt a twinge of regret that she had never shown that feminine side of her nature to him, but then his lips twitched in remembrance of the fire and the passion he had drawn from her. Why should he hunger for softness, when it was the prospect of taming the tigress which excited his blood?

Ruth placed a hand in the hollow of her back to ease her aching muscles as she straightened and stepped away from the bed. An unexpected wave of nausea caught her unawares, and she swayed. A strong arm clasped her waist and she stiffened, drawing a deep breath to combat her momentary weakness.

'I am quite all right, Major. Perhaps you would be kind enough to untie Mr Barcombe's arm.' She regarded him accusingly. 'We have unfinished business to discuss. It is time you told us exactly your purpose in Sussex.'

'As his Majesty's servant, my purpose is the same as yours—to help those wishing to escape to France.'

Ruth regarded him warily. She was about to question him further when from the drive outside came the unmistakable clatter of approaching horses. Her throat tightening with alarm, she glanced at the two servants. Only one group of riders would visit Saxfield on such a foul night—and there, it seemed, the devil himself was looking after his own. At some time during her ministering to Barcombe, the storm and rain had stopped.

Hettie left the bedside and ran to the window. 'Roundheads!' she cried. 'We are lost, mistress!'

Ruth pressed a shaking hand to her brow, her mind racing. Her cousin would not hesitate to search the house, and there was no time to get Barcombe to the secret chamber. And Major Drummond—what was she supposed to do about him?

'If we are to save Barcombe, you must trust me,' Blase declared, accurately guessing her troubled thoughts.

As though to emphasise his words, there was a loud banging on the door below. This time, there could be no compromise: she had to trust him. Dear God, let her not be wrong! Ruth moistened her dry lips, her voice cracked with the strain of the past hour. 'Captain Melville has chosen his moment well. The house will be searched. Nothing would please my cousin more than to be able to imprison Adam by finding Barcombe hidden here.'

'Your brother is not here. *He* is safe!' Blase ground out with heavy sarcasm, but this was no time for Ruth to question his antagonism towards Adam. 'It is you who are in danger, Miss Melville.'

'Captain Melville will not harm me. Does he not see himself as master of Saxfield through our marriage?' Ruth said scornfully. 'But Barcombe and my servants are in danger.'

'There is a way to distract Captain Melville and save Barcombe, but...' For once Blase looked uncertain as he held Ruth's stare. 'I fear it is not a very savoury solution.'

'Anything!' Ruth answered fervently. 'Just as long as it stops them searching the house.

Blase passed a hand across his moustache, obviously reluctant to go on. 'Let Captain Melville's own boasting be his downfall. Instead of discovering treason afoot, what if he were to find the woman he claims as his betrothed in the arms of another man? Would he not appear a laughing-stock in front of his companions? Should he still insist on searching the house, I shall provoke him into a fight and perhaps yet save the day.'

'Mistress!' Hettie gasped with shock. 'Do not listen to him! Your reputation will be in shreds.'

'Is not a man's life worth the tarnishing of my reputation?' Ruth smothered her own misgivings and raised her voice above the hammering on the door.

'It is too dangerous, mistress,' Sam said heavily. 'What Major Drummond suggests is outrageous. It's all right for him—he will not be here to suffer the censure—but the villagers will pillory you for a wanton. And if you are taken prisoner, what of your mask? How do you think they will treat you when they discover the truth?'

'Enough, both of you!' Ruth commanded, her own mind having already traced the same frightening path. 'I shall face that when the time comes. I vowed to Sir Robert that his brother would reach France safely. I will give my life before I break my word. Now go and answer the door before the soldiers break it down. Take Spartan with you.'

Ruth moved across to the tester bed as Hettie left the room, and drew the hangings to hide the figure within.

'Wait, Sam!' Blase rapped out. 'You are right, of course. You stay with Barcombe. Miss Melville and I will meet the soldiers in the parlour. I had no right to suggest that she put her reputation at risk.'

'I do not fear the consequences, Major,' Ruth interrupted. 'Your suggestion is the only one which will stop the soldiers searching the house.'

When Blase and Sam continued to frown, she forced a wry smile, but finding it impossible to hold Blase's burning stare, she walked towards the ante-room as she spoke. 'Besides, those pious bigots will condemn me anyway! Have I not entertained a man in my brother's absence?'

The pounding at the door was growing impatient, and there was the sound of a window being shattered. To her relief, Sam followed her and continued on into the corridor, his heavy tread lumbering down the stairs as he shouted at the soldiers, 'I'm coming! There's no need to batter the door down.'

Ruth walked to the window to look down into the courtyard. The light from the half-dozen lanthorns carried by the soldiers lit up the scene and reflected the steel of their helmets and breast-plates. Clearly, Henry was expecting opposition to his visit.

CHAPTER EIGHT

RUTH HURRIED back into the inner chamber where Barcombe was at last sleeping peacefully. Hearing a measured tread behind her, she covered her nervousness by nodding towards her patient. 'Barcombe had better be gagged.'

Without looking at Blase, she handed him a wide strip of linen and, picking up the bowl of dirty water and the soiled clothes, hid them in a coffer. Satisfied that the room no longer looked like a sick-room and would pass a cursory inspection, she glanced towards the tester bed. Blase had tied the gag over Barcombe's mouth, and after closing the bedhangings, he rounded on Ruth, his face taut with suppressed anger.

'Does your reputation mean nothing to you?' His cynical tone flickered her like a lead-tipped whip.

'Of course it does!' An embarrassed flush stole up Ruth's neck to sting her cheeks. To cover her confusion at what was soon to be expected of her, she moved back into the ante-room, her flesh tingling at the determined way he followed her. 'The only hope we have of saving Barcombe is by this ruse,' she countered. 'We shall be powerless to prevent his men searching the upper rooms if we are held under guard in the parlour. When the soldiers burst in here, we must hope they will be so surprised at finding us together that they will search no further.'

'That depends on how convincingly you play your role.'

He closed the gap between them, the darkness of his eyes fathomless and unreadable as his arms slid about her. In the hall, Sam was arguing with the soldiers, trying to delay them. She ran her tongue over nervously dry lips. To agree to play the wanton to save Barcombe was one thing, but to put it into action was quite another.

'This was your idea,' he said impatiently. 'Have you second thoughts? This is no time to play the coy maid.'

'I know that... It's...' Holding herself rigid, she blurted out, 'My honour and reputation are all that are left me. If my virtue were in danger, I would defend it with my life.' She paused, darting an anxious glance towards the door. On the ground floor, heavy feet could be heard stamping through the baron's hall and solar of the old wing of the house. 'I can learn to live with disgrace,' she added, 'but not the knowledge that a man died because of my false pride.'

'It's too late to hide Barcombe elsewhere. If there were any other way...' The softer note of his voice pierced the shield she was striving to erect against him. 'I pray you will be spared the villagers' ridicule.'

'I am not afraid for myself. And as I have no intention of ever marrying, I shall bring no disgrace to another's name.'

'By heaven, the portrait did not lie!' His voice was sending curious shivers down her spine. 'You are a woman of rare spirit. So, you do not view your cousin's suit kindly?'

'Indeed I do not! I would as soon plunge a viper into my breast as wed him.'

At her impassioned tone, his full lips parted in the disarming smile she had come to dread. Beneath its mystic spell her senses capered dizzily. She was surrounded by danger, yet she had never felt such a burning thrill of excitement. Dimly she was aware of Sam's angry voice carrying to them from the hall below, but it somehow seemed far away and unreal.

'And it seems that I am to play the role of that viper?' He lifted a quizzing brow, his eyes dark and enigmatic.

Then as quickly his mood changed, and he tore off his sword-belt, placing it on a coffer by the side of the daybed. To her astonishment, he shrugged off his green leather jerkin, saying, 'Your collar... Remove your collar.'

She looked at him with horror. Beneath her collar, her gown was far too revealing. 'But that would...' She broke off, her throat cramping with embarrassment as he unfastened the ties at the neck of his own deep lace collar, revealing the swarthy skin beneath the fan of dark curling hair.

'Are we not supposed to be lovers?' His voice was taut, almost angry sounding, as he took her hand and guided her towards the daybed. 'Captain Melville is no fool. Would you have him guess this ruse for what it is, and send his men to search the bedchamber?'

She shook her head dumbly, appalled at what he now expected from her. She had imagined that just to be discovered alone with him in his chamber would be condemning enough, but he was expecting her to act the whore. She swallowed her disgust. He was right, curse his arrogance! How else could they convince the soldiers that no one was hidden in the other room? Her hands shaking, she fumbled with the tapes at her throat.

He brushed her fingers aside, saying softly as he unknotted the ties for her, 'You have nothing to fear from me.'

'Have I not, Major?' Her voice sounded oddly breathless to her ears. This was danger of a different kind. He was stirring emotions, heightening senses of awareness of her own body she had thought forever denied her since Thomas's death.

She steeled herself against the shock of the touch of his cool fingers sliding the collar across the warmth of her half-covered breasts, and closed her eyes against her shame. Her jagged nerves, instead of blotting out the humiliation, intensified the slow, seductive touch of the

lace gliding over her breasts. Shocked, her eyes flew
open. Their gazes linked, held and, without being aware
how it happened, she was pressed down on the daybed,
his arm sliding behind her back. A warning bell sounded
in her mind, but before she could pull free, it was unaccountably stilled. Something strange was happening
to her, something she had no power over and could not
entirely understand. Time was distorted, slowing, until
each sensuous moment stretched endlessly and the
sounds of the house blurred. Her hand trapped against
his chest felt the power and the heat of his body through
the fine linen of his shirt. She found she was waiting—
shamelessly wanting him to kiss her. Spellbound by the
desire shimmering in his ebony eyes, her lips parted invitingly. It is to save Godfrey Barcombe that I am doing
this, she stilled her nagging conscience. Why then did
she yearn for him to kiss her with a need that defied
reason?

For a moment he paused, then his mouth touched hers,
tantalising as a summer breeze. Then he eased back,
gauging her reaction, and as the first booted foot resounded on the stairs, he grinned, his voice ragged
against her ear. 'Never has duty been so pleasurable,
sweet temptress.'

The rogue was enjoying himself! Her sense of moral
dignity rebelled. His instincts of survival were those of
a trained soldier, but was his gallantry part of that role?
Resenting his easy mastery, she pulled back, her sharp
retort withering as she heard the soldiers on the stairs,
the first of the bedroom doors banging open. At any
moment the men would be upon them.

She tensed, too anxious at what was at stake to notice
that he had eased her resisting body down on the cushions
until the muscular solidity of his chest and thighs
partially covered hers. Then his hand slid down to the
hollow of her back, pressing her against him, and his
lips descended, imprisoning hers—no longer gentle, but

fiercely demanding. Her heart thundering in her ears
obliterated the gruff voices of the soldiers. Beneath his
lips, moving slowly down her neck, her flesh tingled,
ever-increasing ripples spreading out from the heat of
his mouth to set her blood aflame. Where his lips led
his free hand followed, tracing the hollows and contours
of her throat, their passage an exquisite agony, building
an indefinable longing deep within her. When his hand
traced the lower edge of her mask, she moved restlessly,
her hip rubbing against his. He drew in his breath
sharply, his hand moving to the neck of her gown,
drawing it off her shoulder.

Instantly she stiffened, conscious of the three coin-
sized scars disfiguring the top of her back. Too late she
tried to push him away, for his hand was already upon
the puckered skin. With a choked sob she twisted her
face into the cushion, her body rigid as she waited for
him to shy away with revulsion.

'Do not turn away.' Firmly, but gently, he took her
chin in his hand and forced her to look up at him. There
was no revulsion, or even pity, in his eyes. When he bent
his head, lightly kissing the tender skin, her eyes misted
with emotion.

'You are a desirable woman,' he murmured. 'Your skin
is soft and delectable and perfumed with the scent of
gillyflowers. Let not a paltry scar or two deny your
womanhood, for you are made for loving.'

She made to protest, but her words were silenced by
his lips playing over hers, their touch reverent, coercing,
until reality fled and she lay relaxed and pliant in his
embrace.

'Put your arms round me,' he urged hoarsely. 'When
Melville bursts in, he must believe that we are lovers—
or Barcombe will be captured and killed.'

Wide-eyed, she stared helplessly up at him. A taunting
smile lifted his full lips. There came the sound of
tramping feet overhead in the long gallery and in the

corridor outside other footsteps resounded closer, the angry shouts piercing her languor, making her remember their danger. The soldiers had found nothing incriminating—yet. If Barcombe was discovered, they could all be hanged as traitors. Their lives depended on her acting the wanton.

Woodenly, she wound her arms about his neck, his mouth again claiming hers with an expertness that scattered her reservations. His hold tightened, causing a flame to leap wildly through her blood like ignited bracken in a forest fire. It was wicked to feel this swirling ecstasy in the arms of a man who was not her husband. Or was it the danger which added to the excitement and set her heart racing? Then, even that thread of coherent thought was conquered as his kiss deepened. Her hands moved upwards, his long hair cool and silken as she ran her fingers through it before they locked behind his neck to bind him closer. She clung to him, a tremor pulsing through her body as a wild impulse overwhelmed her to succumb to the spell he was weaving about her.

The chamber door burst open, slamming against the wall. "Sdeath! What the devil is the meaning of this?' Captain Melville bellowed.

Blase sat upright, his body shielding Ruth's from the prying eyes of the soldiers. 'I ask the same of you, Captain!' he said haughtily. 'This is an outrage—bursting into a man's private chambers. Who is your commanding officer? He shall hear of this.'

'Will he, by God!' Henry spluttered, and beneath the steel face-guard of his helmet his eyes bulged with fury as he took in Ruth's dishevelled appearance.

Ruth pushed herself into a sitting position, concealing her half-naked breasts with an outspread hand.

'Cover yourself, cousin,' Henry raged. 'You shame our house.'

Ruth found her hand captured in strong brown fingers and raised to Blase's lips, the fine hairs of his moustache brushing her overheated skin and, even now, his touch was capable of sending a dart of pleasure through her. For a moment he held her gaze, his dark eyes sparkling with devilment as he handed her collar to her and stood up.

'Take care, Captain, how you speak to my betrothed.'

Henry blenched, then his face turned puce with indignant rage. Ruth's pleasure in his discomfort was short lived as the import of Blase's words sank in. Opening her mouth to protest, she caught the dangerous glitter in his eyes, and fell silent. Was this how he looked when he rode into battle? It was not only her reputation he sought to protect. It went beyond that. To what? Some score left unsettled between Captain Melville and himself?

With courtly grace, Blase raised her, his fingers again claiming hers as his voice rang out with warning. 'Well, Captain! I await your explanation for your disgraceful conduct.'

'You are not pledged to Ruth!' Henry spluttered. 'She is mine!'

'You presume too much, cousin,' Ruth held the collar decorously in place, painfully aware that the tenderness of her lips meant they were swollen from the ardour of Blase's kisses—as he had intended all to see. Had that been part of his plan for revenge upon her cousin? He had not struck her as a vindictive man, yet Henry did not appear to recognise him as an old adversary. What had happened between them? Whether misguided chivalry or vengeance had possessed him to protect her reputation in such a way—this time his arrogance had gone too far! Later she would deal with Major Drummond.

Clearing her throat, she spoke coldly, seizing the opportunity to undermine Henry's position and credulity. 'I never agreed to be your wife. I am my own mistress.' She placed her hand with an outward show of affection upon Blase's arm, but her eyes flashed with warning. 'I could not be forced into a marriage which is not of my choosing.'

'But you hardly know this man!' Henry eyed them malignantly. 'He's staying at the inn, and only arrived in Sussex three days ago. And now you talk of marriage! Do you take me for a fool?'

'You are not my custodian, Henry. I am of age, and free to govern my own life. And this is not a discussion to have before your men.' She looked meaningfully at the four soldiers standing behind her cousin, who were having difficulty in controlling their sniggers at their leader's discomfort. 'The hour is late. If Adam has no objections, my future is no concern of yours.'

'I make it my concern, cousin,' he growled, his be-ringed fingers pompously stroking his small beard. 'Where's that cur of a brother of yours? I have yet to question him as to why Lord Colbourne was found on your land. Colbourne did not travel alone. Three spies were reported in the district.'

'Adam rode into Chichester, and the storm has delayed his return.' Ruth countered stiffly. 'Just what did you expect to find by bursting in upon honest citizens with your soldiers?'

'If Adam is not here, I lay odds he's with those fugitives! He cannot escape justice. I know what treachery he dabbles in.' Henry looked round the chamber, and for a terrifying moment Ruth thought he would insist on the rooms being searched, but his hostility was directed at the Major.

'What's Drummond doing in Adam's rooms—apart from seducing you?'

'Take care what you say, Captain Melville,' Blase grated out. 'The storm prevented me from returning to the inn. I'll have no slur cast upon my future wife's honour.'

'You were being offered more than a room!' Henry laughed coarsely. 'I should know—cousin Ruth entertained me in her bedroom this morning.'

For an instant Blase fingered a ringlet of Ruth's hair, his expression forbidding. He was looking at her as suspiciously as he had looked at Adam the previous evening. Her temper flared. She had no need to prove her innocence to him, but her pride would not allow Henry's insinuations to go unanswered.

'My cousin forced his way into my bedchamber this morning with the same bad manners he has displayed now. My servant was in the room with us at the time.'

Henry snorted disparagingly. 'I recall that your brother was absent then and unable to protect your honour—as he is absent now. At such times, with how many men have you played the whore?'

'You insult my future wife, sir.' Blase stepped in front of Ruth, his hand closing over the sword-belt on the coffer. 'You will apologise, or answer with your sword.'

'I am an officer of the New Model Army. I do not brawl like a common soldier.' A sneer twisted the Captain's thin lips. 'And I do not apologise to any whore.'

'The devil you will!' Blase thundered.

Feeling the tension coiling through him, Ruth linked her arm through his to stop him unsheathing his sword. 'No, Blase, ignore him. He's deliberately provoking you.'

Her hand was roughly shaken off. 'He insulted you. Cousin or not, he will answer for it.'

Before her horrified gaze, Henry drew his sword, his pale eyes now alight with anticipation of a fight. She had to stop it. A duel would solve nothing and would result only in Blase's death or arrest. Inconsequentially, her heart ached that he should risk his life to defend her honour, but at once she quashed the rush of sentiment and rounded on Blase.

'My reputation is already in shreds. Would you make me infamous by provoking a duel? The village tattle-tongues will wag for a year over such spicy gossip!'

Seeing he looked as determined as ever to fight, she softened her voice. Her lips parted in a provocative smile. 'My love, what use are you to me languishing in prison?' She chose her words carefully, reminding him that Barcombe's escape was more important than her honour. 'Do our plans for the future mean nothing to you?'

He stiffened. Pride, anger and the primeval instinct of all men to uphold their sense of justice were carved into his lean countenance. His long lashes fringed his eyes, but when they again lifted to study Captain Melville, their expression was shuttered of emotion.

'Oh, consider carefully your future, sir!' Henry mocked. 'Whore or widow—Ruth will be mine.'

'By Hades, you'll rot first!' Blase snatched up his sword, starting forward. At the same moment Sam's angry shouts rose from the courtyard, the words drowned by Spartan's wild barking. Then every figure in the room froze as Hettie began to scream. The frenzied pitch turning to a thin terror-choked note brought back to Ruth all the horror of another time that the Roundheads had forced their way into Saxfield.

'Dear God!' she cried. 'Those foul beasts have Hettie!'

Everything happened at once with all hell seeming to break loose in the courtyard. Hettie's screams were demented. Spartan's vicious snarling intensified, then a man's shriek of agony and the now muffled growls indicated that the mastiff had sunk his teeth into a victim. Blase at the first sound of Hettie's shrieks had brusquely shoved Henry Melville aside and was running along the corridor, hotly pursued by Henry and his men.

Ruth looked uncertainly towards the inner room. She had to know what was happening below. Could she risk leaving Barcombe? A pistol-shot scattered her indecision, and lifting her skirts, she ran after the soldiers.

Hettie's screaming had stopped; the shouting continued, though, as did Spartan's barking. He must have released his quarry and from the sound of the neighing horses had turned his fury on them.

As Ruth reached the outer door, she saw Blase haul two men off Hettie's prone figure and lash into them with his fists, doubling one over with a blow to his stomach. Whirling round to face the second man, who was fumbling to draw his sword, Blase shot his hand out with deadly accuracy, crashing into the soldier's jaw, to slam him against the wall of the house. Before either of his opponents could recover, he brought up his sword to keep them at bay.

Ruth moved over to Hettie, but as Sam was already helping his wife to her feet, she turned her gaze upon Spartan. The mastiff was darting around the riderless horses' legs, snarling and snapping, making the animals prance and rear, until they broke free of the soldiers pulling on their reins and galloped down the drive.

'Don't stand still, addlepates!' Henry shouted at his men. 'Get after those damned horses!'

Spartan skilfully avoided Henry's outflung foot and loped back to sit at Ruth's side. Absently Ruth stroked the dog's head while looking across at Blase, who stood, sword drawn, but mercifully lowered, as he watched the soldiers running after the horses. After assuring herself that Hettie was shaken but apparently unharmed, Ruth turned her attention back to Blase and her cousin, and her heart contracted with returning fear. They stood like two bear-baiting terriers, bristling and ready to continue their fight.

If their situation were not so dire, she could have seen the funny side of the soldiers running after their horses and Henry stamping and shouting with frustrated rage. But Henry never forgot any slight or insult, and was not a man to be laughed at without seeking reprisal.

Although he deserved the trouncing Blase looked set to give him, she knew it would only make matters worse.

'Henry, tonight has brought one embarrassing incident after another,' she said with false sweetness. 'Diligent as you are in your duty, I fear you have sadly misjudged us.'

'I know what I saw when I walked into that room!' he spat.

'If you burst in upon people unannounced, you must expect to find more than you bargained for,' Ruth maintained. She cast a beseeching look at Blase, praying he would leave the matter as it stood. 'The least said about the incident the better,' she went on. 'You have embarrassed us all by your conduct, Henry. Despite that, I cannot forget that our fathers were half-brothers. Therefore, this time, I shall not report your disgraceful conduct to your commanding officer. Sam will saddle one of the coach-horses for you to ride.'

Sam walked with Hettie to the porch, and as his wife disappeared inside, he moved on towards the stables.

Henry shot out an accusing arm in Ruth's direction, unabashed by her contempt. 'If you think . . .' His voice dried as Blase moved protectively to her side.

'Are you threatening my betrothed?'

Henry stood his ground, the first drops of rain ringing hollowly as they fell on his helmet. He looked sourly from one to the other. 'In Adam's absence, I am protecting my cousin from an unprincipled adventurer. How much longer do you propose to stay in Sussex, Drummond?'

Blase smothered his anger. Later he would settle his score with this pompous ass. 'I am looking to purchase land here,' he said, smiling down at Ruth. 'Although I have much to keep me here at present, regretfully I must soon leave to look at some blood mares. But rest assured, Captain, I shall return.'

Ruth shivered. In the shaft of light from the open doorway, Blase Drummond's stare sharpened like jagged glass. The unmistakable challenge hung in the air between the two men. She rubbed her arms against the chill menace pervading the night air. Unexpectedly, Blase took her hand.

'Inside with you, my dear,' he said tenderly. 'I would not have you catch cold.' He led her back to the porch. 'Ask Hettie to fetch my things. I shall ride to the inn before the storm returns.'

She resented the way he was again taking charge, his hand resting familiarly upon her waist to emphasise their supposed role as plighted lovers. He was deliberately baiting her cousin. She was tempted to shake off his hold, but remembered just in time that she was supposed to be a semi-cripple and instead was forced to lean against him.

The clop of hoofs and Sam's arrival eased the tension in the courtyard. Henry heaved himself into the saddle and threw a bitter accusing look at her. 'Marry him, and you will be a widow before a week has passed!'

As he sped away, Ruth shrugged off Blase's hold and entered the parlour, knowing that he would follow her. Hearing Hettie clearing the table in the dining-room, she crossed to the door, her gaze anxious as it rested on the tiny bird-like figure.

'Are you all right? Did those knaves harm you?'

Hettie did not look up but carried on with her task, her trembling hands belying the calmness she was showing. 'I am well—just a little shaken. It proved a timely diversion, and I was unharmed. You had already done as much by...' Hettie started, knocking over a goblet as Blase loomed at Ruth's side. With a sniff of disapproval the maid glared at him. 'It was you I feared for, mistress, at the mercy of that...'

'Hettie! That will be enough of such talk! You are tired. We all did what had to be done. Leave the clearing away. I shall finish it when Major Drummond has left. Go to bed. It has been a long day. But first look in on Mr Barcombe—the poor man is still gagged.'

'You think of everyone but yourself, mistress,' Hettie scolded, still eyeing Blase with disapproval as she edged past him. She came no higher than his broad chest, but even his forbidding frown could not cower her loyalty. 'If that man had a grain of decency, he would do the honourable thing by you.'

Ruth laughed, its sound brittle in the low-ceilinged room, causing Hettie to look back at her from the door. 'Oh, he has, Hettie! But Major Drummond need not fear that I shall keep him to his declaration.'

Hettie shook her head. 'Heaven save you from the village elders, mistress! Those pious bigots will judge you cruelly.'

A tense silence followed Hettie's departure from the room which was broken by the harsh expulsion of Blase's breath. 'You cannot mean to refuse my offer? Your life will be intolerable here. Those soldiers will make merry sport of your reputation. If you remain unwed, you will be a target for every lecher in the district to force his attentions upon you.'

'Your offer was kindly meant, but I will not have any man wed me out of a misplaced sense of duty.' She tossed back her head. No man would dictate to her. He should be relieved that she had given him his freedom instead of glowering so angrily at her. 'Your gallantry and honour are not in question. I am sure you value your freedom as much as I, and I will not be shackled to a man who would wed me out of pity.'

Blase controlled the fury tearing through him. He had not made his offer lightly. An offer he had made to but one other woman…and had vowed never to make again. Sophia's falseness had cured him of romantic ideals. He took what women offered, giving pleasure but nothing of himself in return. He had no need to marry. His brother, who was also his business partner, had sons enough to continue the shipping line they owned. Nor would he have proposed to Ruth Melville merely to save her reputation, had she not sparked some chord within him. He could not stand by and allow her to be pilloried and thereafter shunned by the village women.

'I do not pity you,' he conceded. 'Why should I? You have the devil's own temper and a contrary disposition to match. I admire your courage. You deserve better than the fate that awaits you here.'

From beneath the mask, her eyes widened. Golden specks, like sunlight spangling leaves in a forest, lit their green depths, the anger of moments earlier fading. Her chin lifted obstinately. 'I will hear no more of the subject, Major Drummond.'

He smothered his exasperation. She stood, tall, proud and defiant. Whatever distortion to her features the mask hid, he knew it would make no difference to his decision. In France he had seen too many beautiful women sell themselves to the highest bidder: his own Sophia had chosen to be the mistress of an ageing French libertine rather than marry a penniless soldier. The vitality in the portrait of Ruth he had seen that first day at Saxfield was ingrained in his mind; to him, she would always be that beautiful wild spirit.

And it was that wild spirit which denied him now. He suppressed the urge to shake her, knowing that once he touched her, his need to make love to her would overcome all else. 'Then I shall speak to your brother.'

'You may speak with my brother, Major, but I assure you that in this I know his mind as well as my own. He will never force me to marry a man not of my own choosing.'

The mention of Adam Melville brought a return to sanity. He had almost forgotten why he had come to Sussex. So much of the evidence pointed to this woman's brother being guilty. Captain Henry Melville's visit had been no mere chance. Someone had informed him that Barcombe was here. Did that not make Ruth's future in Sussex even more precarious?

His thoughts broke off as Sam Rivers appeared, carrying his pistol, sword-belt and jerkin. He dressed quickly, and as he re-sheathed his sword, he saw Ruth holding out a thick black woollen cloak.

'Wear this, Major,' she said, 'You cannot ride out in such weather unprotected. At least the storm seems to be holding off.'

'Is that all you can say?' Blase fired back at her.

'There is nothing more for us to say. Your offer was generous and given with the best intentions, but I cannot accept. We are strangers. I will make no man a prisoner of convention to save myself.'

'Your pride will be your downfall,' he said darkly. 'However, I see no reason, since Captain Melville believes that we are to wed, to disabuse him of the knowledge, even though the actual event is unlikely to take place. It will give you some protection from censure from the villagers. Also, any visits I make to Saxfield will not be questioned. Barcombe must be got away as soon as he is strong enough.'

A becoming rose-tinted flush crept up Ruth's cheeks as she held his steady gaze. 'To that I will agree, Major Drummond. And I thank you for your consideration.'

She cursed the sudden leaping of her heart at his insistence. In his guise as her betrothed he could visit Saxfield frequently—that in itself presented a greater problem. He had not betrayed Barcombe, but that did not mean he was a Royalist...and he was deeply suspicious of Adam. Despite all that had happened tonight, she could not yet trust her brother's life to his hands. She must continue to play her dual role, and there must be no repetition of the familiarity with which he had treated her upstairs. That had been for the benefit of cousin Henry. She held out her hand, her voice coldly formal. 'I bid you Godspeed, Major Drummond.'

He took her hand and bowed over it, his lips warm and lingering as his dark enigmatic gaze held hers. Then he smiled, his stern countenance transformed by the provocative tilt of his lips.

'Tomorrow is Sunday,' he said, straightening but retaining his hold upon her hand. 'Ostensibly to accompany you to church, I shall ride to Saxfield in the morning. If Barcombe is fit to travel, arrangements must be made for him to leave tomorrow night.'

'I shall welcome your company at the morning service. It is unlikely that Adam will return until after midday.'

The cynical twist returned to his lips as he settled the cloak about his shoulders. 'Both Adam Melville and your neighbour Daniel Fowkes are adept at being far from any confrontation with the Roundheads when they are most needed.'

His statement was softly spoken, but the accusation behind his words struck her like ice. He had made no secret of his distrust of Adam and herself at their earlier meetings; did he now suspect Daniel Fowkes?

'Trust no one.' Adam's voice rang through her mind as clearly as though her brother were in the room, and it unnerved her. The bond of their birth, which somehow allowed her to interpret Adam's thoughts, was a phenomenon her mother had called the devil's work. Now it seemed that Adam was warning her. What if Blase had saved Godfrey Barcombe earlier, knowing that at any time he could hand him over to the authorities?'

'How easily you condemn, Major,' she said reprovingly. 'Your own habit of appearing and acting the knight-errant so close upon the Roundheads' heels could also be considered as too much of a coincidence. Some would construe that you are in league with them!'

'The devil I am!' His voice rang with affronted honour. 'I came to Sussex to ensure that no more Cavaliers would be played false. Fowkes is supposed to be for our cause, yet he turned Lord Colbourne from his house. As a result of that act, Colbourne was murdered by the Roundheads.'

'It is unjust to blame Daniel for that. If you are who you say, you would have investigated that incident. Therefore you know that a troop of Roundheads had billeted themselves at the Grange that afternoon. Where were you, sir, when Lord Colbourne was murdered? Are you not to blame for his death?'

Blase picked up his hat, his knuckles whitening as he gripped its brim before jamming it on his head, his voice gruff with barely controlled fury. 'I bid you goodnight, Miss Melville. I believe, tomorrow, the success or failure of Barcombe's escape will force every man, or woman, to show their true colours.'

CHAPTER NINE

THE NEXT morning was well advanced as Ruth hurried
to the parlour window, thinking she had heard a horse
upon the gravelled drive. It was deserted. She glanced
up at the cloudless sky and, lifting her veil, touched a
rosewater-dampened handkerchief to her neck and
throat. The cool relief was momentary in the oppressive
heat of the August morning. Her agitation mounting,
she looked across at the family coach waiting under the
shade of the oak at the far corner of the courtyard to
take her to church. Blase Drummond was late.

She clasped her hands together to still their nervous
movements. In another five minutes she must leave, and
it looked as though she must face the censure of the
villagers alone. She dragged her gaze from the empty
drive, her temper flaring. What was she doing standing
here as nervous as a lovesick maid just out of the school-
room? She did not want or need Blase's protection. The
strain of the past days was telling on her, culminating
in the near disaster of the Roundheads' visit.

With the implications and events of the previous
evening jostling through her mind, she had spent a
sleepless night and now her nerves were frayed almost
to breaking-point. She picked up her brother's clay pipe
which lay beside his favourite chair, and her heart twisted
with anguish.

'I need you, Adam. Never more so than now,' she
said raggedly. 'Where are you?'

Her thoughts were jolted back to the present by
Spartan's rising and padding out of the door, his ears
pricked and alert. She glanced through the window and

saw a lone rider approaching the house. It was Blase
Drummond. Her palms were suddenly slippery with
panic. Had she been a fool to believe his silvery words?
What had prompted him to offer her marriage? Not
chivalry! He was an accomplished gallant who clearly
enjoyed the company of women. Although bold in his
advances, his consideration of her feelings proved he was
not an inveterate rake, as were so many of the Cavaliers
who emulated the young King Charles in his pursuit of
Venus. With a start she realised how the turn of her
thinking was linking him with the king.

'Remember Adam's warning.' She spoke her thoughts
aloud. 'Trust no one!'

She watched Blase leap from his mount, pause a
moment to pat Spartan, then toss the reins to Sam, who
led the horse to the stables, followed by the mastiff. She
must remain on her guard. Blase had helped them last
night, but her overriding impression was of the hostility
he had shown towards Captain Henry Melville. Somehow
their paths had crossed in the past. And what of his
reasons for protecting her? If he were a government spy,
he would lose nothing by playing such a role. He could
pretend to be Ruth's friend and still take Barcombe
prisoner when they plotted his escape. By so doing, he
would also catch other Royalist sympathisers. Instinct
told her that he was no novice at this work. If she played
along with his schemes, she must be on her guard at all
times.

Hearing his deep voice exchange a greeting with Hettie,
a quiver of apprehension sped down her spine, and, adjusting her veil, she turned to face the door as Blase
strode into the parlour. He swept his hat from his head
and bowed to her. Used to seeing him in the worn leather
jerkin, she was disconcerted at the richness of his grey
velvet doublet and breeches trimmed with black and
silver braid. If he did live in exile, he certainly was not

penniless, for the lace at his throat and wrists was of the finest quality.

'Your servant, Miss Melville.' His gaze swept appreciatively over her black taffeta Sunday gown with its high neck and deep white collar.

Again apprehension rippled through her, and her cheeks flamed as she recalled the ardour of his kiss a few short hours ago. Stiffly she acknowledged his greeting, noting with relief Sam's giant figure in the hall. Hettie was at his side to help him on with the buff coat with its red-banded sleeves Sam always wore when he drove the coach. There would be no further liberties such as she had been forced to permit Blase the night before. Sam would protect her.

'Your pardon for my late arrival.' He raised a mocking brow at her frigid manner, his voice spiced with sudden menace. 'I learned this morning that Captain Melville has moved his quarters to an inn at Shoreham overlooking the river mouth. From the information I received, he intends to remain there to assist the government ship patrolling the coast.'

'Then another route must be found to get Barcombe away,' she replied, searching her mind for a plan.

Sam appeared at the doorway, his expression grave. 'Barcombe is too weak to ride. This is no time to be taking unnecessary risks.'

'You cannot afford to delay. Time is short,' Blase rapped out. The intensity of his glare seemed to strip away the grey veil beneath her high-domed hat as he continued harshly, 'Has your brother still not returned?'

Ruth moved to the table, where her cane and prayer-book lay ready. Taking them up, she schooled herself to show an outward calmness she was far from feeling as Blase fell into step beside her and they left the room. This was no time for argument. If they did not leave at once, they would be late for the service.

'We have dealt with such situations before,' she said coldly. 'My brother will not fail you. I expect his return within the hour.'

They stepped out into the courtyard, and as Sam held the coach door open, she laid a hand upon his arm, her eyes sharp with meaning beneath her veil and mask. A slight flicker of his eyelids showed her that Sam had seen her warning. While they were in church, he would check that Captain Melville was indeed now at Shoreham and also whether a government patrol vessel lurked in the coastal waters.

Ruth settled back on the velvet-upholstered seat, spreading her skirts wide to avoid too close a contact with her companion. To her dismay, instead of sitting to one side of her, he sat opposite, crossing his long legs and leaning back relaxed and at ease, as the coach rolled forward.

'Can you not dispense with your veil? Will it not seem strange to the villagers that you continue to hide your face from your future husband?' he disconcerted her by saying. 'Or are you hiding something more than your scars behind that veil?'

She controlled a bitter laugh, recalling her bruised cheek beneath her black satin mask. 'We are not unobserved,' she answered coolly, nodding to the family of farmers walking to church. 'My veils have protected many a Cavalier from the prying eyes of the locals. Would you have me discard such a ruse to appease your own suspicions?'

A slight twitching of his lips showed his amusement, but it did not reach his eyes. 'I have never doubted your loyalty.'

'But you do my brother's!' she bristled. 'And without good reason. In this, Adam and I are as one.'

'So you do deny that you are hiding something from me?' His expression was forbidding. 'You are too fervent in making excuses for your brother's absences.'

Ruth coloured self-consciously, glad of the veil to hide her confusion. Just what had he guessed? Her mind raced to defend Adam, but as she saw the unrelenting harshness of her companion's face, she felt an inexplicable need to justify herself in his eyes. The notion was as absurd as it was dangerous, and she turned her head to look out of the window, disdaining to rise to his baiting.

'Is it true that Godfrey Barcombe is too weak to ride?' Blase asked.

'The fever has gone, but it has left him weak.'

'If he sleeps the day through, will he be strong enough to travel?'

'That remains to be seen,' she said heavily. 'If not, his escape must be deferred.'

'No! It must be tonight.'

At his unremitting tone, Ruth gripped her prayer-book more tightly. A trickle of fear slid down her backbone. What was so important about tonight? Had he laid a trap for them? The doubts and suspicions returned in force. 'Barcombe is safe where he is. Saxfield has already been searched. They will not do so a second time—unless someone has betrayed us.'

'Do you discount that possibility?' he fired at her.

'No.' Her voice trembled. Looking into his handsome, enigmatic countenance, she did not want to believe he would betray them. Why, then, did he never answer a question openly?

'Barcombe must be moved,' Blase went on less curtly. 'My information is that Captain Melville has asked for reinforcements. It will be too dangerous to leave Barcombe another day.'

How reasonable his words sounded, but there was a guardedness about his expression that could not allay her suspicions. She was treading on thin ice. He knew too much of Saxfield's secrets. But Henry could order another search of Saxfield at any time, and if she refused to co-operate with Blase and he was the spy she believed, he would still have Barcombe arrested. This way, there was a chance that Barcombe would escape.

The coach drew to a halt before the village church, where another ordeal awaited. There would be little charity in the villagers' speculations surrounding the rumours of her betrothal. Blase opened the door and leapt to the ground. Lowering the carriage steps, he held out his hand to assist Ruth as she stepped on to the grass. A dozen or so villagers turned in her direction as they walked towards the lich-gate, where the Clerk, wizen-faced and stooped with age, waited to greet them. Ruth acknowledged his greeting and moved on as quickly as her pretended limp allowed. When several of the village women turned aside to avoid greeting her, the pain of their censure cut deeper than she had expected. A hot wave of humiliation stung her skin, adding to the discomfort of the suffocating veil in the hot sun.

'Pay the old hens no heed,' Blase whispered, squeezing her hand. 'You are worth ten of any one of them.'

After the friction between them in the coach, his unexpected compliment flustered her. She was saved from replying as they entered the coolness of the church porch, and the burly figure of the Rector, Mr Tilford, dressed sombrely in black breeches and coat and white linen bands turned to address them.

'May I introduce Mr Drummond?' Ruth deliberately avoided using his rank, knowing it would cause further speculation. 'Mr Drummond—Mr Tilford.'

'I believe we are to congratulate you on your good fortune, sir.' The Rector fixed them both with his short-sighted gaze. 'The news of Miss Melville's sudden betrothal has come as a surprise to us all. Considering the circumstances of its announcement, I trust you wish the banns to be posted immediately?'

Ruth stared at him aghast. 'There is no need for unseemly haste, Mr Tilford. Mr Drummond's family have yet to be informed.'

Blase's hand tightened over hers, his assured voice cutting across her faltering speech. 'My family is large. It is more likely that we shall be wed from my home.'

Mr Tilford's thin lips set primly. 'I protest, sir! If Miss Melville's father were alive, you would not be so dilatory in your duty. He was a God-fearing man, for all his misplaced loyalty to Charles Stuart.'

'Mr Tilford, you did not know my father,' Ruth replied briskly. 'It was Mr Waters who served our spiritual needs in those days.' She paused significantly, her own thoughts winging to the proud and dignified Rector who had been dismissed from the parish for refusing to follow the dictates of Parliament and change the familiar liturgy. For many an hour Mr Waters had been closeted with her father as they argued the various points of the service, her father preferring a simpler mode of worship. Yet throughout they had been friends, and her father would have been shocked at the way Mr Waters and his family had been cast out to fend as best they could. 'Had you known my father, you would know that I would do nothing to shame his name!'

'Your position at the Manor does not put you above God's judgement.' Mr Tilford spoke with icy deliberation. He drew an outraged breath to go on, but as his glance fell upon Blase's chiselled features, whatever he read in that ruthless expression caused him to clamp his lips shut and turn aside to greet another worshipper.

The Rector's warning rang through Ruth's mind as Blase led her into the small church. The usual fidgetings and murmurings of the congregation stilled, all heads turning in their direction, and the single word 'Jezebel' was muttered darkly as Ruth took her place in the Manor pew. She lifted her head proudly, staring back at the gathering, her flesh shrinking with unease at the hostility in the older women's eyes and the open leers upon the faces of several of the young men. Blase moved forward, turning his body sideways so that his broad back shielded her from the congregation.

Gratefully her gaze sought his and, seeing the tautness of his face, she smiled, saying softly, 'I appreciate your concern, but I must face these people some day. Better now and be done with it.'

'You will not face them alone. Not while I can help it.' His dark eyes flashed with the disconcerting gleam she had seen before. 'The Christians were dealt with more mercifully by the lions than the way those bigots would treat you. Even your so-called friends are ready to condemn you.' He gestured towards the opposite pew, where Daniel Fowkes and his family were settling themselves.

Ruth looked across the chancel, her greeting freezing on her lips. Daniel dipped his head as though embarrassed to acknowledge her, while his mother pointedly ignored her, and after a warning hiss at her three daughters, slapped the youngest girl's wrist when she smiled shyly at Blase. The four women remained engrossed in smoothing the skirts of their gowns until Mr Tilford climbed into the pulpit and all knelt with heads bowed for the opening prayer.

Ruth murmured the appropriate responses, puzzled that Blase was hesitant in them. His unfamiliarity with this form of service brought a crowd of questions leaping to her mind. The first that he was a Papist, she discounted, for no Catholic would set foot in a heretic church. So that meant that either he was not a regular worshipper, which was too shocking to contemplate, or he had not spent much time in England in recent years. Would not the latter prove him to be the king's man? Her heart leapt with momentary gladness, and she nudged his arm that extended the open book between them. Their shoulders touched as he leaned closer, their heads so intimately near that she could smell the fresh tangy scent of his skin. The words of the liturgy choked in her throat, her mind blanking out everything but the physical awareness his nearness aroused, his briefest touch sending a sizzling heat through her.

To stop the wayward path of her thoughts, she reached forward to replace the prayer-book on the ledge. It slipped from her nervous fingers to her lap, and fell open at the title page. Her eyes misted at the sight of her father's bold inscription, the ink already turning brown.

> *To my beloved daughter Ruth. Follow God's law and your conscience, and let no man lead you from the path of righteousness. John Melville, 1642.*

It had been her father's parting gift before he rode out to join the king's army when war with Parliament had become inevitable. Yet the words sprang at her now. Were they a recrimination or a warning? She had followed her conscience, but had she strayed from the path of righteousness by so doing? The words of the service dimmed in her ears. Wherever she looked in the unadorned church, which had long since been stripped of all its finery, she met accusation and condemnation in the eyes of the congregation. Even Daniel Fowkes looked sullen and ill at ease if she chanced to meet his glance.

All at once she realised there was a change in Blase's relaxed manner. He sat stiff-backed, his sharp profile rigid, and the black moustache drawn down over lips compressed with fury. Only then did the words of the sermon, which after an hour seemed no closer to drawing to an end, penetrate her wandering thoughts. Looking up at the pulpit, she, too, stiffened with outrage as she realised that Mr Tilford, his sallow cheeks flagged with high colour, was pounding the pulpit with one fist while his fanatical glare rested on the Manor pew.

'. . . and I say unto you, fornicators and their whores will be denounced. The ungodly will be driven from our midst. They are the instruments of Satan who would corrupt the innocent and...'

The Rector got no further. Blase rose to his feet, his deep voice resounding high into the rafters. 'This is no sermon, but a deliberate incitement to turn these people against an innocent woman. Sir, you shame God's house by spreading malicious lies!'

A shocked gasp went through the congregation at his audacity in challenging a preacher in his own church. Beneath her veil, Ruth's cheeks flamed, and she wished she could melt into the high back of the pew and disappear from sight. Mr Tilford's sermons regularly fulminated against women and the temptations of Eve who lured innocent men into sin, but today he had deliberately pointed at her.

'This is the Lord's house. I will not have it...' the Rector choked out, his face darkening, and he seemed about to suffer an apoplexy as Blase savagely cut across his protest.

'That is exactly why I speak. Where is more appropriate than the Lord's house to speak the truth? I tell you all now that these rumours are false, besmirching the good name of a virtuous woman who has honoured me by agreeing to become my wife.'

'Little choice you had in the circumstances, as I heard it!' a matron piped out.

'That's if he hasn't got a wife already,' a farm labourer said above the coarse laughter of his fellows.

'With respect to this worthy congregation,' the sardonic note was back in Blase's voice, 'I would no more give my name to a harlot than I would walk away from defending my honour, or that of my chosen lady. The virtue of Miss Melville is above reproach. Any man who says otherwise will answer to me. And I hold every man here responsible for the silence of his wife's tongue.' He turned to the pulpit and bowed to the Rector, his handsome face set and forbidding as he sat down, a stunned silence falling upon the church.

Mr Tilford cleared his throat several times, and then brought the service to a speedy resolution. Throughout the exchange, Ruth sat rigid with disbelief. In recent years she had sought anonymity behind her veils, and now Blase had made her the centre of attention and the most shameful speculation. Yet when she looked defiantly over the congregation, few people were looking in her direction. Had Blase Drummond truly silenced their condemnation?

The tight bud of tension that had been with her all morning unfurled, a chink appearing in the barriers she had sworn to erect against him. Had she not known him for what he was, she could consider his defence of her honour as vehement as that of any lover. He could afford to be generous: had she not told him she had no wish to marry? And that was true! So why had his speech caused her heart to beat so wildly? She must harden herself against his easy charm and remember that he was an expert in both his profession and the ways of the world, where she was but a novice.

Her troubled glance fell upon Daniel Fowkes in the opposite pew, and she was startled by the anger darkening her friend's face as he glared at Blase. A sharp word from Mrs Fowkes brought Daniel to his feet as his family filed out of their pew behind the Rector and Clerk, who were moving in stately procession to the west door. Blase took her arm to follow, and at the door the Rector mumbled a few inconsequential words to them, clearly unwilling to provoke Blase further.

Once outside in the bright sunlight, Daniel barred their passage to the coach. His mother and sisters were some distance away, speaking with the Rector's wife. 'A word, Ruth, if you please,' he said, glancing over his shoulder at his family.

'Anything you wish to say to my betrothed, Mr Fowkes,' Blase's voice sliced through the air like a sword-thrust, 'you may say before me.'

Ruth jerked her arm free, her voice laced with sarcasm. 'By your leave, sir, I shall speak to whom I wish. The role of jealous lover ill suits you.'

Immediately, Blase's expression became shuttered. Have I touched a raw nerve? she wondered. What woman caused him to erect such barriers against all others? Aware of several curious glances, she had no wish to provoke a scene. It was not her way to plead, but she felt she owed Daniel an explanation. Forcing a lighter note in her voice, she went on, 'Daniel is my friend. A few words is all he asks. Is that so unreasonable?'

'Your pardon, my dear,' Blase surprised her by demurring. He stooped closer, his breath rustling her veil as he said, for her ears alone, 'But even to a friend you would be wise to guard your words.' With that, he stepped several paces back, apparently absorbed in watching a flock of ducks flying overhead.

'I cannot believe it is true,' Daniel began, distractedly. 'You cannot mean to marry that man.'

At his stricken expression, she almost blurted out the truth, but something about his manner stopped her. Throughout her conversation with Blase he had refused to look in his direction. Why had he not stood up to Blase Drummond? A year ago he would have done so.

'Captain Melville's troop searched Saxfield last night,' she explained. 'If it had not been for Blase, Godfrey Barcombe would now be in prison, and so would I.'

Daniel paled, his blue eyes darkening with horror. 'Melville at Saxfield! But that could not be! I mean, surely he could not suspect *you*.' His voice took on a strange inflection, and he seemed incapable of holding her gaze. 'While Adam is away, you must let no Royalists into the house. And send Drummond away. He's up to no good. I don't trust him.'

'I shall do what must be done to save Godfrey Barcombe. I am indebted to Major Drummond for his actions last night.'

'Major Drummond, is it? In whose army, pray?' Daniel scowled. 'You have fallen prey to that rogue's charm. Can you not see that he has deliberately compromised you? Is it not strange that he's always around when there are Roundheads about? He's likely in league with them! Dammit, Ruth, I thought you had more sense than to be taken in by a handsome face.'

Unaccountably Ruth felt her temper rising and was defending Blase before she realised what she was about. 'I could not have saved Godfrey Barcombe last night. Major Drummond did, by his quick thinking.'

'Bah! Young Barcombe is small fish—he knows little,' Daniel sneered. 'What excuse did Drummond give about abducting Sir Robert? There's been no news that he is safe.'

Everything Daniel said echoed her own doubts, and suddenly she was again uncertain of Blase's motives. She looked across to where he seemed to be engrossed in reading an inscription on a gravestone, but she could sense the barely checked impatience as he glanced back at them.

'He has offered to help Barcombe to escape to France tonight,' she said worriedly. 'I have no choice but to trust him in this—he knows too much of our plans.'

Daniel fidgeted with a golden tassel on the pale lemon sash about his waist. 'How do you plan to get Barcombe away? The Roundheads are increasing their patrols. You cannot risk the river, and the beach is too open for a rowing-boat to put ashore undetected.'

Ruth nodded. 'Sam will have made the necessary arrangements. Although it means a longer ride, I expect we shall meet a boat at Broadwater Creek.'

'Then let Drummond go alone.' He sullenly studied the toe of his boot.

Ruth sighed, saddened at Daniel's apparent jealousy. They had always been friends, but it could never be more than that. 'I shall be on my guard.' She suppressed a shudder of unease, dreading parading as Adam. In the last days, Drummond had been with her often, so would her disguise be convincing enough? 'It could be that he is one of us,' she added, more to convince herself than Daniel.

'If that is so, why has he no knowledge that Adam was on that ship?' Daniel pressed. 'Especially if your brother was carrying information to the king of those ready to fight for him in Sussex.'

The midday sun beat down on her head and shoulders and the air was suddenly stifling behind her veil. Just as she had begun to convince herself that Blase was not the government spy, Daniel was telling her that he was. How neatly Blase had trapped her! He had found her at her most vulnerable and had not hesitated to strike. The yew trees interspersed amongst the gravestones began to dance and weave in an exotic rhythm, She fought for breath, but the veil was smothering, and to her horror she felt her body begin to sway. Instantly a strong arm was clamped about her waist, the familiar deep voice gruff against her ear.

'You have talked long enough. Ruth is tired,' Blase snapped. 'As a friend, you show little consideration for her needs. I suppose you were safe at home when she was in peril yesterday?'

'How could I know that Saxfield would be searched?' Daniel was sweating in the hot sun. 'I would give my life for Ruth. I was sure Saxfield was safe.'

'Daniel has his mother and sisters to consider,' Ruth intervened, making excuses for Daniel's jealousy which was making him act so strangely.

Several people were wandering in their direction, their glances openly curious. The Rector's wife, her thin face prim with outraged propriety, was bearing down upon them, looking like an angry coot in her black gown and plain white linen cap. In the heat, Ruth was in no mood to listen to whatever lecture Mrs Tilford would deem it her duty to inflict. Leaning more heavily upon Blase's arm, she gave way to her exasperation.

'If you two have differences to settle, pray do so at a more appropriate time. We are being watched, and I have no wish to encourage further gossip.'

Daniel touched his hat to her, his leave-taking stiffly formal as Mrs Tilford's shrill voice set Ruth's nerves jangling.

'Miss Melville! If you please, I must speak with you.'

Ruth resignedly turned to face her, and without pausing she launched her attack. 'Really, you must see that a wedding must take place without delay.'

'I am touched at your concern in the interest of my betrothed,' Blase intervened, sweeping his hat from his head and bowing to Mrs Tilford. 'But only the guilty wed in haste. I trust that my sentiments and the high esteem in which I hold Miss Melville will be conveyed to the other gracious ladies of the village. I will not have the villagers counting upon their fingers the months until our first child is born.'

'Oh! I did not imply... I mean... We never thought...that she was...!' Mrs Tilford came to a flustered halt, her thin body giving a pious shudder.

Ruth had never known the Rector's wife at a loss for words, and the woman had many a time reduced many a burly farmer's son to shamefaced submission. Now, seeing her mortified expression, Ruth bit her lips to still her amusement. Although she resented Blase's domineering manner in the church, she now reluctantly admired the bold way he had turned the tables on their accusers.

Before the shocked stares of the older villagers, Blase took Mrs Tilford's hand and raised it to his lips, his smile at its most disarming. 'It grieves me that I must

leave Miss Melville so soon after our announcement, but
I shall rest easy, knowing that her reputation is guarded
by so worthy a woman as yourself, dear lady.'

To Ruth's astonishment, instead of Mrs Tilford's
blasting Blase with her tongue, she smiled, her long thin
face softening and, when he released her hand, it fluttered with almost girlish confusion to push a stray wisp
of hair into her cap. Had Ruth not seen it with her own
eyes she would never have believed it possible that Mrs
Tilford was capable of simpering beneath a man's
flattery. Blase had completely won her over.

When they were again settled in the privacy of the
coach, she lifted her veil and could no longer control a
chuckle. ' For shame, sir,' she admonished him as the
coach set off. 'You have completely put Mrs Tilford out
of countenance!'

He tipped his hat further back, and his black eyes
regarded her steadily. 'Not so you, sweet Ruth. You did
not approve of my declaration in the church, but it had
to be done. At the very least, the Rector would have
demanded that you spend a morning in the stocks, if
not that you be whipped publicly as a wanton.'

'Thank you for sparing me that,' she acknowledged
with a shiver. 'But it will be harder now for us to extricate ourselves from this arrangement.'

Blase lifted a dark brow enigmatically, the husky
timbre returning to his voice. 'Then, my dear, I must
remedy the situation to your satisfaction.'

Her breath stilled expectantly in her throat. His words
sounded more like a challenge than a reassurance. She
held his gaze, her pulse quickening in anticipation of
pitting her wits against his.

'To begin with, you could tell me something of
yourself. Times are not easy for the king's supporters.
You spoke of your years in France—but before that,
where was your home?'

'I lived in Bristol.' She sensed his withdrawal, even as he continued flatly, 'But since our house, together with the other properties my father owned, was either fired during the siege or sequestered by the government, my parents have now settled in France. We lost everything.'

'Then how did you live?'

His brow darkened at her persistence. 'My father was a merchant. He imported spices from the east, Venetian glass, Chinese silk—he had contacts all over the world. Some years ago my sister married one of these—a French banker. My parents live with them on a small pension provided by her husband.'

His story echoed that of so many of her father's friends...if he spoke the truth. After Daniel's insinuations, she could not afford to take anything Blase said at face value. 'Did your father not resume his business?'

A spasm crossed his face. 'A week after he arrived in France, he suffered a seizure. He has been partially paralysed ever since. Does that satisfy your curiosity?'

'I am sorry that your father was so stricken.' She refused to back down from the coldness of his tone. He did not want to talk of his life in France. Although she could understand his not wishing to speak of his father, as to the rest of his time abroad, if he had nothing to hide, why should it trouble him? 'To be honest with you, Major, it does not. Until a few days ago, we had never met. Now you know the secret of Saxfield, and expect my brother to entrust Godfrey Barcombe's life—indeed all our lives—to your protection.'

'How well you cloak a woman's curiosity with common-sense.'

Despite his taunting, his voice hardened, warning her that he disliked being questioned. Undaunted, she persevered, knowing that they would shortly reach the Manor and he could take his leave before she could question him further. 'Your own career was surely ex-

ceptional. You must have earned your rank at a re-
markably young age?'

Blase rested his elbow on the carriage window,
thoughtfully running his forefinger across his moustache
for some moments before he answered. He had put those
years of disillusionment behind him. Instead of anger,
his admiration for Ruth Melville grew. Only a fool would
put his life on the line to a virtual stranger. He gazed
into the almond-shaped eyes looking up at him from
beneath the tilted brim of her hat, and his usual reservations crumbled.

'I was nineteen when I joined Prince Maurice's troop.
Most of us were young, hot-headed and inexperienced.
Like our commander, we sought to emulate his brother's,
Prince Rupert's, dashing cavalry. The battles were
bloody—our officers leading the charges were struck
down like flies. I was promoted to captain after Edgehill
and major three years later at Naseby. After our defeat,
I followed my parents to France.' The dozen images
evoked by those words leaped into his mind: the twisted
face of his father, his mother's frailty, the debauchery
of the exiled courtiers. Sophia—beautiful, beguiling and
so treacherous. Damn her wanton hide! He crushed the
vision, the images flashing on in time to the battles he
had fought as a mercenary until the sight of blood and
death had sickened him.

The coach bumped over a rut as it turned off the
chalky track into Saxfield's drive. His expression
hardened, his tone sardonic. 'Those were misspent,
wandering years, without purpose.'

Ruth digested his words in silence. There was so much
he had not told her, but she wanted to believe him. It
was the same story so many of the Cavaliers told, but
her misgivings would not give her peace. A government
spy would long ago have perfected such a background.
This had just the right touch—his father's affliction had
roused her sympathy. He had been modest in outlining

his exploits in battle, and the hint of wistfulness about his supposed years of exile would melt the sternest heart.

Through the coach window, Ruth saw Hettie waiting by the entrance porch. Her suspicions concerning Blase were not so easily allayed. To add to her confusion, he was expecting to meet Adam when they returned from church. She smothered a sigh at another round of deception she must play. She had just witnessed the ease with which Blase could twist a formidable woman like Mrs Tilford round his finger, and to her chagrin, last night had proved that she herself was far from immune to that lethal charm. All the more reason to pay heed to Daniel Fowkes's warnings.

CHAPTER TEN

THE COACH drew to a halt, and Sam had barely time to open the door for them to alight when Hettie hurried forward. Blase stepped out of the vehicle, looking askance at the maid's apparent distress.

'You have just missed Master Adam.' Hettie wrung her hands in her large white apron. 'He stayed only long enough to change. He conveyed his regrets to you, Major Drummond, but said you would understand that there was not a moment to be wasted if he was to arrange for a fishing-vessel to take Mr Barcombe on board tonight. He will be back before nightfall.'

Ruth could have hugged Hettie for her quick thinking, but from Blase's tight-lipped expression he was far from pleased. Curtly he asked Sam to have his horse brought from the stable. At a nod from Ruth, Hettie disappeared into the house and as Sam drove the coach through to the stableyard, she continued the lie Hettie had begun.

'I am sorry Adam could not wait, but as you have been so quick to point out that he is dilatory in serving our cause, I trust his prompt action has your approval?'

'It has, providing, that is, he has indeed gone to secure a passage to France.'

Must the man question everything? He had shown clearly enough that he had little confidence in Adam, or, rather, her impersonation of Adam. Unaccountably that hurt. She had done nothing in that guise to earn his censure. Possibly Adam would have acquitted himself better in the fight when Drummond had abducted Sir Robert, but spy or not, Blase by then was already showing suspicions concerning her brother. Dare she follow her instincts and trust him?

It was on the tip of her tongue to tell him the truth: that Adam had been shipwrecked. But her dual role had become so interwoven, and her need to protect Adam too ingrained, to be discarded so easily. From deep inside, as though Adam were in the courtyard with her, she heard him cautioning her—'Trust no one.' Adam was alive and lying injured somewhere—she could feel it. The bond of twinship could never be severed without her feeling that part of herself had withered and died. The bond had weakened when she had felt that strange floating sensation, but at night before she drifted into sleep, it was still there, quickening, growing stronger with each day. To protect Adam, she must say nothing.

Blase Drummond rode back to Saxfield Manor in the gathering dusk, his mind troubled by doubts. Would Adam Melville be there? The man had been damned elusive these past days. On nearing the house, he saw two horses saddled and waiting and quashed his disparaging thoughts. Tonight he would learn, without doubt, how loyal Adam Melville proved to be.

A light was snuffed from inside the entrance hall and moments later the slim figure of Adam Melville appeared, his body stooped under the weight of Godfrey Barcombe, who was leaning heavily against his shoulder.

'At last we meet again Mr Melville,' Blase commented drily. 'Do we make for Broadwater Creek, as your sister suggested in your absence?'

'We do, sir.'

Blase mastered his irritation at the way Melville kept his hat pulled low down over his face and refused to look directly at him. At seeing how unsteady Barcombe appeared on his feet, he rapped out, 'Barcombe will ride behind me while you lead the way, Melville.'

Adam Melville seemed to stiffen at the sharpness of his tone, but made no protest. He was nervous, and apparently spineless—all the signs of a turncoat. When Sam Rivers ambled out of the Manor towards the second horse, Blase's hold upon his temper slipped.

'The servant remains,' he ground out. 'Would you leave your sister unprotected again? Good Lord, man, it is no thanks to you that she's not incarcerated in Lewes Gaol for giving refuge to a Royalist!'

Servant and master exchanged a long look. The giant stared at Blase, his great fists clenched with anger. Blase checked his disdain. He had witnessed Sam's fierce protectiveness towards Ruth. Did Adam also expect the servant to take up his fights for him?

'The Major is right, Sam,' Adam Melville said in a voice rather too emphatic to ease Blase's rising distrust. 'I doubt the Roundheads will return, but for their own safety my sister and Hettie should not be left alone.'

Ruth steadied her apprehension as Blase settled Godfrey Barcombe in the saddle behind him and brought his horse level with hers. His expression was forbidding. The difference in his manner towards her as a woman, which had been courteous and considerate, and now in her guise as Adam, was proof of the distrust in which he regarded her brother. The next hour or so would not be easy. She despised having to take a subservient role, knowing well that Adam would have spoken out. For every word she uttered she had to deepen her tone. If she allowed her temper to rise, her voice would betray her.

Following the tense interchange, they rode in silence, and all the while, Ruth felt Blase watching her every move. Did he plan to jump her and ride off with Barcombe as his prisoner, once he had identified the fishing-craft? She maintained her guard as she led them in the fading light. After the heat of the day, the mist clung damply to her loosened hair, and she was glad of

the warm worsted jacket and breeches borrowed from
Adam's room. She halted at the edge of the trees at the
foot of the South Downs. Ahead stretched the flat plain
leading to the pebble beach. Scanning the grey ribbon
of sea, she could see the fishing fleet setting sail from
Shoreham, a cluster of tiny dots in the distance. To her
relief, there was no sign of the large government lugger
patrolling the coastline.

'All goes well, so far,' Drummond commented drily.

Ignoring him, Ruth looked anxiously at Godfrey
Barcombe, who was hunched over with pain.

'God willing,' the young man gritted out, 'it is not
much further.'

'Not far,' Ruth encouraged. 'Look! Against the
skyline a mile west from here you can see the square
church tower of St Mary's, Broadwater. The vessel is
sheltering in the creek.'

They moved on westwards, hugging the base of the
grass-domed hills as the darkness closed in. Absorbed
by the shadows, they stole through the mist, becoming
part of the night itself, until Blase suddenly snatched at
her bridle, pulling her horse to a halt. He held a finger
to his mouth, gesturing silence. She tensed. Was this the
moment she had feared? Her hand closed over her pistol-
butt, but he made no move to attack her, merely studying
their surroundings. The mist obscured the overhanging
willows, ghostly apparitions that could conceal a troop
of Roundheads lying in ambush. It looked deserted, but
just visible was the outline of the small fishing-craft.
Ruth shivered in the chill air. There was no sound, no
movement, yet something intangible was warning her of
danger. She started when a duck flew up from the reeds,
squawking in alarm. Had a fox disturbed it, or a human
form? She followed suit when Blase drew his pistol, but
the only sounds to disturb the night were natural ones.

Blase walked his horse forward, beckoning for Ruth
to stay close at his side. Her glance darted all about them.

They were so close to success that they could not fail now. Suddenly a pale face rose out of the reeds.

'Have you come to try your hand at fishing, gentlemen?' The man gave the password.

'A large catch for deep waters,' Ruth replied appropriately.

'Then make haste, sirs. The mist is dispersing and the moon uncomfortably full.'

The fisherman unlooped the mooring-rope and leapt aboard. Blase dismounted, threw his reins to Ruth to hold, and helped Barcombe to the ground. When the wounded man swayed unsteadily, he heaved him over his shoulder and carried him to the boat. Settling him in the prow, Blase jumped back on shore and pushed the vessel away from the bank as the sail unfurled and filled with wind.

'May the Lord speed them safely to France,' Ruth said, watching the small craft make its way seawards.

'Amen to that.'

Blase took the reins Ruth handed to him, his expression less harsh. She relaxed—her fears had been groundless. Then, as he turned aside to mount, the stillness was shattered by the crashing of horses through the high meadow grass.

'They're getting away! Fire on that boat!'

Ruth recognised her cousin's voice from further up-stream. Blase leapt into the saddle, and together they made a wild dash towards the trees, the last of Captain Melville's words almost lost amid the pounding of horses' hoofs.

'You men spread out, I want the men who helped them to escape!'

Behind, Ruth heard several shots. They were firing on the fishing-craft. Dear God, let Barcombe get away! she prayed. Then a shot, much closer, warned her that she, too, was in danger of capture.

'Make haste, man!' Blase shouted. 'This way!'

Crouching low over the saddle, she instinctively obeyed his authoritative tone and urged her horse to keep up with his black gelding as more shots were fired. They had reached the edge of the trees when her mare shuddered, pitching her forward on to her neck as she stumbled. Her cheek slammed against its shoulder and, to her horror, Ruth felt the hot stickiness of blood. Her mare had been shot! Already she could feel the animal weakening, and the thundering of hoofs behind was closing by the moment.

'Drummond!'

Her cry was cut short by a gasp of shock as the mare suddenly crashed to her knees. Reaction made Ruth kick her feet free of the stirrups and she leapt to the ground before the horse could roll on its side and crush her. She stood up, shakily. The mare was dead.

'Quickly, up behind me!' Blase thrust a gloved hand towards her. She gripped it, his strength hauling her upwards as she sprang on his mount. Giving her barely time to adjust her balance, he set off at a furious pace, the Roundheads almost upon them.

At least there were no further pistol-shots, as the Roundheads were too intent on running them down to pause to reload. To stay on the horse, Ruth had no choice but to keep her arms round Blase's waist as he wove the horse in and out of the trees. Although the sound of pursuit was further away, it was still nail-bitingly close. From the crest of the hill, just perceptible on the sea was the outline of a small craft. Thank God, Godfrey Barcombe was safe!

As they sped on down into a narrow coombe between two hills, it seemed that at last they were gaining on the Roundheads. She sat stiffly behind Blase, their legs rubbing together as they rode, each contact of his steely muscles against her inner thigh sending a spiral of heat curling up to the pit of her stomach. His broad back was disquietingly near to her cheek and the impulse to

lay her head against those strong shoulders almost overwhelmed her, but she fought against it. She was acting
with the instinct of a woman, whereas tonight all her
thoughts and deeds should be a man's.

Despite her resolve, her physical awareness of him
became more acute. Twice now he had saved her from
certain arrest. The impulse to confide in him and lessen
the burden of secrecy she carried was a temptation becoming harder to resist. How close they had come to
losing their freedom tonight! Too close!

She tensed, an insidious thought breaking through the
spell Blase was again creating. How had Henry known
where to look for an escaping Royalist? Had it been coincidence, or had they been betrayed? But by whom?
Only three people beside the fisherman and herself knew
of their plans—Sam, Daniel and Blase. No! She would
not believe it of any of them. Especially Blase—not now.

'We shall never escape the troop riding double,' he
said over his shoulder, scattering Ruth's confused
thoughts. 'Our only hope is to jump, and trust that the
horse leads them far from us.'

Ruth studied the oval outline of the hill ahead. Their
flight had taken them to the outer ramparts of the Iron
Age fort of Cissbury Ring. Rising to her right in the
valley was the four-gabled tower of Sompting Church.

'Swing round towards the church,' she suggested. 'If
we are to jump, there is a curve in the track just ahead.
The slope is covered with bushes.' She braced herself as
they pounded round the bend and Blase slackened the
gelding's pace.

'Jump!' he ordered.

Hearing the Roundheads close on their heels, Ruth
flung herself from the horse, her heart leaping to her
mouth. Fiery agony shot through her shoulder as she hit
the ground and began to roll down the steep slope, the
hilt of her sword digging into her hips. When she col-
lided with a bump into a blackthorn bush, the prickles

scratching her face went unheeded as the pain seared her shoulder. A yard to her right, she heard Blase roll to a stop. Gritting her teeth to prevent herself crying out, she lay still while the Roundheads rode on without faltering, following the riderless horse.

She let out her breath in a rush, and a gasp of pain was torn from her lips.

'Up on your feet, man,' Blase said tersely, towering above her.

'I—I cannot.' Ruth cursed the high pitch of her voice. 'My shoulder...'

'Have you been shot?' She tensed as he knelt at her side. Her hat had come off in the fall, and he was peering at her pain-twisted face intently.

'No,' she answered raggedly.

'Stay very still.'

Stripping off his gloves, he ran his fingers along her shoulder. The pain was excruciating.

'You've dislocated your shoulder,' he said, less harshly, his expression taut and unfathomable in the moonlight. He took a kerchief from his jacket and held it against her mouth. 'Bite on this. When I push the joint back into its socket, it will hurt like Hades.'

She did as he bade, knowing that a scream would bring the Roundheads back. He gripped her arm in one hand and placed the flat of his other palm against her chest. Briefly it pressed against her full breast and a flicker of shock crossed his lean face before his palm moved upward and his other hand rotated.

Ruth bit down as a firebrand seemed to gouge into her shoulder.

'Ruth!' Blase gasped, his voice sounding far off.

Then mercifully there was darkness.

Blase stared at the unconscious woman in his arms, incredulity giving way to an inexplicable anger at the danger she had placed herself in. Then, as quickly, that too dissipated into wonderment as he gently brushed back a tendril of hair from her brow, his fingers encountering a ridge of scar tissue going back into the hairline. He frowned at the livid bruise on her cheek, but there was no other disfigurement on her heart-shaped face. The pale moonlight played over her high cheekbones and long slender neck. She was more beautiful than the portrait, ethereal and beguiling. No wonder he had thought Adam Melville effeminate! It was *her* he had met on each occasion. Memories crowded back, appalling him. He had been scathing, demeaning her remarkable courage. An iron band constricted his chest when he recalled that he had nearly run her through during their sword-fight! Yet, even then, something had stopped him.

Her eyelids flickered open, alarm sparking at him. His hold tightened, pushing her back on the grass when she struggled to sit up.

'You little fool! Are you trying to get yourself killed? Why are you impersonating your brother? Where the devil is he?'

'I wish I knew.' Her voice broke, the first sign she had shown of any weakness. She hesitated, lowering her gaze, indecision flickering across her face as she fought an inner battle. With a shaky sigh she looked up at him, the words seemingly dragged from her lips. 'I believe he was on a ship that was sunk by a government vessel in the River Severn. Adam is alive... It's like a sixth sense we have between us, which tells me that. He's wounded, though, or he would have returned.' Unshed tears sparkled in her eyes like crystals and her hand was trembling as she raised it to her brow and inhaled deeply. Fearing she was about to faint, Blase lifted her into a sitting position, his arms locked about her waist. Her chin tilted defiantly as she forced herself to continue. 'I could not turn the Royalists away from Saxfield. And I learned during the war between king and Parliament that men do not take kindly to entrusting their lives to a woman. It is not the first time I have done this.'

Instinctively Blase checked their position before answering. They were well hidden by the tall stems of the wild flowers. Should the Roundheads return, it was as good a hiding-place as any. 'I suppose you did not trust me enough to tell me of this before.'

Her silence was more condemning than words, but she did not look away. A slight tremor shook her body, her mouth parting tantalisingly as she breathed, 'You did not hide your contempt for Adam. How could I be sure you were not using me to trick him? It was not merely to buy land that you came to Saxfield. What kind of a man would tie himself to a scarred cripple, if it were not for gain?'

'Scars that are not as you would have us believe,' he told her.

Ruth drew a quavering breath. He had moved closer, his hold about her tightening as he spoke in a seductive whisper. 'You are more beautiful than your portrait, yet beauty is but a shell. Nothing could equal or dim the fierce spirit lighting your eyes. You belittle your charms, my dear.'

There was bitterness in his tone, and she wondered fleetingly what woman had made him so cynical. Above his dark head, dozens of stars shone like diamonds on black velvet, and the scent of wild honeysuckle filled the air. Her breathing stilled. Danger sharpened her senses, her pulse racing now that the need for pretence was over. Her fingers coiled about his arm, absorbing his strength and vitality. She should push him away and stand up, but captivated by the intensity of his appraisal, she was powerless to move.

'Beauty, wit, courage, innocence and honour,' he said hoarsely, moving her sword aside where it had fallen between them. 'A potent combination, my sweet warrior. You never cease to amaze me.'

With a sinuous twist of her body, he drew her across his lap, a low sigh sounding deep in his throat. He gathered her close, her breasts pulsing with an aching fullness as they were crushed against his solid chest, and his lips caressed hers with a tenderness that sent the blood clamouring. She clung to him dizzily, heedless of the dampness of the grass soaking into her clothing. The strength of his arms and the hardness of his figure as he lay across her brought a new and exciting warmth to her body while the kiss lengthened and deepened profoundly.

'You are an exceptional woman,' he said softly, drawing back. His expression enigmatic, he took her hand and kissed it, then rose in a single fluid movement to his feet, raising her to stand beside him. 'Too much a woman to hide yourself away, or parade in men's clothing. It is time you discovered your own capabilities, sweet Ruth.' He grinned rakishly. 'But, regrettably, this is not the time or the place to convince you.'

His kiss had held such sweet promise, but his words were a blatant challenge, plunging her into deeper confusion. It frightened her that he could so bedevil her senses. She had witnessed the way he manipulated other women, and *she* would not be so used! Besides, the distrust, although alleviated, was still there between them.

'And, no doubt, you see yourself as the very man to teach me!' Instead of the scathing set-down she had meant to deliver, her words sounded oddly breathless.

'Are we not betrothed? A situation I find more agreeable as each day passes.'

She wished her heart would not somersault so wildly at the intimation behind his words, and to defend herself against the emotions he aroused, she went back on the attack. 'You have not told me what brought you to Saxfield. There was a time when I thought you were a government spy.'

When he shot her a fierce look, her heart plummeted. Had she been right all along—was he the spy? Then his expression cleared and he gave a low chuckle. 'As *I thought* your brother had been betraying our cause. It seems I must now seek my quarry elsewhere. That is why I came to Sussex. To discover who is betraying us.'

How desperately she wanted to believe him, but she made herself continue cautiously, 'It is a question that has troubled Adam for some weeks.'

'Why did your brother sail north?'

Ruth tensed at his leading question. Yet, in the circumstances, was it not natural enough? Impatient at her inability to judge him for what he truly was, she gave in to her instincts and growing need to trust him. 'He had no intention of doing so when he left the house that evening. He was guiding two Royalists to a ship. But it would not be the first time he has discovered information that must be passed on without delay.' She paused to draw a deep breath, her legs and lungs aching from the steepness of the hill they were climbing. 'Adam was waiting for word of the numbers who would support the king when his Majesty's standard was raised in England.'

'Such information is vital.' Blase nodded gravely. 'And in order that your brother's absence is not commented upon, you pretend to be him.'

'Until now, the ruse has worked well enough.'

'Which says much for your ingenuity and play-acting! It was you who planned Barcombe's escape. What deception will you surprise me with next, I wonder?' A spate of pistol-fire from the coppice towards which they were headed ended their conversation. 'The troop at the creek could never have guessed that our route lay in this direction,' Blase said darkly. 'We were betrayed!' His voice broke, and he took a step forward, his face twisted with such fury that Ruth backed away in alarm. 'I should have guessed!' he raged. 'You're the spy!'

His hand moved to his sword-hilt as another shot from directly behind her drowned the rest of his accusation. She spun round, expecting to see the traitor. No one was in sight. 'It's not true,' she said, turning back to confront Blase. To her horror, there was a dark line vivid against the paleness of his wide brow as he swayed and, knees buckling, crumpled to the ground.

For a moment she was too stunned to move, but he did not rise. When she threw herself on her knees, cautiously touching his head, her fingers came away tacky with blood. He could not be dead! Frantically she touched his throat, and sighed, feeling the pulse beating as strongly as ever. But he did not stir, and she peered closer at the wound, which, although long, was not deep—that chance shot had knocked him unconscious. Her anger at his accusation withered as fear replaced her shock. How badly was he hurt? She had to get him to safety. She stiffened at a nearby sound, then drew her sword.

'Ruth!' a hushed voice called out from some way in front of her. 'Are you there, Ruth!'

'Daniel?' she answered, disbelieving her ears.

He appeared from behind the rocks. 'Praise God! I have found you and you are unharmed.'

'Blase has been wounded.'

Daniel cast a cursory look at the fallen man. 'Do not waste your sympathy on him. He planned for Adam to be captured tonight.'

'That's not possible! Blase saved me when the Roundheads shot my horse from under me.' Ruth defended him stoutly. 'Barcombe is safely away. Blase is not the government spy.'

'Blase—Blase!' Daniel interrupted sharply. 'All I hear is Blase. He's bewitched you. I know what I saw this afternoon in the village tap-room. Drummond was speaking to Sergeant Carter from your cousin's troop, and very secretive he looked, too!'

Ruth shook her head, refusing to believe what he was saying. 'He is not a traitor, Daniel! Help me to get him to safety.'

'I will not lift a finger to save this treacherous dog!' he spat. 'If he did not betray you, who did? Who else knew of the plans tonight?'

Disillusion started to take over her perplexed thoughts. Surely Blase had not betrayed them, not after that tender moment on the hillside? But until then, he had believed she was Adam. Why then had he saved 'Adam' when her horse had been shot? Her head reeled. With all her heart she wanted to believe in Blase, but Daniel was right. Who else had known of their plans for the escape? Indeed, had Blase not insisted that the escape must be *tonight*? Daniel had risked everything to protect her, so why should he lie? He was her friend.

Daniel's dark cloak had fallen back, the moonlight clearly picking out his pale yellow and gold tasselled sash as he glanced anxiously at the ridge of the hill, his voice urgent. 'I followed you tonight, suspecting something like this might happen. Did you really think I would allow you to ride into danger and not help you? We must make haste. The Roundheads are combing the far side of the hill and they will be upon us at any moment.'

'I will not leave Blase,' Ruth protested stubbornly. 'Whatever he is, or has done, he always treated me with honour and has twice saved me from being arrested.'

'Good Lord, Ruth, what does it take to convince you? We shall all be arrested if we stay here. If that stray shot from the Roundheads had not struck him down, I would have shot him myself. He was leading you into a trap.'

'No, he was not,' Ruth said emphatically, her heart aching as she looked down at Blase's still figure. 'He was doing all in his power to save me. He would not betray me—not after what he said.'

'Said what?'

Ruth's eyes misted, her voice too choked to answer as she knelt at Blase's side and, taking his hand, willed him to regain consciousness. His wound had stopped bleeding, and her hand lingered upon his brow as she sought to blot out the suspicions Daniel had rekindled. Blase had lost no opportunity to question her about Adam's movements. She snatched back her hand, clenching it with disgust at her naïvety. How close she had come to giving her heart to this rogue!

'So, that's the way of it!' Daniel fumed. 'You have begun to care for that heartless scoundrel. And tonight he saw through your disguise. Well, I suppose even he has scruples when it comes to sending a woman to hang. Not to mention becoming a laughing-stock among his companions because you had duped him for so long. It's Adam he wants, not you.'

There was an angry shout from the far side of the hill. 'Spread out, fools! They cannot be far away.'

Ruth shivered, recognising Captain Henry Melville's impatient voice. 'I will not leave Blase to fall into their hands. He will be at their mercy.'

'He's one of them,' Daniel scoffed. 'They will not harm him. To take him with us will slow us down. Drummond is too valuable to them—they will take care of him.'

'But he helped Barcombe to escape,' she persisted.

'And, by so doing, won your confidence. How else would he gain access to others who work for the cause?'

She could hear the tramping of feet perilously close on the other side of the hill, but still she hesitated to leave Blase to their mercy. Too much of what Daniel said made sense. Deceit and seduction came too easily to Blase, she had seen that for herself, so why should his manner to her be any different? She was just another woman to be charmed and won over. Had he not proved his deceit by this last accusation against her? He had actually thought she was a turncoat!

'Think of Adam,' Daniel whispered impatiently. 'Your loyalty is to him, not to this traitor! If you are caught, dressed as your brother, you condemn him, and Saxfield will be lost. Henry Melville will be triumphant.'

But what if Blase were innocent? She continued to be tortured by doubts. It would be impossible to carry him away now without all three of them being discovered. At least if she were free, and Daniel had been mistaken, there might be a chance to rescue him if he were taken prisoner.

'Make haste!' Daniel urged. 'Do you want us to get caught?'

Swiftly she pulled off her own dark cloak and laid it over Blase's still form. That would protect him from the cold, and the Roundheads would probably follow them when they heard them escaping.

'For Adam's sake I shall go with you, Daniel. Lead on!'

'My horse is hidden in the thicket yonder.'

She stumbled after Daniel in the darkness, stopping once to look back but was unable to see any shape that looked like a man lying on the ground. She should hate him for the way he had tricked her, but the gnawing ache within her breast was not hatred.

Blase stirred, and clutched at his head, a fiery, vicious pounding seemed to split his skull in two. He blinked several times to clear his blurred vision. Ruth! The memory of their last moments together flooded back. Shock and realisation had made him speak without considering his words. She was in danger! He dragged himself on to his elbow. She was nowhere in sight. Gruff voices carried to him from a short distance away. Melville's men! He was too groggy to risk a confrontation with them tonight, and dazedly he cast about for a means to escape, but the hill was almost bare of cover. When he tried to stand, the pain in his head made him

grimace and fall back. Those rocks would be the first
place they would look, but one of the boulders jutted
out just above the ground, and the gap should be large
enough for a man to wriggle under. Wrapped in his cloak,
he might pass detection. He touched the second cloak
placed over him. The look of horror on Ruth's face when
he had issued his challenge returned to plague him. Yet
still she had left him her cloak for warmth.

The pain in his head was making it difficult to reason
as he hauled himself along the ground. The soldiers were
almost at the ridge. He had to reach the shelter of the
overhanging rock.

CHAPTER ELEVEN

'MISTRESS RUTH, wake up!' Hettie gasped, still in her nightgown as she hurried into the bedchamber.

'What's amiss?' Ruth raised her head from her arms, startled to find she had dozed as she sat by the window during an interminably long and anguished night. She stared across the dark room, puzzled that Hettie carried no candle. Wrapping her robe about her chilled figure, she grimaced at the soreness in her bruised shoulder. The sky was lightening, but it was not yet dawn.

'Have you not been to your bed?' Hettie shook her head, concern for her mistress momentarily diverting her. 'Little good it will do to worry over that rogue Drummond! Mr Fowkes is below and in a rare taking. Not like his usual self at all. He insisted to Sam that you came at once.'

Ruth sprang to her feet, hope flaring in her breast. She was half-way to the door before she realised it was unlikely that Daniel would bring her news of Blase. 'Is Mr Fowkes alone?'

'Yes, and friend of the family though he is, I trust you do not intend seeing him in your nightrobe,' Hettie said, groping for a gown on its hook in the closet.

Ruth moved to where a candlestick stood on a coffer and picked up the tinder-box.

'No lights, mistress,' Hettie warned. 'Mr Fowkes was most particular that no attention should be drawn to the house. He came to the kitchen door below our bedroom window, drawing Sam's attention by giving the secret bird-call Master Adam always used. Once Sam admitted him, he insisted on setting Spartan loose in the grounds to give us warning of any prowlers.'

Alarmed, Ruth threw off her robe and stepped into the gown, her fingers drumming on her hips as she impatiently waited for its back to be laced. She almost waved aside the mask and veil, but years of caution made her take them up, although she did not put them on.

'Mr Fowkes is in the kitchen,' Hettie surprised her by saying as they hurried to the back of the house.

Ruth froze in the doorway, her fear intensifying at Daniel's haggard expression. He sat forward on the wooden settle, his elbows resting on his knees as he stared down at his hands hanging despondently between his parted legs.

'Daniel! What has happened?'

He was on his feet at once, his face clearing. 'Ruth, my dear, there's news of Adam at last! He was found unconscious on the banks of the River Severn by a servant cutting rushes, and was taken to an apothecary's house in Tewkesbury, which fortunately is sympathetic to our cause. Apparently he was feverish for some days and they had no knowledge of who he was.'

Ruth beamed, her voice shaky with relief. 'That's wonderful news, Daniel.'

He crossed the floor to look gravely down at her. 'Adam cannot travel. He cracked several ribs, and a night in the river left him weak with a fever.'

'Then I must go to him. He needs me.'

'It's too dangerous. I shall go, of course. I stopped here first to put your mind at rest and let you know he is safe.'

'If Adam is wounded, how will you get him home? We cannot keep his absence secret much longer. Major Drummond knows everything. What if he discovers where Adam is? He was insistent upon our betrothal to suit his own ends, so now we can use that against him and get away. Blase's family lived in Bristol. All I need are papers to say I am travelling to Bristol to be married.'

Daniel looked at her sharply. 'I would have thought you would wish to forget everything about Drummond, but what you say makes sense. There's a man at Shoreham who forges papers.'

Ruth threw her arms around Daniel's neck and hugged him. 'You have never failed me, my friend.'

His pale eyes glittered with a disturbing fervour, and self-consciously she stepped back as he said, 'Not only shall I save Adam, but I shall convey the information he learned to his Majesty. I learned this evening that the king and a Scots army of some 12,000 men have marched across the border. Two days ago on the ninth of August, Carlisle was occupied.'

'Then indeed we must not delay! If Blase were to learn the names of the Royalist supporters here, they would be imprisoned before they could join the king.'

Daniel moved to the door, saying curtly, 'I shall return within the hour with the necessary papers. Be ready to leave.'

'Daniel!' she called after him, unable to hold back the question that had been plaguing her all night. 'Have you heard whether Blase was captured?'

He glared across at her, and his voice quivered with rage. 'From what I hear, the Ironsides took no prisoners. It is as I expected: they had no quarrel with Drummond and could afford to let Barcombe go. His escape meant that Drummond could safeguard his cover, and thereby still be able to enter Royalist households and betray them. I have spread the word to others to warn them of him.'

Sick at heart, Ruth threw herself into preparing for her journey. She had dreaded hearing that Blase was a prisoner or, worse, dead. That he remained free could only confirm Daniel's words. And she, naïve creature that she was, had fallen for his expert persuasion. He

had spoken easily of his background—perhaps too easily.
Had it been a carefully rehearsed speech? He knew she
would have no way of checking his story. And how
poignantly she had fallen beneath his spell—had even
allowed her guard to slip and allowed herself to believe
that he cared what happened to her. It was all lies! Where
torture would have failed, a lop-sided smile and a hint
of promise in ebony eyes had broken her resistance, and
she had told him everything of Saxfield's secrets and her
brother's involvement with the Royalists. How soon
would it be before he sent someone to discover Adam's
whereabouts and arrest him?

'Curse you, Blase Drummond!' she gritted out through
her agony. 'Should our paths ever cross, I vow you shall
never again betray our cause!'

Blase stared furiously at the shuttered windows of
Saxfield Manor. Several minutes' banging on the door
had aroused no warning barking from the huge mastiff,
and a search of the stables had shown that the coach
and horses were gone. Saxfield was deserted. Fowkes
had something to do with this, he was certain! Yet,
knowing Ruth as he did, he was convinced of only one
thing that could at this moment have driven her from
her home: she had learned of her brother's whereabouts, and he needed help. He returned to the inn where
he was lodging.

The landlord bustled out, grinning lewdly. 'Why, Mr
Drummond, I did not think to see you back here for
some weeks. It is the talk of the village that Miss Melville
has left to meet your family in Bristol before your
wedding in a few weeks.'

Blase's expression was stony. Had the wench deliberately tried to make a fool of him? The bitter memory
of Sophia's betrayal speared him, making his tone sardonic. 'I shall join my betrothed on the road tomorrow,

for I still have business to conclude here and the coach travels slowly.'

'Not the way they were speeding.' The landlord laughed coarsely. 'According to Sergeant Carter, who checked their papers at Bramber Bridge, she looked in a desperate hurry to be wedded and bedded!'

Minutes later Blase was in the saddle and galloping towards the Grange, where a haughty major-domo informed him that Mr Fowkes was not at home. At Bramber Bridge Sergeant Carter, still on duty, told him that Ruth and her brother had been travelling in the coach, but that the maid-servant, Hettie, was going only as far as her sister's farm a mile further on. They also had a three-hour start on him. Ruth and her brother? What game was she playing now? He would wager a year's income that Daniel Fowkes was the one behind those veils. He should have seen the danger earlier and taken steps to prevent it.

For hour after hour, Blase pressed his flagging horse on until the tired mount stumbled and, checking its pace, he grimaced at the pain shooting through his temple. His head pounded from his wound but it was not the agony of that which gave him no peace. Did Fowkes not know that every mile of the roads to Bristol was infested with parliamentary troops? Each mile would take Ruth further into danger.

He knew that her brother's ship had been sunk in the River Severn as she tried to slip up-river past Gloucester. Ruth had made it clear she had no intention of becoming his wife, but she had not hesitated to use his name and family to gain her own ends. His mouth turned down cynically. He had thought her different, yet she was as treacherous as Sophia had proved. It would not happen a second time, for in the eyes of the world, Ruth Melville was promised to him. He must overtake her. Once past Bristol, she would need new papers, but that would not deter her. Then he must discover the where-

abouts of Adam Melville and learn what information
had been so important to take him from Sussex. Blase's
eyes narrowed. There was also Fowkes to be dealt with.
He was a weakling. If the odds turned against him, he
would go only so far to save Ruth...

By noon the next day, when he clattered out of the
courtyard of a roadside inn five miles past Winchester,
he knew he had missed their departure by less than a
quarter of an hour. As he came on to the road, he
swerved abruptly to avoid being ridden down by a galloping rider.

'Damn your eyes, man!' Blase growled. 'You'll kill
that horse and yourself riding like that!'

'Major D-Drummond!' the red-faced rider stam-
mered shame-facedly. 'Corporal Pyke at your service,
Major. Lord Woodford recognised you when you rode
through Winchester and sent me after you.' The young
soldier went on, fumbling in his jacket and producing
a crumpled piece of parchment, 'Orders, sir.'

Blase scanned the document, his eyes lifting regretfully to the road ahead where Ruth was so close. Duty
came first, and with Cromwell's army assembling at
Coventry in preparation to meet the Scottish invasion,
he could not ignore this summons.

For Ruth, the coach journey to the apothecary's house
in Gloucestershire seemed endless. Over the next four
days they were stopped and searched every few miles.
Even Sam's expert driving could not prevent their being
forced off the road by a large detachment of Roundhead
troops with their accompanying baggage train, and the
resulting broken wheel had delayed them for half a day.
Once out of Sussex, where it was unlikely that Daniel
would be recognised, she resumed her role behind the
veils while he impersonated Adam. At Bath, a further
day was lost while Daniel procured new papers before
they could continue to Tewkesbury.

Although she was impatient to be at her brother's side, each mile they travelled from Sussex intensified the ache in her heart for Blase. From their first meeting she had been aware of him in a way that no other man had affected her, and now his absence gave her no peace. However much she might rail against him—she loved Blase Drummond! A love that must be conquered, for she would never allow her feelings for an enemy to place the cause at risk. Better for her heart to be broken than for England to continue to suffer under Cromwell's yoke.

Daniel muttered an oath just below his breath, dragging her thoughts back to the present. 'That's your fourth sigh in as many minutes,' he commented sourly. 'You're thinking of Drummond, aren't you? After all he's done, you still wish he was at your side and not me.'

'I could not have made this journey without you,' she prevaricated. 'I'm worried about Adam.' She broke off, frowning, as the coach rattled past a village green where yet another troop of buff-coated Roundheads were watering their horses at the pond. 'Cromwell's Ironsides are everywhere.'

'They are reinforcements. After the king's success in the skirmish yesterday at Warrington bridge over the River Mersey, it is likely he will make a bold dash on London. But we, too, need every man, since the recruits are not being raised as hoped for.'

'And I am keeping you from joining them.'

'Time enough,' Daniel shrugged. 'If Adam is too weak to travel, I must be certain that the information he carried has been delivered to those concerned. Naturally, I shall join his Majesty's forces as soon as I am able.'

There was a stiffness about Daniel's manner that left her uneasy. Of course he would be eager to join the king's army! Her troubled gaze returned to the coach window. In the near distance the pinnacled tower of Gloucester Cathedral rose majestically over the tree-tops. Before nightfall, the good Lord willing, she would be reunited with Adam.

Fate at last was with them, and by late afternoon they were travelling along the riverfront at Tewkesbury. Ruth, having earlier discarded her mask, swept back her veils and stepped down from the coach, her heart racing with excitement and apprehension as she entered the dark interior of the apothecary's bow-windowed shop. What would she find within? Would she even be welcome? Daniel's hand on her elbow was warm and comforting as he waited at her side. Rows of labelled bottles stood on shelves, and the air was sweet with the scent of herbs and a host of exotic ingredients she could not put a name to.

Behind the high counter, a pretty dark-haired woman a year or two older than Ruth put down her pestle and, wiping her hands on the large apron covering her russet gown and heavily pregnant figure, looked up enquiringly, her eyes widening. 'I am Mary Willetts. You must be Ruth—your likeness to Adam is astounding!' She smiled warmly and nodded to a pimply young apprentice to take over her task, before stepping from behind the counter. A dimple appeared at the corner of her mouth, and her brown eyes, bright as a mischievous spaniel's, dispersed Ruth's fears that she might be imposing. 'I shall take you to your brother. He's resting and is still weak, but with each day he grows stronger.'

'Thank you, Mary, but I fear my coach is blocking the street. I must first send my servant to take rooms for us and Mr Fowkes at an inn.'

'If my husband were here, he would insist that you and your servant stay.' Her face darkened. 'But I regret there is no room for Mr Fowkes.'

Daniel stepped forward, all smiles. 'I would not dream of it, Mistress Willetts. After I have spoken to Adam, I must join the king, who has need of every man.'

'You will stay and eat with us, of course, Mr Fowkes?' Relief showed behind Mary's bright smile. 'My husband has been called to a meeting,' she lowered her voice meaningfully. 'It is to raise money for his Majesty.'

Ruth nodded to Daniel to give instructions to Sam about the coach and horses. Removing her cloak, she handed it to a red-cheeked maid before following Mary through the shop into a comfortably furnished parlour and out of a side door leading to a high-walled garden. A rose-arbour festooned with yellow and red flowers was bathed in sunlight, where a man sat reading.

'Adam!' When he heard her cry, he looked up and, with a delighted shout, laid down his book. He rose to his feet, his shoulders slightly hunched against his pain as Ruth ran into his arms, careful to restrain her welcoming hug, but even so he winced beneath his breath.

'Come and sit down; you should be resting,' she admonished him gently, her anxiety growing as she saw the bandage about his tawny locks.

Adam took her hand and led her to the bench, but not before she had caught the grin he exchanged with Mary. 'My nurse insists that my crown remain bandaged, although the wound has healed well enough.' He dismissed her alarm. 'The best medicine I could have is the sight of you, dear sister!'

Frowning, she touched his gaunt, pale cheek, but meeting his forthright stare, she smiled and ran her fingers across a flourishing light brown mustache. When he pulled her close and kissed her brow, the tickling sensation was a disturbing reminder of the touch of Blase's mouth. Her face-muscles stiffened under the strain of holding her smile, and she forced a light note into her voice. 'How fortunate that you had not cultivated so fine an appendage before you left Saxfield, for I would have failed lamentably in impersonating you!'

His green eyes darkened with concern. 'You have been in danger—I could feel it once the fever left me. Dear God, Ruth, I have never felt so weak and useless!'

A snort of laughter from Daniel came from behind, 'Together we triumphed over danger—did we not, Ruth?'

Adam shot an accusing look at his friend, his expression hardening. 'What possessed you to allow my sister to travel the roads at such a time?' he raged. 'And in this danger... Was Saxfield used as a safe house while I was away?'

Ruth had never seen her brother turn upon Daniel in such a manner. She gripped his hands, her chest constricting as she sensed something deeper than the constant pain which was eating into Adam. There was uncertainty and, more puzzling still, hostility towards his friend. Why?

She spoke quietly to reassure him. 'Daniel has proved himself a worthy friend. I was set upon finding you, and he was kind enough to offer me his protection. Since you left, much has happened in Sussex. Cousin Henry has returned, and he is more determined than ever to see you convicted as a Royalist sympathiser.'

'Your sister's life was in danger at Saxfield,' Daniel said stiffly, the tension again flaring between the two men. 'If Captain Melville were not enough to contend with, there was a government spy poking around, and Ruth had a wounded Royalist in the Manor.'

'Tell me of this spy, Ruth?' Adam insisted.

'I was suspicious of the stranger at first, but later, when all seemed about to be lost, he did everything in his power to help me.' She drew a shaky breath, each word dragged painfully from her aching breast. 'He saved me from imprisonment when Henry raided the house. I see now it was but a ruse to win my trust, and that he was hoping to learn more which would condemn others.'

'The man's name?' Adam demanded, his almond-shaped eyes cat-like as he glared at Daniel.

'Major Blase Drummond,' Daniel snapped.

Adam passed a hand across his temple, irritably pulling off the bandage to reveal a fist-sized yellowing bruise and a jagged barely healed cut. 'Well, Daniel, was Drummond of that lowly, despicable breed who spy on those who trust them?'

Daniel fidgeted with the tassels of his wide sash for a long moment before answering, and did not meet Adam's stare. 'Ruth omitted to tell you that she is promised to Drummond. Captain Melville caught them in compromising circumstances when he was searching Saxfield for the Royalists. She is infatuated with the scoundrel.'

She was about to challenge Daniel's words but, noticing how darkly circled with pain Adam's eyes had become, she deferred. Now was not the time to pursue the matter. She had come to Tewkesbury to speed her brother's recovery, not to weaken him with worries for her safety. 'You exaggerate the matter, Daniel,' she said determinedly. 'Adam is tired. He should rest. Mistress Willetts will not thank us if we undo all her good work.'

'Ruth is right, my friend,' Daniel declared warmly, placing his arm about Adam's shoulders. 'You must recover your strength. I leave at first light to join his Majesty, but first,' he looked apologetically at Ruth, 'I must speak with Adam.'

'I, too, would like some moments alone with Daniel,' Adam intervened before she could protest.

Ruth looked pointedly at Daniel. 'Pray do not overtire my brother.'

Inside the kitchen, she found Mary Willetts preparing some mulled wine. 'My husband has returned and awaits you in the parlour.'

Ruth paused at the door of the inner room. Nicholas Willetts looked more like a prosperous city merchant than the apothecaries she had ever seen, who were usually pale and stooped from long hours mixing potions. Although some ten years his wife's senior, he was sandy-haired, bluff and hearty, the high colour across his cheeks showing his fondness for wines and ales.

'Come forward, Miss Melville,' he beckoned. 'We have heard much of you. I suppose you have come to take your brother home, but it would not be wise for him to travel for another week at least.'

'I have a coach, sir, for I would not have our family a burden upon you.'

'Talk not of burdens! Mary has little chance to relax and enjoy another woman's company. We are honoured for you and your brother to stay as long as his ill-health requires.'

An angry shout came from outside, and as Mary and Ruth moved as one towards the window overlooking the garden, Ruth saw Daniel striding angrily towards the house. She ran out into the passage to block him, her glare questioning as he stormed through the house.

Daniel inhaled harshly. 'That wound to your brother's head has addled his wits! He will not entrust me with the names of those who will support the king in the south. The information is vital. These men should be summoned at once!'

'Let me talk to Adam,' she begged. 'We have all been under a strain of late, but we should be together in this, as we have in all things in the past.'

He looked over her shoulder to where Adam leaned heavily on the doorpost, glaring at him. 'Give my good wishes to Mistress Willetts, but I shall take my meal at the inn.'

'Mary!' Nicholas Willetts cut through the interchange. 'Help Adam to his room. He should rest for an hour before we dine.'

Daniel left the house, and Mr Willetts drew Ruth aside as Mary helped Adam to the stairs. 'Every care must be taken that your brother suffers no relapse.'

Ruth nodded, and when Adam spent a night again beset with fever, Daniel was denied visiting him before he left Tewkesbury. With Daniel gone, Adam's fever abated. When she challenged him over his argument with Daniel, he shrugged her questions aside, his expression hardening as he stated flatly that a messenger had already ridden south. Ruth was saddened by the growing rift between the two friends. There was no disputing that Daniel had changed since his father's death, his once easy laughter replaced by an excess of fanaticism for the cause. He was obsessed with knowing every last detail of their plans. She sighed, wondering why Adam was not more sympathetic towards his friend. But he, too, had changed: the fever and constant pain from his injuries frayed his patience and there were times when she tried to call upon the strange power that gave her insight into her brother's feelings, only to find him somehow blocking it. What was he keeping secret from her?

Fussed over by both his sister and Mary, Adam grew stronger each day. The Willetts took Ruth and Adam to their hearts, and a week sped by with Ruth cocooned in a sheltered world far removed from the danger of the previous days. Only when Adam questioned her about Blase did a nagging uncertainty pierce her emotions. She evaded his probing with a frivolous banter that belied the emptiness of her heart.

The fragile shell of her cocoon burst abruptly when Nicholas Willetts burst in upon them from the shop, his face crimson with outrage. 'The king has been denied entry into Shrewsbury! The army rides to Worcester.'

Adam sprang to his feet, his tone resolute. 'His Majesty has need of every man. I must join him.'

'No!' Ruth cried. 'You are not strong enough.'

'While I breathe and there is strength in my sword-arm, I will not fail our Sovereign.' He turned to Nicholas Willetts, ignoring Ruth's protests. 'I thank you and your family for all you have done, but it is time for us to leave. I, to the king, and my sister to return to Sussex.'

'With respect, Master Adam.' Sam Rivers came to the parlour door from where Adam's raised voice had carried to him in the kitchen. 'Putting aside the question of your own health, Mistress Ruth faces ridicule and possible arrest at Saxfield. She needs your protection.'

Nicholas Willetts raised a silencing hand. 'Ruth is welcome to stay here, but Adam is right. The king needs every man. I shall prepare a pain-killing potion for him if he is determined to fight.'

Ruth strove against a rush of panic—loyalty to the king and sisterly devotion tearing through her. 'If you go, so do I. I have proved that I can fight as well as any man!'

'You have done your part, Ruth,' Adam said fiercely. 'Stay here with the Willetts and I shall return when I can.'

'I shall not!' Ruth clenched her fists with rage. 'I have the right to fight. Am I less his Majesty's subject than you?' She drew herself up to her full height, her eyes burning with fury. 'And do not dare to insult me by saying I am but a woman. I would rather die for what I believe in, than live a prisoner shackled by these long skirts.'

Adam wiped his hand across his brow, then held it out in submission. 'I know the folly of arguing with you, once your mind is set! Retire early, for we leave at dawn.'

The crow of a cockerel roused Ruth from her sleep, and she scrambled from the bed. Pulling on the breeches and doublet she had worn when she first fled Sussex, she snatched up her sword-belt from her travelling chest and, carrying her deep-cuffed boots, crept down the stairs to meet Adam.

'Good morning, Sam.' She smiled at the servant eating a chunk of bread at the kitchen table. 'Is Adam not down yet?'

'He's gone, mistress. He left last night after you fell asleep.'

'Gone! Without me!' Ruth dropped her boots with a thud on the floor, her eyes wide with disbelief. Impotent fury raged through her. Adam had lied to her—tricked her into staying! 'I will not be treated like a child! It changes nothing. I shall follow him. Adam is still weak—he may have need of me.'

'He loves you and would know you are safe,' Sam counselled.

'Your servant is right.' Nicholas Willetts spoke from behind her. 'A battleground is no place for a woman. The horrors of Edgehill and Marston Moor still haunt me. Adam is proud of your courage and bravery, but he would spare you that.'

She spun round, her throat working against the agony clawing at it. 'Adam is all I have. As he is so set against it, I shall not fight, but I must be near him. Do not fear for my safety. I know how to protect myself, and I shall have Sam.'

'And what of Saxfield? Does that mean nothing to you?' Nicholas Willetts questioned.

'If the king's cause be won, Saxfield will be safe. If Cromwell triumphs, Saxfield will be lost to us.' She glanced beseechingly at Sam, willing him to support her. He nodded resignedly, and she went on with greater fervour. 'You know our story, Mr Willetts. Should I return unwed and Adam remains absent, they will know we duped them. My cousin will seize the chance to have my brother attainted of treason.'

'Adam warned me that you were strong-willed. The king is heading towards Worcester. If I cannot dissuade you, I can at least give you a note of introduction to Elizabeth Willetts. She is my cousin's widow and, never being blessed with children, she will welcome your company. She lives in Glover Street, Worcester.'

Ruth stared out of the coach window at the passing countryside, her spirits at their lowest ebb. The farewells to the Willetts family had been harder to make than she expected after so short an acquaintance. Her days with them had been happier and more carefree than she had thought possible in these troubled times, and she had been able to cast aside her disguises. The close unity of family life had shown her the emptiness of her own existence, making her more determined than ever that Saxfield would again prosper. The king must regain his crown . . . only then could she dispense with her disguises for good and consider marrying and raising a family.

The unexpected path of her reasoning startled her. Since the fire she had been resigned to spinsterhood, indeed the thought of marriage and the curtailment it would bring to her independence had left her cold. Blase had changed all that. Unbidden, the image of his lean, swarthy face filled her mind, his ebony eyes aglow with sultry promise. There was an animal sensuality in every line of his powerful body, drawing her inexorably like a lodestone. She gasped, her heart suddenly feeling that it had been squeezed dry. Blase did not care for her—he had manipulated her and then betrayed her. He was her enemy—she must learn to hate him! The taunting vision of his handsome face could not be banished, mocking her words, but she would never be so deceived again by any man, especially by him.

CHAPTER TWELVE

As THE coach rolled down the steep slope of a wooded hill, Ruth leaned out of the window. Before her the high city walls of Worcester rose stark and defensive, their stones scarred from the sieges of less than a decade earlier. Above them the cathedral dominated the skyline, and Ruth's pulse quickened as they sped through the gate. 'The faithful city', Adam had once called it. It was less than three miles from here at Powick in 1642 that the first encounter between Royalists and Roundheads had occurred. Now, nine years later, both armies were converging here. Throughout the troubles, Worcester had remained fervently loyal to its Sovereign, and Ruth caught the air of excitement rippling through the streets as the people again prepared to honour their king.

The coach halted before an overhanging timber-framed house in Glover Street, and Sam jumped down to help her to alight. The front door opened, and a short plump woman looked askance at Ruth as she stepped from the coach.

'Are you Elizabeth Willetts? I come from your cousin, the apothecary in Tewkesbury. I need somewhere to stay.'

'Nicholas sent you!' Elizabeth's Willetts's round face lit with pleasure as she stepped back for Ruth to enter the house. 'My friends call me Bess. You are welcome to my home. The hostelry along the street will take care of your coach and horses. Have you come to see the king? He will ride into the city tomorrow.'

'My brother is with the king's army.'

'Then you are doubly welcome, my dear. And you will have news of Nicholas and Mary. How is she? There

can be only a month now before the child is born.' Bess
threw up her hands in mock horror. 'Listen how I rattle
on! You must be tired. We shall have time enough later
to talk.'

And talk they did, throughout the evening and long
into the night. Although Bess was several years older
than herself, Ruth immediately felt an affinity with her
and although she was usually reticent, Bess wheedled
her story from her, laughing with delight at the way she
had impersonated Adam and tricked the Roundheads.
She patted her hand with understanding when she spoke
of the fire, and Ruth found herself confiding in her, as
she would have in her own mother, at the complexity of
her emotions roused by Blase.

'It is a real man you have lost your heart to,' Bess
sighed. 'What family is not pulled apart by this con-
tinual conflict? My father and my two younger brothers
fought for the king at Edgehill. Father was slain. My
eldest brother is a major under Cromwell, and my sister
is married to a member of Parliament. As children we
were close, and although our family is split, I cannot
hate them. There is precious little love and tolerance in
our world today. Sometimes we have to listen to our
hearts. It is the men who do not always find it so easy
to compromise. But love conquers all—eventually.'

There was a strange comfort in Bess Willetts's counsel
that lulled Ruth to a dreamless sleep. The next morning,
accompanied by Sam and Bess, she waited expectantly
among the crowd, all jostling for a better view. The cathedral bells rang out their welcome as King Charles II
and his weary and dejected-looking army marched into
Worcester to the accompanying beat of drums. The
crowd went wild, the men throwing their caps into the
air while the women scattered flowers in his Majesty's
path. The young king, slim and tall, his complexion
darker even than Blase's, smiled graciously at the
cheering crowd, the lines of worry easing from his face.

When he received the keys of the city from the mayor on the Guildhall steps, he knighted the man on the spot, then paused to receive the good wishes of the people. There was a majesty in every inch of his long figure that came not from arrogance, but from an empathy with his people. Ever since she could remember, Ruth had upheld the cause of the Stuarts and now felt humbled before the presence of her Sovereign.

When the king was led away by his counsellors, Ruth searched the columns of riders for a sign of Adam, but as the beat of drum and stamp of feet faded, she turned away unable to recognise him anywhere. For three days she and Sam roamed through the army encampments and the streets. No one they spoke to had seen Adam, but as she had met with the same blank response when also asking after Daniel, she was not disheartened. The king's army numbered 14,000 and the chance was slim that she would meet someone who knew them. At last, foot-sore and weary, she chanced upon her brother escorting several carts of freshly-cut timber to the construction work being carried out for the new Fort Royal on the existing earthworks outside the Sidbury Gate.

'I should have known you would not stay at Tewkesbury!' he said sharply. His darkly circled eyes crinkled with exasperation as he ordered the troop to continue. 'You know that Cromwell's forces are no more than a dozen or so miles from here at Evesham. You should have returned to Sussex. There'll be a battle any day, and our troops are vastly outnumbered.'

'That's not much of a greeting!' she said gently. 'I have been searching for you for three days.'

He dismounted and hugged her hard for a long moment, then held her at arm's length, the tawny stubble along his jaw making him look haggard and much older. 'This is the last place you should be.' His voice sounded weary, but it was something more than that—a note she had never heard in it before, which clutched at her heart—the note of defeat.

'Ay, defeat, Ruth,' he answered her thoughts as though they had been spoken aloud. 'The recruits we need do not answer the call to arms. Go home. One of us should be at Saxfield to carry on the fight. There is much to be done here before the battle. Best we say goodbye now.'

Icy fear prickling her spine, she threw herself into his arms. 'Do not talk like that! You will ill-wish yourself. You are tired and over-fanciful. I'll not leave Worcester. We shall win the battle. We have to!'

He kissed her brow and released her, swinging up into the saddle. 'I shall visit you when I can, but promise me, if the battle goes against us and there is danger of the city falling to Parliament, that you will leave at once.'

During the next four days the city took on the semblance of an army camp. Apart from when Ruth took a pre-pared lunch to Adam, now promoted to major, she had seen him only once, when he came to the house in Glover Street. Bess Willetts was involved in various works or-ganised by the women in sewing for the king's army, and despite finding such mundane work stifling, Ruth sat plying her needle, only half listening as they gossiped of the trial of the spy William Guise, who had been hanged. The proceedings had cast a gloom over the Royalist camp, for Cromwell's forces were increasing daily, and in an attempt by the Royalists to put the Roundheads' guns, which were now trained on the city walls, out of action, a surprise night attack had been decided upon. Unfortunately, the plans had been overheard by the tailor, William Guise, and when the Royalists attacked, their advantage was lost, and they had been driven back. Ruth had seen for herself the dejection of the Royalists, but it was the air of defeat that continued to afflict Adam which filled her with dread. She put her sewing aside, needing reassurance. She must talk to Adam, and it was almost time to take him his midday meal.

With Sam at her side they walked out of the city to the Commandery, where the Royalists had set up their Headquarters. The grounds were filled with drilling pikemen, and all along the walls were sounds of intermittent musket-fire as snipers picked off the enemy troopers. Her thoughts were taking a turn towards the melancholy as Sam led her to a room overlooking the street.

'Wait here, mistress. I shall enquire where Master Adam is.'

Ruth nodded and wandered over to the window. There still had been no sight or word of Daniel, and Adam had been terse when questioned about their friend.

'You need not fear for Daniel,' he had said sharply. 'He's not been near Worcester and has probably skulked back to Sussex.'

'That's unjust, Adam! If Daniel has returned to Sussex, it's because he is worried about his family. But, even so, I cannot believe he will desert the king. He is probably working hard in the outlying villages trying to bring in recruits.'

Adam had looked at her searchingly. 'You are always so loyal and sometimes too trusting.' He appeared to check himself, but when she lifted a quizzing brow, he smiled wryly. 'Look how you were mistaken in Drummond.'

Try as she might, she could not banish Blase from her thoughts. Often during the last days she had found herself studying the back of a tall Cavalier, her heart leaping erratically, but each time it had been a stranger when he turned to face her. She was a fool! Worcester was a Royalist stronghold, and the last place she would expect to find Blase.

She was about to turn away from the window when a tall figure detached itself from a group dragging a

cannon up to Fort Royal. She stiffened, every pore on
her body tingling with awareness. Although his back was
to her, that long, loose-legged stride was unmistakable—Blase Drummond *was* in Worcester! With one
spy already hanged, it looked as though the Royalists
were about to be infiltrated by another. He had to be
stopped. Heaven knew what information he could already have learned of the defences! Running out of the
room, she was dismayed to see no sign of Sam, but she
dared not delay. Blase was already walking towards the
cathedral, and at any moment he could be swallowed up
by the crowds.

Dropping her basket of food, she ran out into the street
and in the direction Blase had taken. Whistles and calls
followed her progress from a group of Cavaliers, far in
their cups, emerging from a tavern. Breathing heavily,
she hurried towards the river. Suddenly from behind a
hand clamped across her mouth, smothering her scream,
as she was dragged into a doorway, the deep all-too-
familiar voice grating against her ear.

'Ruth! What in God's name are you doing here?'

She had no need to turn, for her whole body was op-
pressively conscious of him—of his body, hard muscled,
against her back. His hand over her mouth smelt of
horse-leather and gunpowder, and his hair blowing
forward across her cheek was permeated with cannon-
smoke—all powerful reminders of war and that they were
on opposing sides. She could just imagine the haughty
set of his Roman nose and the full curving lips—lips
that had set her body aflame, but which now would be
compressed and forbidding. She knew his secret—she
could destroy him!

Blase kept his hand over her mouth as he slowly turned
her to face him. Without her mask or veil, her face,
framed by two feminine clusters of dark gold ringlets
falling to her shoulders, was revealed to him clearly for
the first time. Seeing her thus, it seemed impossible that

this beautiful woman had tricked him into believing that she was a man—had ridden at his side, defying authority, her courage and sharp wits winning his admiration. Yet she had shown a duplicity only a woman could be capable of, or a Melville! He must not forget that. Warily he lowered his hand.

'You dare to call on the Lord's name,' she seethed, 'when we both know it is the devil's work that brings you here!'

Angered by her vehemence, the sharp retort never reached his lips, for at that moment the heavy stamp of soldiers' feet and the sudden flaring in Ruth's eyes alerted him. Fowkes had turned her against him. Taking no chances, he moved swiftly as the first of the soldiers marched into view. He held her head still in one hand and clasped her tightly against him with the other, pushing her up against the wall as the soldiers went past. Her hands beat against his chest and the muffled groan deep in her throat was one of fury, not passion, goading him to overcome her resistance by kissing her. He ran his hand down the hollow of her back until he felt a tremor pulsate through her body, and her lips parted in supplication as the soldiers disappeared from sight. The sweetness of her mouth and the tantalising pressure of her body against his roused a hunger such as no woman before had done. He drew back reluctantly and hooked his thumbs over his waist-sash, startled to discover that his hands were trembling. No woman would have that hold over him again!

Finding herself so abruptly released, Ruth flattened herself against the wall, shocked, despite all her resolution, that she had responded to his kiss. Her scathing glare took in his self-assured figure leaning against the opposite wall. He had tipped back his brimmed hat, its white ostrich plume curling round his broad shoulders, but his long lashes carefully guarded the expression in his dark eyes.

'Devil's work, is it?' he ground out coldly, as though the wild moment when she had felt him respond to her with equal passion had never existed. 'Do we not serve the same cause? Fowkes has done his work well!'

'What has Daniel to do with us, or what you are?' she flared. 'Daniel is a true and loyal friend, while you— you force yourself upon me when it suits your purposes. You twist the truth and everything else to suit your own ends. I despise you!'

'Is that why you left your cloak covering me on the hillside?' A dangerous edge entered his voice. 'Or was it guilt because you ran away and left me to my fate? It was a poor reward for saving your honour and your life.'

His expression was inscrutable as he put a hand on her shoulder to draw her closer. She shrugged it off with a shudder, as she would a loathsome snake.

'You think you have but to smile and flatter, and all women jump to your bidding! You are so careless with your kisses, Major, that they mean nothing. I despise you for what you are. Women to you are just a means towards your own gratification or manipulation. Perhaps such creatures do not deserve your respect, but *I* will not be so abused.'

His straight brows drew down formidably, and his hand snapping over her wrist was as unyielding as an iron fetter. 'You know why I was in Sussex: to bring to justice the enemies of our cause.'

'Which cause is that, Major?' she asked bluntly. 'You played your part well, but I know now that you sought to denounce my brother.'

'Drummond!' A furtive voice wheezed close by. 'Three pieces of silver you said would pay for word of...'

'Silence, man!' Blase rasped, his eyes glinting savagely, as he ignored the ragged creature and glared down at Ruth's bristling figure. 'So, my vixen, you show your claws—like all women's, they are sharpened with spite,' he sneered. 'The city is beleaguered and duty calls me.

But I shall not forget that you and I have a reckoning to settle.'

His arm brushed hers as he moved past, the casual touch branding her flesh. At the doorway he pulled the brim of his hat over his brow, his eyes shadowed as he shot her a last challenging glare.

The encounter left her shaken—he had not denied her insinuations that he was a spy. And what information had he purchased from that man? Was it her duty to denounce him? She felt sick with indecision, her heart and mind warring against each other. How could she condemn the man she loved? Yet the damage the traitor William Guise had done to the king's cause had cost them a major triumph over the Roundheads, and because of their failure, the army was demoralised. Blase was a trained mercenary, and whatever information he could collect about the town's defences would be invaluable to the enemy. However, she knew she could not denounce him—not without irrefutable proof to uphold her suspicions.

Heavy-hearted, she turned away, and was hailed by Adam with a worried-looking Sam at his side. 'What possessed you to take off like that?' he demanded. 'No woman should walk the streets alone, for many of the soldiers are in their cups and looking for sport. Do you want to be accosted as a whore?'

'I thought I saw Blase Drummond, and followed. If he is a spy, he cannot be allowed to pass on knowledge of the city's defences.'

'Was it he?'

She looked away, unable to meet his gaze, and made a pretence of lifting her skirts from the garbage littering the gutters.

'Traitors do not deserve your loyalty!' He accurately gauged her distress. 'He was not worthy of your love. Forget him!'

Ruth raised her tortured gaze to his. That Blase had never loved her—even that he had tricked her and abused her confidence—was unimportant. For all his falseness, he had made her feel like a woman again, and she would go to her grave grieving for him. 'I had not thought I wore my heart so readily upon my sleeve.'

'You do not, but you cannot hide such an emotion from me. I am your twin. It is more than that, is it not?' He took both her hands as they halted by Bess Willetts's house. 'You hesitate. Are you convinced that Drummond is a spy—or did Daniel persuade you?'

A burst of fire from Cromwell's cannon outside the walls sent a shiver through her. 'I want desperately to believe that he is innocent, but how can I deny the circumstances that bear out Daniel's words? Can you make discreet enquiries of others who have spent the last years in France? You must judge if he is a spy or not.'

'I shall search the city for word of him. First, though, I must return to my post, for Cromwell's men under cover of those cursed guns are already constructing a bridge of boats across the river. Tomorrow we shall fight, so leave Worcester now, while you can.'

She shook her head. 'I shall go to the cathedral and pray for our victory. For you, and—God help me—for Blase Drummond's innocence.'

Ruth sat alone at the oak table in the candlelit parlour, her hand idly twirling the stem of a pewter goblet as she stared wretchedly into it. Earlier, she had declined to join Bess Willetts at a friend's house, and when Sam had left to visit Adam, she had been glad of her own company. Now, her nerves were strained as she awaited word from Adam. Dear God, let Blase be innocent of spying! It was impossible to extinguish the image of him from her mind. She forgot he was a traitor, remembering his lazy smile, the laughter in his ebony eyes which could darken to the velvety blackness of a midnight sky.

So tall—so assured—a giant among men, and not in stature alone. She gripped her arms against a wave of torment, her nails digging through the ribbons tying the slashed sleeves of her gown.

'Could it be that my ice-hearted maiden is showing signs of remorse at having the city scoured for news of me—my name blackened by your brother and servant?'

The deep mocking drawl made Ruth whirl round so quickly that she had to clutch at the table to prevent herself from overbalancing. She stared in astonishment at the figure silhouetted in the doorway. 'Blase! How did you find me?'

'I, too, have my accomplices.' He stepped forward into the light, his voice and face implacable. He did not wear the buff leather coat of the New Model Army, but was dressed in black, the candlelight reflected on the steel gorget beneath his lace collar, proclaiming his officer's rank. 'You have much to answer for.'

'Do I, sir? I would say the same for you. You made no secret of your low regard for Adam, and I have seen the ruthless way in which you cajole women to gain your own ends. Why should I trust you?'

'*You* presume to accuse *me* of manipulating *you*? The speed you set off for Bristol, allegedly to our wedding, made a mockery of my name and the protection I offered.' The lethal coldness of his voice struck her like a December wind. 'Were you a man, you would answer with your sword for that. Do you think that, because you are a woman, I hold you exempt?'

'What is it you want of me, Major? Say your piece and begone, quickly, before I call the night watch.'

His rage turned inward upon himself as he stared down at her beautiful, defiant face and was no longer sure why he had come. When he had first heard the questions Adam Melville was asking about him, he had raged against her treachery, reviling her for being another such as Sophia. It was madness to want her after all she had done, but want her he did, with an intensity that defied reason. He had come here tonight to teach her a lesson and lay his own ghost to rest. She had intrigued him for too long. With a battle due tomorrow, he could not afford such distractions. Once he had possessed her, she would cease to haunt him.

'I would tame you, my warrior maid. I would show you that it is the man who is always the master—show you that you are a woman capable of passion.'

Guessing his intent, Ruth stepped back, but was brought up short by the chair that lodged hard against the table.

'You cannot fight me and win, sweet Ruth,' he challenged. 'You are too beautiful to deny yourself the pleasures of love.'

'That will be for my husband to teach me, no other!'

He lifted a brow provocatively. 'Are we not promised to each other?'

'Out of necessity,' she parried, her stomach tightening with alarm. She had never seen him like this. Outwardly he played the taunting lover, but threaded through each word was the threat of a ruthless predator. He had come here intent upon seducing her, and nothing would sway him from his course. She fought to control the quiver in her voice as she felt the situation slipping from her grasp. 'You do not love me! I am grateful that you saved my life, but from the outset I made it clear that I would not hold you to so absurd an arrangement.'

His black eyes sparked like tinder upon dry kindling. 'Grateful! You have a strange way of repaying your gratitude, by holding my name to ridicule.'

'As you would seek revenge by treating me like a whore! I would rather be flogged than so shamed.'

The look he shot her was like a dagger-thrust straight to her heart. The candlelight played over his swarthy face, deepening the tense hollows of his cheeks, their angular planes outlined by the bluish tinge of his beard-

line. This was how he would look, cold and merciless,
as he was about to deliver the death-blow to his enemy.
His eyes glazed as his hands circled her neck, his thumbs
tracing its slim outline. Stiffening, she held her breath,
intuition telling her that it was not her he was actually
seeing, but someone else who had once dealt him a soul-
destroying blow. She met his stare unflinchingly and his
eyes cleared, their expression quickly guarded as his lips
twisted into a devastating smile.

His hands moved to her jaw, the play of his thumbs
drawing light circles over her skin as he gently eased her
head back. 'Would a man kiss a whore like this?' With
cold calculation, his lips touched each eyelid and the tip
of her nose, skimmed across her cheek in a sensuous
trail before fastening upon the lobe of her ear. Her taut
muscles relaxed and a gasp leapt to her throat as darts
of pleasure shot through her. His arms went round her,
hungrily pressing her closer. 'Or like this?' he murmured, giving her no surcease as his warm lips stroked
her skin with a tantalising slowness that made the blood
sing in her ears. A strange languor possessed her body,
and her lips parted unconsciously as his mouth laid siege
to them. His kiss deepened, his tongue teasing the soft
inner flesh, and with a last grain of remaining sanity,
she flattened her hand against his chest, intending to push
him away. Beneath her palm the strong pounding of his
heart drummed out a wild, pagan beat, matching the
quickening rhythm of her own. Somehow she found the
strength to wrench her lips from his.

'No, Blase! Please, not this way—not with anger and
hatred in your heart.'

'I am not cold-blooded or mercenary,' he said
hoarsely, his smouldering gaze willing her to obey him.
'Tomorrow I ride into battle, but tonight I would forget
the horrors and carnage of war in the arms of a beautiful and desirable woman. I want you, Ruth, and I know
you want me, but I shall not take an unwilling woman,

however misguided that reluctance may be. Tell me to go, sweet Ruth, and I shall.'

She opened her mouth to order him from the house, but no words came. Her eyes widening, she gazed at him. She could not deny the clamouring of her blood. What did it matter whether he were Royalist or Roundhead? Tomorrow he faced death on the battle-field, and she loved him! That was all that mattered at this moment. She had sent her first betrothed away to war without ever knowing the completeness of their union, and during the empty years after his death, she had regretted her purity. Love had come to her a second time, with all the intensity and blossoming passion of a woman.

Then his lips were upon hers with an ardour that left her breathless and sent her senses whirling. Placing a hand in the small of her back and behind her knees, he swept her up into his arms. 'Neither Sam or Goodwife Willetts will return for another hour—perhaps two,' he said, determinedly walking towards the stairs. 'Which room is yours?'

'The second on the right,' she heard herself saying, her voice seeming to come from a great distance. How often in her dreams had Blase appeared to lift her in his arms and carry her off. She must be dreaming. She would awake and find the house empty. But as Blase stooped to avoid knocking his head against the low lintel of her chamber door, the heat of his lips lingering upon her brow and the cool silkiness of his long hair falling across her face could not be conjured in a dream, or the musky scent of the orris root he used. As she sank into the soft mattress, she tensed, her ardour cooling at the enormity of what she was about to permit. Blase struck a tinder and lit the candle at her bedside, the soft, seductive light adding to her embarrassment. He had already removed his hat and sword-belt and unfastened his doublet. The bed sank beneath his weight as he leaned across her, and she fearfully clutched at his hand as it closed over the ribbons securing the front of her gown. 'Blase, I . . .'

He eased back, watching her intently. He was so devastatingly handsome, and the way the bright moonlight silvered his face brought back a flood of memories of their escape from the Roundheads. She had trusted him then until Daniel had opened her eyes to the truth. Yet each night she had been plagued by guilt that she had left him wounded on the hillside. Somehow he had escaped, he was alive, and he wanted her. Whatever midsummer madness was overtaking her, she could not deny him.

Her arms slid round his neck to draw his head down, then his lips were on hers, captivating, demanding, the touch of his hands gentle as unhurriedly he untied her laces. In a whisper of silk her gown and petticoats were removed, leaving her naked. When, instinctively, she tried to pull the edge of the pillow down over her scarred shoulder, her hand was caught and clasped tightly against his chest.

'Do not be ashamed of your body,' he said softly, his fingertips slowly caressing her shoulder. 'You are beautiful. More beautiful than my wildest dreams, Ruth.'

Her breath escaped in an ecstatic sigh as his hands stroked the hollow of her spine, then forward, exploring the curve of her hips, feathering a sensuous path across her flat stomach and up to close over her breasts, sending a cascade of white-hot bubbles coursing through her veins. His lips followed the trail of his fingers, spreading the fire within her until she was shaking so much that she clung to him fiercely, unable to silence a gasp of pleasure. 'Oh, Blase, I never knew—never dreamt—it could be like this.'

'This, my adorable innocent, is just the beginning.' He, too, sounded shaken. 'There is so much I shall teach you.'

He began to pull his shirt from his breeches, but she reared up, her hand closing over his. Pushing it aside, she removed his doublet and shirt, her hands as eager as his had been to know every muscle and sinew of his body. He drew in his breath as her hands ran through the dark curling hair of his chest and down over his taut stomach. At the waistband of his breeches she hesitated, too shy to go further. With a soft chuckle he swept her hand aside and divested himself of the remainder of his clothing. 'You are an apt pupil, my sweet. I shall not hurry you.'

He drew her back into his arms, the touch of his warm skin fanning the flames of her awakening desire. His mouth fastened over hers, supple, beguiling, transporting her to giddy, breathless heights, until a wildness consumed her in her need to express her love by responding with a fervour to answer his. Hungrily his lips sought her breasts, his tongue tantalising them to a throbbing urgent fullness. Her feverish kisses tasted the saltiness of his skin, her hands seeking the hairroughened contours of his thighs as his body covered hers, instilling a delicious, aching sweetness that craved release. She gasped raggedly as his hands parted her legs, then his mouth locked upon hers and she moved sinuously to accommodate him. A sharp stab of pain tensed her muscles, then with a second thrust it was gone and his possession was complete, the cadence of his breathing and his rhythm building to take her out into the heavens, her own passion making her move with him with an instinct so primeval that it needed no teaching, until she cried out as her senses soared to a crescendo.

He clasped her to him, the tempo of his kisses slowing to a deeper reverence so that her body shimmered in the after-glow of their lovemaking, and leaving her so weak that she scarcely had the strength to return his kisses. He levered himself up on an elbow, his eyes dark and intense as he stroked a damp tendril of hair on her brow. 'My wild, sweet enchantress, you are ravishing!'

'I love you, Blase.'

Her dreamy world of contentment evaporated as she saw the shutter falling across his expression. 'I know,' he said huskily. 'And I am honoured.'

She bit her lip, fighting to control the sickening dread pitting her stomach. She had not meant to say those words. It was obvious that he did not love her. 'I should not have spoken. It changes nothing. It was just that it was special—you were special. I would not have you think me wanton.'

His lips twisted as he took her hand and raised it to his lips. 'It was special for me, too. You are a very remarkable woman, and I respect you too much to insult you with false words that could have no meaning for me.'

Pulling the coverlet over her nakedness, she drew back. 'You are brutally honest!'

His hold tightened over her wrist. 'Honest, yes! But I had not meant to be brutal.' He kissed her with lingering tenderness but without a resurgence of passion, then with a sigh put her from him. 'The hour is late. I would not compromise you further. I must be gone before Mistress Willetts returns.'

While he dressed, she stared miserably at the coverlet, frightened that he would leave her now, never to return. She heard the clatter of his sword as he adjusted it over his hip, and forced herself to look up. He tipped his hat in salute to her.

'You have won my respect, sweet Ruth. It is a higher and more lasting accolade than love.' His expression hardened. 'Leave Worcester. Your place is at Saxfield. You can do nothing here but cause your brother anxiety as to your safety.'

He spun abruptly on his heel, bent his long body to pass through the door, and was gone, the sound of his boots echoing down the stairs. He had left with no word that he intended to see her again. She closed her eyes against the onrush of pain, but they flew open instantly. How could she have forgotten the impending battle tomorrow? Would it not be on his mind that he would be among the many who would not return to their lovers? Dear God, let it not be so!

CHAPTER THIRTEEN

THE NEXT day was overcast, the grey clouds dismal and gloomy, duplicating the bleakness of Ruth's mood. Hourly the tension grew, becoming a tangible living thing in the scared, hollowed eyes of the inhabitants, as Worcester reverberated to the boom of Cromwell's cannon and crack of musket-fire. When Ruth entered the street, the sultry oppressiveness of the threatening storm clutched at her throat and her ears rang to the shrieks of the frightened women and children and, worse, the screams of wounded horses and men. All around her was chaos, confusion and fear.

Sam touched her arm. 'If we are to leave, it must be done now, mistress. Already it is too late to risk using the coach.'

'How can I leave, when so many of these brave and loyal people must stay?' she answered heavily, adjusting the weight of the water-skin she was carrying on her hip. 'I must do what I can to ease the suffering of the wounded. The battle is not yet lost. The king is rallying our men.'

Ruth looked up at the cathedral tower from where earlier the king had been watching the progress of the battle. When a short time later his graceful figure, weighted with half-armour, galloped towards the gate, she feared the battle was going against them. Was it true what she had heard—that the Scottish cavalry had not ridden to support the infantry?

Through the clouds of acrid smoke settling over the streets, distorted figures appeared, reeling and battle-dazed, as the Royalists were beaten back, and her dread intensified. She sank back against the shuttered window of a half-timbered house as an ox-cart loaded with more wounded rumbled past. Although she closed her eyes against the hellish sights, nothing could shut out the clanking of harness, hoofs ringing out on cobblestones and the awful cries of the wounded. Suddenly a shaft of agony drove into her side, and as she clutched her ribs, she heard Adam cry out so clearly that she looked along the narrow street, expecting to see him. The ox-cart had vanished, and although Adam was nowhere to be seen, his voice continued to echo through her mind. 'For God's sake, Ruth, escape! All is lost... Save Saxfield!'

As the pain in her side faded, she knew Adam had been wounded, that it was his agony she had felt as he tried to warn her. Panic filled her, but refusing to admit that he could be dead, she began to push her way through the frightened scurrying townspeople seeking shelter in their homes. Outside the city walls, the sound of fighting was now building in ferocity, and shouted commands by officers were drowned by wild, unearthly battlecries rending the air.

'Mistress, come away!' Sam urged. 'It is too dangerous here.'

The street ahead was blocked, and, disgusted, Ruth turned along a side street, the windows of the houses around her shaking from the thundering of the guns. At the sound of hard-ridden horses behind, she flattened herself against a doorway to allow the riders to pass.

'Godswounds, Ruth!' Blase ground out from above her on his lathered black horse. Startled, she looked up into his furious face. His hair was caked with sweat and dust, and the lace collar over his dulled and dented breastplate was ripped and splattered with blood, but mercifully not his own. 'Why have you not left the city? The army is in retreat. Go now while there is still time!'

She was too stunned to question the strangeness of his being within the city gates. He wore no distinguishing uniform, and the blue officer's sash about his waist was neither the yellow of Parliament nor the crimson most commonly favoured by the Royalists. There was no sign of the tender lover in the haggard lines of his face, only the ruthless determination of a soldier whose mind was centred upon war. This was a stranger. His face was forbidding, his eyes bloodshot with fatigue and glazed with the futility of war. She shuddered as a cannonade of fire shook the nearby wall. 'I cannot leave. I must find Adam.'

'Fort Royal has fallen. They fought to the last man.' Blase's expression was harsh and unreadable as he swung down to stand at her side. He glared daggers at Sam as though condemning him for exposing her to danger, but as he turned to her, his voice cracked with regret. 'I saw Adam struck down in the last foray. He's dead, Ruth.'

She stared blankly at him, his swarthy face streaked with sweat and gunpowder misting before her eyes. She swayed, then, conscious of his arms about her waist, it needed all her willpower to resist the need to bury her head against his shoulder and weep. His life, too, was in danger. She should despise him for the Roundhead he was, but as she gazed into his ebony eyes she saw... Frustration? Impatience? Torment? Her heart could not, even now, deny her love. The cause was lost—too many men had died today. She could not bear it if he were killed, and she drew herself up. She had delayed him long enough and increased the danger to him. 'I cannot leave—not yet.' Her voice rustled like dead leaves. 'Adam's body... I cannot leave him here.'

Sam gripped her shoulder, drawing her away, his expression distrustful upon Blase. 'Mistress, there is nothing you can do, not now. Bess Willetts will do what has to be done. She has proved a good friend.'

'Take her back to Saxfield, Sam,' Blase ordered.

She looked up at him, noting his impatience to rejoin his men. Was it fear for her safety that caused his anger, or that she had not heeded his warning? The grief of her brother's death left her too numb to analyse his feelings. Blase did not love her, so what did she expect from him? Her future had been with Adam and her duty to the cause. Both were lost to her now. A vision of Saxfield filled her mind, sustaining her, and with it Adam's last words.

'I shall go to Saxfield,' she said hollowly. 'It is all I have left. Somehow I shall save it.' Her gaze held that black inscrutable stare, her love bridled beneath her grief. He made no mention of joining her in Sussex. 'God go with you and keep you safe, Blase, although we do not serve the same master.' She turned from him, her head held proudly.

'Ruth, I . . .' Blase bit back his words, startled by the accusation in her parting. The words of comfort he was about to offer and the hot rush of anger were swept aside by the urgency of his mission. Ruth was safe enough with Sam protecting her. Already he had delayed too long, and sprang into the saddle. With duty commanding him, he pressed his horse into motion, thrusting aside the image of Ruth's pale, beautiful face setting into a rigid mask as she mastered her shock and grief. This was no time for distractions, however beguiling— years of soldiering attuned his instincts for survival. The Royalists were defeated but not crushed, and although the battle was lost, the fighting would probably continue until nightfall as the Royalists sought to escape rather than be captured. His duty was clear: he must rejoin his men.

Forcing their way through the streets rapidly filling with retreating Royalists, Ruth and Sam finally reached Glover Street. The house was empty, and pausing only long enough to strip off her gown and petticoats and pull on her brother's doublet and breeches, Ruth sought out Bess Willetts, who was comforting an elderly neighbour next door.

'Will you not come with us, Bess? We could accompany you as far as Tewkesbury. If the city falls to the Roundheads, they will deal harshly with the faithful people who made it such a stronghold.'

'This is my home, as Saxfield is yours,' Bess said emphatically. 'Go quickly. My thoughts and prayers will be with you.'

Ruth kissed her friend's cheek and ran out to the street, where Sam had procured two saddled horses. Mounted, she led the way through the street, where fighting between the two armies had already broken out. Over the heads of the men, she saw the tall figure of the king galloping out of the city, and her heart sank. He was in flight . . . The battle was lost!

'Make haste, mistress,' Sam demanded, grabbing her bridle and increasing their pace. 'There's a long ride ahead of us if we are to escape capture and imprisonment.'

The miles sped by in a blurred haze as Ruth followed Sam's lead across country and away from the main highway. There was an emptiness inside her, a void left by Blase's absence. Yet deeper was her feeling of incompleteness at the loss of her twin, which blotted out her lover's betrayal. She pulled her mind back to the present, and what Sam was saying as he slowed his horse to a walk.

'There's an inn ahead. Do you wish to rest? I had rather we had passed Oxford before stopping, though.'

'We shall stop, but only long enough to change the horses.' Through her numbing grief, reason reasserted itself. 'We must reach Saxfield without delay. And it will be Adam who returns—not Ruth. No one must suspect that Adam died at Worcester. I will not see Saxfield fall into Henry's hands without a fight.'

Sam flashed her a look which held a dozen arguments, but then, seeing the setness of her expression, he shrugged. 'Would that it could be done. But you cannot deceive Captain Melville indefinitely.'

'I must. You forget that I left Saxfield on the pretence of getting married. How can I return? I have done with my veils and mask. In this way I can live without constraint. The villagers will believe that Adam has just returned from his sister's wedding in Bristol.'

'Nay, I doubt they will be so trusting. Think on it carefully, mistress. There's many a pitfall to such a plan.'

Those cautious words of Sam's had proved uncomfortably true, Ruth reflected a fortnight later as she drew Adam's grey gelding to a halt. Already she was feeling the strain of impersonating Adam under the close scrutiny of people who had known him all his life. She was as much a prisoner in this role as in that of the veiled cripple. Even though she had first shown herself in the village less than a day after the Battle of Worcester—and several hours before the full account of the king's defeat had reached so far south—the local people had been markedly sullen and suspicious of Adam's return.

Apart from her early morning rides, she took care to avoid contact with the villagers, rarely leaving the sanctuary afforded by Saxfield. Sundays were the worst. It was impossible to escape the church services unless she wished to cause further censure and speculation. Without her concealing veils, she felt naked and exposed. Although she was always the last to arrive for the service and the first to leave, she could not relax. Throughout the service she was conscious that she must not only control the timbre of her voice, but emulate her brother's mannerisms and the way he held his body. Slowly she was beginning to feel that her femininity was being smothered. She was neither Ruth, nor Adam, but a disembodied stranger who must think and act with the aggressiveness of a man while inwardly longing to be true to the woman Blase had awoken.

Her grief for Adam pressed down upon her like a giant yoke. She missed him desperately, and had never needed his strength and guidance more. She was so alone—so isolated. There was no one she could trust apart from

Sam and Hettie. Two pheasants flew up out of a coppice some way below and Spartan lumbered into sight, his heavy body flattening out as he sped up the hill at her whistle.

'I still have you, my faithful friend,' she said, wearily turning her horse for home. 'If only Daniel were here. It would be so much easier. I had not realised how much I relied on his company when Adam was away.'

It had been a shock to discover that Daniel was not at the Grange when she needed him. His mother had been evasive when questioned by Sam. Was it true he was now in London? What dangerous game was he playing now? He, who had always urged caution, seemed to have walked into a hornets' nest.

Her morose gaze rested upon a large poster nailed to an oak by the side of the track. Snatching it from the tree, anger pierced the lethargy which had overtaken her, her chest burning with indignation as she read its bold script: *'£1000 Reward for information of the fugitive Charles Stuart, a tall black man upwards of two yards high.'* Screwing it into a tight ball, she flung it to the ground. Each day rumours grew that the king was still in England. Thank God, he was still free! Was Daniel risking everything in a last bid to help his Sovereign to escape?

And Blase... Where was he? The oft-repeated question caught her unawares, refusing to be silenced. Each night her dreams were haunted by his memory and each dawn brought with it a fresh determination to cast him from her heart. How, in good conscience, could she love him when he served that king-butcher, Cromwell? As the only survivor of her family from this bitter conflict, would she not be betraying them if she allowed herself to weaken?

The stableyard at Saxfield was deserted as she swung down out of the saddle. Knowing Sam had duties enough to keep three men busy, she led the grey gelding into his stall, unsaddled him and, stripping off her doublet, rolled up her sleeves and began to rub him down. The long sweeping movements across his sleek back built to a steady rhythm, the routine task bringing a comfort of its own. Then the mastiff's low growl alerted her to danger. Hastily placing a blanket over the grey's back, she grabbed her doublet from the side of the stall and was just shrugging it over her shoulders when a figure blocked the light from the doorway.

'How well you fit the role of groom, cousin,' Captain Melville sneered.

Ruth stiffened, quickly lacing the heavy doublet, her blood running cold at the narrowness of her escape. A moment or two earlier, and her ruse would have been discovered. Her glance swept disparagingly over his buff coat and breastplate. He carried his steel helmet under his arm, and his waving blond hair was bleached almost white from the sun. There was a great swagger to his step, which showed all too clearly how Cromwell's Ironsides saw the Royalist cause totally crushed.

'What brings you to Saxfield, Henry?' she answered coldly. 'I thought you were now garrisoned at Lewes.'

'So I was, until I learned of your return. That was some ride—from Worcester to Saxfield in a day!'

'Your wits have gone begging, I returned at a leisurely pace from my sister's wedding in Bristol,' Ruth countered.

'Without the family coach, it would appear. That was somewhat careless of you, was it not?'

Her heart thumped painfully with deepening fear. In the confines of the stable, the smell of brandy was heavy upon his breath. In his cups, Henry's mood was usually belligerent and his temper unstable. How much did he know or guess? 'The coach was a wedding present to Ruth. I had little enough to give her by way of dowry. The taxes have seen to that!'

Henry glowered, his pale complexion suffusing with colour as he pompously twirled his moustache, a sign that his temper was about to erupt, but she forced a smile. There was no point in antagonising her cousin without need. Jamming her hat low over her brow, she moved past him into the courtyard, lengthening her stride to a manly gait as she called back over her shoulder, 'Come into the house, Henry, you must be parched after your ride. What is this talk of Worcester?'

A sneering grunt acknowledged her remark, but Henry was not to be daunted. 'You are looking pale and frailer than when last we met. A fever, perhaps? Sea voyages can be such a peril. Did you not take ship from Shoreham some weeks ago?'

A knot of nausea lodged in her throat, preventing her from answering. Henry missed nothing, devil take him! 'Sadly, I had no such good fortune. You know how I love the sea. It must be my buccaneering blood. How I envied our great-grandfather his years at sea.'

'That's not what I meant,' Henry snorted as they entered the kitchen, his gruff voice startling Hettie into dropping a copper pan. 'Too many questions concerning this household have been left unanswered.'

'Mis—Master Adam,' the maid hastily corrected. 'I did not know Captain Melville was here.'

'We met in the stables. Possibly my cousin was making an inventory for his future use,' Ruth retorted. 'He seems to be labouring under the impression that I fought at Worcester.' At Hettie's horrified expression, Ruth relented, but her voice remained sharp. 'Bring ale to us in the parlour.'

Ruth strode through the house and stood aside for Henry and Spartan to enter the parlour, then moved to stand with her back to the window, her features deliberately shadowed. Neither spoke as Hettie, flustered and ill at ease, brought in a tray and two tankards and a pitcher of ale. Presenting one each to Henry and Ruth, she hurried from the room, calling for Sam.

'Your maid would summon your bodyguard!' Henry jeered. 'But, as you see, I came alone without my troopers.'

'Then I am honoured that you pay a social call upon us,' Ruth said warily. 'My sister told me that your last two visits were both offensive and of an unseemly nature. What did you hope to gain by your bullying?'

'Every house in the district was being searched. Saxfield was no exception.' He drained his goblet and, without asking, refilled it before continuing. 'What I found here was... I was shocked by Ruth's wanton conduct. I need say no more.'

'There I beg to differ.' Ruth's temper flared. 'Earlier that week you had pushed your way into my sister's bed-chamber. Had you hoped for a repetition of such conduct? You have made no secret of your designs upon her. Was it your aim to shame her into marriage with you?'

To her amazement, Henry turned away, ignoring her provocation. Again he refilled his emptied goblet, his voice beginning to slur. 'The purpose of this visit is not to question my conduct, but yours!'

He spun on his heel, eyeing her stonily. Beneath those pale almost invisible lashes, the brown cast in his blue eyes was disconcertingly evil and sinister. He saw Saxfield within his clutches, and would be merciless in destroying her. 'It is nearly a month since Ruth left Sussex. A rushed marriage, was it not? I thought you would have coun-selled her to allow a decent interval. What does she know of Drummond anyway—or of men, for that matter, since she has been shut away here?'

She downed a manly measure of ale, inwardly grim-acing at its bitterness. 'Ruth knew her own mind,' she said defensively, convinced that Henry's show of concern was a false lull before he turned his full vengeance upon her. Anger stung her blood at the way he had boasted he would have her, promoting a counter-attack. 'She fell in love with the rogue, and would have him and no other.'

His eyes smouldered with hatred before his drooping lids concealed his thoughts. Unlike his behaviour on previous visits to the Manor, Henry contained his temper, but hostility oozed from every line of his stocky figure as he gritted out, 'I know you were at Worcester. There are prisoners aplenty eager to win their freedom by informing on others. I shall have my proof, and when I do...' His gaze travelled possessively around the room. 'Saxfield will be mine. How sweet will be my revenge for the years your family scorned me! I had the foresight to choose the winning side. While you—misguided fool that you are—gambled everything on a hopeless cause. You do not deserve Saxfield. First your father, and then you, brought it down by misplaced loyalty. Edmund Melville was my great-grandfather, too.'

'And my father was your guardian when your parents died from the plague. For ten years he treated you as a son, yet how did you repay him?' Ruth whipped her indignation at the pain her father had suffered at Henry's wild, unruly ways. 'You ran away to sea. We had no word of you for two years.'

'I was never wanted here. Your father gave me a home out of duty. It was you and Ruth he doted upon. I was the one at the end of his sermons. I could never do anything right. He was glad when I left.'

'That's not true! Father was strict. He was deeply religious and saw clearly what was right and wrong. You resented his curbing your wildness because he was not your own father. He was just as strict with—with Ruth and myself, until the war took him away.' She took a steadying breath, nervous that her anger had made her stumble over the names. At every moment she must be on her guard.

'Now at last that war is ended.' Henry slammed the tankard down on the table, his lips curling back into a malicious snarl. 'And prison or exile will be your fate, while I return Saxfield to the greatness it knew in Edmund Melville's time.'

Ruth was stunned into silence. She had always believed Henry to be totally mercenary in wanting Saxfield for himself, but he spoke as though he loved the old house. At least she could understand that. Saxfield was now the only thing which gave purpose to her life, and she had no intention of relinquishing it.

'You have no proof against me, Henry. Or any claim upon Saxfield. Should I die without heirs, the property is unentailed and comes to—goes to—Ruth or her children.'

'Ruth is as guilty as you. By marrying Drummond, she has sealed her fate.'

'What do you mean by that?' She struggled to keep her voice from rising with surprise. 'Drummond is Cromwell's spy.'

This time, it was Henry who looked taken aback. A strange expression twisted his ruddy face. 'After all the abuse she hurled at me, she married him, believing that? Then she truly does love him, but the little fool has played into his hands.' He gave a bitter laugh. 'Blase Drummond hates all Melvilles. He had vowed to destroy any who bear that name.'

'That's absurd! He did all in his power to save my— my sister's reputation.' She had almost betrayed herself there, and it needed all her willpower to retain her manly poise. 'Why should he wish us harm?'

Tipping the last of the contents of the pitcher into his tankard, Henry flopped down into a chair, his mood turning maudlin. Ruth waited, stilling the questions crowding her mind. As a child, Henry would never own he was in the wrong and would brood for days after being lectured on his conduct. Guilt was making him morose now, and she sensed that she was on the brink of learning something important about Blase.

'I should have remembered who he was when I first saw him,' he said at last. 'But after so many battles, so many deaths, you harden yourself against the past. Marston Moor was something we all wanted to forget. We all knew the king's cause died that day. Oh, there would be other battles, but it was at Marston Moor that the tide turned against him, and upon every man's lips was the name of General Oliver Cromwell and his New Model Army.' He waved his goblet in drunken salute to an invisible figure. 'Until that time, I was as loyal to the king as the rest of you. That is until I, and three others, were cut off from the Royalist army. Suddenly I found myself·looking down the barrel of the enemy's pistol, and all I could think of was that I was nineteen and did not want to die.'

He broke off, staring into his goblet. Somehow Ruth held her tongue. Although repelled by his craven act of changing sides, after the horrors she had seen at Worcester, she could understand, even if she did not condone, the terror that had driven him. She stood very still. If she spoke now, he would turn even more unpleasant and she would never learn the truth.

'Marston Moor!' He spat the words out like a profanity, his speech laboured. 'The men I was with were strangers to me, and in truth I had long forgotten their names. What were three more deaths among so many? I have slain a score or more in battle. But, in truth, those men haunt me still. Ay, Drummond has reason enough to see me dead and us all brought down.'

Ruth's spine prickled with foreboding. Just what was Henry telling her? Her skin turned cold and clammy as she waited for him to go on.

He slammed his goblet down on the table with such violence that the silver base dented. 'As the Lord is my witness, I was out of my mind with fear and said the first thing that came into my head. I condemned my companions as Royalist spies. Lionel Drummond was one of those men. He was Blase Drummond's brother and even younger than myself. They were hanged.'

Turning aside, she bit back her exclamation of horror, gulping painfully. She wished she could close her ears to her cousins's words, but once started, the flow tumbled from his lips.

'It was to humiliate me that Drummond betrothed himself to Ruth. I never thought he would actually marry her.'

'I think you had better leave, Henry,' she forced out through clenched teeth. If he did not go quickly, she was certain she would betray herself. Adam would never have felt so weak and faint. She closed her eyes, willing the room to stop dipping and rising like a storm-tossed ship.

Henry rose unsteadily to his feet. 'So reproving—just like your damned father!' His fist clenched aggressively as he moved towards her. 'What would you know of Marston Moor? You were too young to fight and stayed safe at home.' A warning growl from Spartan halted Henry, but not his recriminations. 'What would you know of loneliness, of being looked on as an intruder? You and Ruth were always together like each other's shadow. You did not even have to speak, but would suddenly burst into laughter, sharing some kind of secret jest. I was an outcast in this family, but Saxfield was my home. It will be so again.' His voice sharpened with hatred. 'Your days of freedom are numbered. When next we meet, it will be across a courtroom table. No Royalist will keep his property should it be proved that he fought at Worcester!'

Sam appeared at the doorway, where he had stood out of sight but ready to protect Ruth. He was pushed rudely aside as Henry strutted out of the house, mounted, and set his horse galloping down the drive.

''Tis a nasty piece of goods, that one!' Sam rubbed a meaty hand over his shiny head. 'I feared this would happen. He always hated Master Adam, but he would not turn you from the house if he knew the truth.'

For a long moment Ruth was motionless, wearied and shaken by this fresh conflict too cruel to be endured. 'He hates us, Sam. And Adam and I are to blame. Apart from being older than us, Henry was always moody and aloof. Adam and I had each other, and with the self-ishness of children did not see his unhappiness. There is much of great-grandfather in all of us. For all we revere his memory, he was a cold-blooded buccaneer, who may have served Good Queen Bess, but who served his self-interest first. Is Henry so different?'

'How can you ask that?' Sam raged. 'It is the woman in you making excuses for his youth. No Melville worthy of the name would condemn others to save himself.'

'No wonder Blase despised us,' she agonised, slumping into a chair. 'And all the time it seems likely that he was a Royalist. Dear God, I believed the worst of him. I even abandoned him, and he could have been captured by the enemy.'

'You have no proof that he is a Royalist. Many have changed sides,' Sam said, less harshly.

Desolation swept through her. 'No, not Blase. I should have known he was too honourable. But Daniel was convinced...'

'With respect, mistress, Mr Fowkes's feelings towards you are—well...dare I say, possessive. He saw Major Drummond as a rival, so naturally his opinion would have been biased, and...' Sam broke off, frowning.

She conquered the despair that threatened to engulf her as her thoughts settled upon Blase and the rift that was now forever between them, to ask, 'What is it, Sam?'

He hesitated. 'There have been some strange rumours concerning Mr Fowkes. That he is in London serving his own cause, not his Majesty's. Why was he not at Worcester? I believe he, too, has his eye on Saxfield to enlarge his own estate.'

'Daniel would never betray Adam!' Ruth cried, aghast.

Sam shrugged. 'All I am saying is that Master Fowkes has changed in the last year. The Royalists are routed. Any man who wishes to keep his freedom and his property must swear allegiance to the Commonwealth. If Mr Fowkes was not at Worcester, he has no proof that Master Adam fought there, or that he is dead. Since you are determined to take your brother's place, it is better that no one knows the truth.'

Ruth rubbed her hand across her eyes. 'But Daniel is our friend.'

'Trust no one, mistress. Is that not what Master Adam warned you?'

Ruth nodded absently; she could understand Sam's warning, but she could not believe that Daniel would betray her. Besides, she was too sick at heart upon learning that Henry was responsible for Lionel Drummond's death to dwell upon lesser matters.

Apparently satisfied, Sam left the room, and without warning, Ruth's eyes filled with tears. She blinked them angrily away. She could not afford to show weakness. Now, more than at any time, she needed her strength. With a soft whimper, Spartan laid his head on her lap.

'At least you, my friend, are exactly what you seem: loyal and faithful. Has the world gone mad that we are all playing out some elaborate masque? I needs must be Adam. Henry for all his faults is not quite so mercenary as he seems. He truly cares for Saxfield. While Blase... What further injustice have I served upon him? Is he Roundhead or Royalist?'

Her hand stilled from ruffling the mastiff's ears, and she stared unseeing into his large trusting eyes, her thoughts far away. Had she been so coloured by her suspicions that she had not seen the truth? It was too late now. All her life she would cherish the memory of their night of passion when she had given her love unstintingly and become truly a woman. Surely those tender moments had not stemmed from vengeance on Blase's part, but he had been so cool and reserved when he left her. What had been in his mind? There were so many misunderstandings, but deeper than those, Lionel Drummond's death was irrevocably between them. Even if he had begun to care for her, could he ever forgive her for being a Melville?

CHAPTER FOURTEEN

RUTH THREW down her quill pen and pushed aside the leatherbound estate book she had been working over for the last hour. Crossing one booted leg over the other, she flicked the fall of lace from her sleeve over her wrist.

'You will ruin your eyesight by working in this gloomy light,' Hettie admonished her, placing a candle on the table.

'The taxes are long overdue, and the repairs after last night's storm must be done before winter sets in. But how shall I find the money?' she answered heavily.

Rising, she walked across to the library window and leaned against the side of the casement. September had given way to a wet and windy October, and, too restless to settle, she flung herself away and walked out into the long gallery, her heart wrenching at seeing the devastation. The far end with its secret chamber was crushed by the great oak that had been uprooted and had crashed through the roof.

'There's little left to sell apart from the land,' she went on, more to herself than the maid, 'and I have not received an offer that approaches anything like half its true value. For all their pious talk, those crop-headed Puritans would bleed us dry! It looks as though the coach horses will have to be sold so that the roof can be repaired, at least. Adam's grey gelding will be kept, of course. I shall go to Bramber, where the wheelwright's son Ned is a reliable worker and his charges are not extortionate.

'We shall manage to raise the money,' Hettie said. 'We always do! But it's not just the repairs that are making you so low. Major Drummond will come, mistress. You must not torture yourself so, or pay heed to the feud Captain Melville spoke of.'

'No, Hettie, it is nearly six weeks since I left Worcester, and there has been no word from him. Blase does not love me. I was a diversion, a means of safeguarding his cover in Sussex. If he has survived the battle, he will be safe in France by now.'

'Or in hiding, as is his Majesty!'

Ruth stared unseeing at her. News was slow to filter through to Saxfield, but she had heard that the Royalist prisoners were being transported to New England. At least the king had not been captured, for if rumours were true, he was still in England, in disguise as a servant. Her thoughts turned to matters closer at hand. There had been no further threats from Henry as yet, but Sam had told her that several of those involved in running safe houses had been arrested and were being questioned.

'Is there still no word from the Grange?' she asked worriedly. 'It is a week since Daniel returned. Twice I have sent Sam to the house, asking him to come here. Why did Adam and Daniel quarrel? Do you think Daniel is deliberately avoiding me, or rather Adam?' The sound of the entrance porch door slamming and the ring of spurs upon the floorboards halted her.

'Adam!' Daniel Fowkes's voice rang out. 'Where the devil are you, man?'

Ruth sped to the top of the stairs, but instead of waiting for her to descend to greet him, Daniel bounded up the steps, two at a time, his face thunderous. Dragging off his scarlet cloak, he flung it at Hettie and stormed past Ruth into the long gallery before rounding on her.

'So, Adam Melville, you have now taken to summoning me like a common lackey! We have said all there is to say to each other. I came only to find what the devil had happened to Ruth.'

The welcoming smile froze on Ruth's face. She had never seen him like this before, and it made her uneasy. Menace sparked in the air. Just why had Adam and Daniel quarrelled so violently at Tewkesbury? An uncomfortable feeling cautioned her to keep her identity a secret from him, but that was absurd. He and Adam had been through so much together. 'Trust no one', Adam had warned. But he could not have meant Daniel, could he?

Clearing her throat, she deepened her voice. 'Ruth is staying with Mary Willetts until the birth of her child.'

'Then why has the rumour about her marrying Drummond been allowed to spread?'

'It is why she left Sussex. How else could her reputation be safeguarded and also all we have worked for?'

Daniel stripped off his gloves, slapping them against his open palm, his eyes narrowing. 'Then there is no truth in the rumours?'

'You know why Drummond was in Sussex as well as I . . . or do you?' She needed to convince him that Blase was innocent. 'We wronged the Major. He was no spy, but loyal to the king, or so my cousin Henry declared.'

'What would Captain Melville know?' Daniel scoffed. 'He wants Saxfield, and will do or say anything to get it.' For a long moment he chewed his lip, his eyes glinting in the reflected sunlight. 'I have no need to ask if *you* fought at Worcester. That was a remarkable ride to return here so fast.' Ruth remained silent, matching his assessing stare. He dropped his gaze first and, pacing the room, said sharply, 'The cause is lost!'

'But the king is still free and in danger. We cannot rest.'

'So you intend Saxfield to remain a safe house?'

'While I have breath in my body,' Ruth declared passionately. 'Yet, sadly, the secret chamber has been destroyed.'

Daniel turned to survey the damage behind him. That he had not mentioned it earlier showed a callousness that disquieted her. 'Had you the money, you would do better to tear the old house down and rebuild.'

'Tear Saxfield down?' she jerked out, shocked. 'I would rather tear out my right arm!'

He looked at her strangely, and for a moment she thought he had seen through her disguise. 'You and Ruth cling to the past too much. England is changing. It is the future we must look to. But I had not wished to sound unfeeling.' His manner remained cold, despite his more courteous tone. 'But back to the matter in hand— the question of assisting fugitives. There are rumours that his Majesty was denied passage to France from Lyme some days ago, and that is but two days' ride. Such rumours abound, but if they were true...'

'Is it likely that his Majesty will come this way?'

'We must be prepared. Noll Cromwell's Ironsides are searching for him all over England. It will not be said that Sussex men so failed him, if his Majesty should come to us. What other houses can we call upon if needed? Whom can we trust? Our numbers are precious few. We face death if caught giving help to so important a fugitive. Which sea-captain could be relied upon at such a time?'

The questions were fired at her with the ruthlessness of an interrogation. She stiffened, her instincts warning her that Daniel was hiding something. Surely, if Adam had taken him into his trust, he would know the men who would give their lives for their king. Caution prompted her to choose her words carefully. 'Should the need arise, the usual safeguards will be taken. In these uncertain times, my friend, whom can we trust but ourselves?'

Daniel bristled with affronted pride, unsettling her further, although her disguise must be more effective than she had thought. There was a new aggression in his stance and, something else, a swaggering confidence that had been lacking this past year. Unaccountably, she wished Spartan were in the room and not out hunting rabbits with Sam. She looked out of the open door to where Hettie sat in a window embrasure in the long gallery, the pistol from Ruth's bedchamber on the sill at her side. The maid too had sensed the danger of Daniel's mood.

'You always did set yourself above me!' His pale eyes glinted savagely. 'I have not forgotten Tewkesbury. We shall see who proves himself the better man.' Abruptly he spun on his heel, snatched up his cloak and strode to the door.

'Daniel, about Tewkesbury...?' Ruth broke off as he swung round, his face rigid with fury.

'If you mean to apologise, it's too late for that. You made your feelings plain enough. We have nothing more to say to each other.'

Shaken by the violence of his outburst, she watched him go. In his rage he had been deaf to the feminine plea which lightened her voice. She could not tell him the truth now.

'Mistress, you look pale.' Hettie hurried to her side. 'You should rest awhile.'

'How can I rest?' Ruth paced the tiny study. 'Apart from Sam and yourself, I dare trust no one. I am frightened.'

'You are not yourself, mistress. No one could have come through these past weeks unscathed. Likely you are sickening for something. Shall I bring you a honey posset to revive you?'

Ruth's stomach rebelled at the thought of the sweet spicy drink. The nausea brought a return of a growing suspicion. This was not the first time in the past week she had felt queasy, and usually it was upon waking in the mornings. 'Sam was right: I should never have pretended to be Adam. Where will it end?'

'You have deceived Captain Melville and Mr Fowkes, so the worst is over. No one will suspect you now.'

Ruth laughed mirthlessly. 'You cannot deceive nature. Heaven help me, Hettie, I believe I am with child!'

Hettie nodded sagely and without reproach. 'I guessed it was so. Once Major Drummond learns...'

'No, Hettie, this is my problem, not Major Drummond's. I want nothing from him which is not given willingly. I am the last of my line. Saxfield needs an heir, but I do not need a husband. I shall marry no man out of misplaced duty.'

'You are too proud. Major Drummond has the right to know that you are to bear his child.'

'What right is that—the right of conquest? Have you forgotten how his brother's death lies between us? If he loved me, it would be different.'

'Well, Saxfield will have its heir.' Hettie looked at her doubtfully. 'But what of you? Once your figure starts to thicken, I suppose you could leave Sussex and have the child in secret. When you return, it will be said that it was Mistress Ruth's child and that your poor sister died in childbirth. I am sure you will think of some explanation for why Major Drummond placed it in your care.'

Ruth walked back into the library, but Hettie would not be silenced. 'You talk as though Major Drummond hated you. The way I saw him looking at you, even in your mask, had nothing to do with thoughts of vengeance.'

Ruth blinked away a rush of scalding tears. Did Hettie not know how much she wanted to believe Blase would come to her? She sniffed, her voice gruff with determination. 'The web of deceits spreads wider. We shall face each hurdle as we come to it. Saxfield is important, but not if I must sacrifice the well-being of my child.' Protectively Ruth covered her stomach with her hand. 'I had not realised how much I wanted a child—no harm must come to it.'

'Then why suffer the poor mite to be born in shame?'

'He will be born of love, Hettie—my love for his father. That is enough.' Seeing Hettie's worried expression, she hugged her close. 'It will all come right in the end.'

'Amen to that, mistress.'

Unable to bear Hettie's anxious scrutiny, she tidied the desk she had been working at. 'There is much to be done. I shall ride to Bramber at once and arrange for the repairs to the house.'

'I'll go and summon Sam to accompany you.' Hettie was already half-way to the door.

'That will not be necessary,' Ruth called after her. 'Sam has his own work to attend to.'

A doubtful look entered the maid's kindly eyes. 'Is it wise to go alone, mistress? Some of the men were casting surly looks at you in church last Sunday. And wasn't it at Bramber that Master Adam used to visit the widow...?'

'I shall take pains to avoid any of my brother's women companions. Spartan should deter them from accosting me too openly. My mind is made up. I shall leave at once.'

An hour later, Ruth tethered Adam's grey gelding to a post and entered the wheelwright's yard. Immediately she felt dwarfed by the rows of ash planks seasoning in stacks. Huge elm logs filled another corner by the saw-pit. Both the yard and saw-pit were empty, as was the open shed housing the forge. Hearing the ring of a hammer upon chisel, she squeezed past a partly re-painted pony-trap and several broken wheels towards the single-storey hovel used as a workshop.

'Good day to you, sir,' a voice boomed from the gloom within. 'It is Mr Melville of Saxfield, is it not? How can I be of service?'

Ruth took a moment for her eyes to accustom them-selves to the darkness, and coughed, her throat catching in the dusty air. A lantern on a roof support threw its light on the rows of chisels lining the walls and, more sinisterly, upon an upright coffin. The wheelwright served the community as undertaker and painter, as well as carpenter when required.

'It is Ned I came to see. We need him at Saxfield. The
gale last night brought a tree down through the roof of
the house.'

The wheelwright, his round face red and sweating with
exertion, wiped his hands on his leather apron. 'I'm sorry
to hear of your misfortune. Ned is working over at
Steyning today. He'll come to Saxfield tomorrow to inspect what is to be done. With a job as serious as that,
he will start right away.'

Ruth sighed with relief. 'That is good news! I feared
it would be longer. I shall expect Ned tomorrow.' Her
business done, she returned to the street.

'More ale, landlord!' An impatient shout drew her
attention to the ale-house at the far end of the village,
where a troop of Roundheads noisily blocked the road
as they took their ease. 'Landlord! A pox on you,
laggard!'

The cry was taken up until the landlord staggered out
of the inn, his arms full of pottery jugs to replenish the
soldiers' cups. 'Make haste, man! We would toast the
health of Noll Cromwell.'

Idly, Ruth's gaze travelled over the timber-framed
cottages; some small and squat with little beady eyes for
windows, others taller, fuller bellied and festooned with
climbing ivy. Before starting to untether her horse, she
noticed a group of horsemen riding past the broken castle
wall and down the sloping narrow street into the village.
Suddenly a high-pitched squealing rent the air, and a
lanky swineherd, dressed in a rough homespun jerkin
tied at the waist with twine, waved his arms and shouted
in a drunken frenzy as several pigs ran through the legs
of the Roundheads and their horses.

Spartan, who had been lying at their feet, sprang up,
ears pricked and legs braced ready to bound forward.
Ruth stared at the sight, amused by the reeling antics of
the swineherd, which added to the chaos started by the
runaway pigs. She blinked, foolishly, her heart somer-
saulting between joy and shock. Was she dreaming? The

tall shambling figure, as graceless and witless as a village idiot, was disconcertingly familiar, for all his hat partly obscured his features. Just what was Blase doing here and in such a role?

Every particle of her being screamed out for him to turn and notice her. His name burned upon her lips as she stopped herself from calling to him. He was moving deliberately towards the Roundheads. Why was he in such a disguise? Her heart stilled. Whatever happened next would surely show her where Blase's loyalties lay! A jeer went up from the soldiers as Blase stumbled, his leg catching a large sow on the rump as he recovered his balance. Squealing in outrage, the sow lumbered forward, scattering the orderly line of her companions into a snorting, squealing stampede straight towards the soldiers.

Puzzled by his strange behaviour, she looked towards the four riders pushing their way through the shouting soldiers and let her breath out in a rush of surprise. No wonder Blase was acting so strangely! He had need indeed to create a diversion. In the riders' centre, his long body hunched in a servant's dirty breeches and coat, rode someone else she recognised. The black curling lovelocks were now jagged and shorn above his shoulders, the shabby hat pulled low over the olive-skinned face of the most wanted fugitive in England.

She glanced anxiously at the Roundheads. Had any of them recognised the king? Most were abusing Blase as their tethered horses began to shy, their eyes rolling in panic at the pigs rushing through their legs. Her doubts fled. He was a Royalist! Her heart lifted, ringing a re-sounding peal of exultation. In this, at least, they were not enemies. Nothing could lessen the shameful part her family had played in Lionel Drummond's death, but now she had been given another chance to work with Blase, this time truly united in the same cause. Fear made her hold her breath at the risk he was taking. He was known in the district. What madness possessed him to play the fool and draw attention to himself?

Two burly soldiers had closed about Blase, cutting him off from the horses and any attempt he might make to clear a way through the street for the king's party. He must be acting as vanguard, or decoy, to them. To create a diversion at a moment such as this, when the king's freedom was threatened, undoubtedly he was a trusted companion of his Majesty! Even as the thought winged through her mind, she was alarmed to see one of the soldiers stare curiously at the king. At any second he could be recognised.

'Go, Spartan!' she urged him, knowing that he would chase the pigs.

As the dog sped forward, barking and scrambling between the soldiers' legs, the Roundheads, nervous of the snapping jaws of the huge mastiff, alternately laughed and cursed as they shuffled to keep out of his way. But the jeering was fast turning to angry shouts, and Ruth saw one of the riders, whom she recognised, bring his horse to a halt. With a quick nod of his head, the king urged him to continue. If they turned back now, Ruth reasoned with sickening dread, their action would surely arouse the Roundheads' suspicions. Hemmed in as he was, Blase could do little, and already the attention of several of the soldiers was beginning to wander. Blase's freedom, as well as the king's, was at stake!

Impulsively Ruth lunged at a pig that had broken free of the confusion. The heavy sow rammed against her legs, knocking her to the ground, drawing a great roar of laughter from the soldiers. Their attention now centred upon herself, Ruth stubbornly hung on to the sow's foreleg, her face pressed into the dirt, the sow's squeals almost deafening her. She rolled aside from the animal's hoofs and came up on to her knees, and locking her free arm about the sow's bristly body, managed to turn her about before loosing her. To her delight, the incensed creature ran straight back into the swarm of soldiers.

As she dusted herself down, she noted that the soldiers had moved away from the edge of the road, but it was still partially blocked by their horses, and the king's party had been forced to a halt. She glanced at Blase, who was now haranguing a red-faced soldier standing nearest to the horses. Clearly he needed another ruse to get the horses out of the way, but how to do it without drawing attention to the king? Feigning indignation, she snatched off her plumed hat, its feather hanging down forlornly after her tumble.

'A murrain on that clod-pated swineherd!' she shouted, marching towards Blase as he clutched a struggling pig to his chest. The grinning soldiers parted to let her through, their eyes glittering at the expectancy of a fight. She slammed her full weight into Blase from behind, striking him across the head. 'Bumbling jackanapes, one of your pigs had me in the dirt!'

She met the impact of a piercing ebony stare from under his frayed hat-brim. His eyes crinkled in surprise at recognising her and she inhaled sharply, stilling the nervous fluttering in her breast, noting in the space of a single heartbeat the change in his appearance. His dark hair was cut short above his plain linen collar, his height disguised by the reeling drunken stance he affected. He had shaved off his moustache, and as his gaze swept over her indignant figure, his full lips twitched in a ghost of a mocking smile. His stubbly face, scored by lines of weariness, bore little resemblance to the self-assured visage she had first laid eyes upon.

'I meant no disrespect, sir,' he mumbled in a thick Sussex burr as he tugged his forelock ingratiatingly. 'When a pig takes it into its head to go rummaging, there's nothing on God's earth will halt it.' He thrust his face closer, and rubbed his chin in puzzlement. 'It is a young sir, is it not? With so much lace and ribbons on that fine doublet, I thought for a moment 'twas a woman.' His voice dropped to a low whisper. 'What the devil are you doing still parading as Adam?'

She had not expected him to speak words of love, but this was so cold, so removed from the passion they had shared, that her pride rose in defence. 'I had no choice,' she murmured. 'Should I have returned as a jilted bride to be ridiculed, as well as losing my home?'

His expression closed. 'Is that what you think? Dear God, spare me a woman's reasoning!'

'Go on, young sir,' a prim-faced soldier urged Ruth, preventing them from saying more. 'Give the insolent cur the thrashing he deserves!'

Blase swung round, falling heavily against a horse which moved aside to allow the four riders to push their way through the gap. Nodding sagely to the soldiers who were grinning widely at his gibes, he pointed to their sober buff uniforms, continuing where he had left off. 'I meant no disrespect to the young master.' Blase tugged his forelock. 'The lad can't help his looks. He's pretty enough to be a woman.' He sniggered, knowingly rubbing the side of his nose with his finger. 'God knows, there's many a horse-faced doxy between here and London who could pass as a man.'

A stout soldier laughed coarsely. 'Ay, there's fat Annie at the Swan on the Horsham Road for one.'

Ruth took her lead from Blase: the longer they could keep the soldiers' attention on themselves, the better chance the king had of escaping. 'What would you know of women, swineherd?' she shouted above Spartan's barking, as the mastiff continued to chase the pigs. 'That sow you clutch so ardently to your chest is probably the only female to nestle against you in years! Not only do you reek of the sty, but your manners shame the creatures in your charge.'

Ruth cast a furtive glance at the king, who was on a level with her, and met, sidelong, his dark eyes, full of mirth despite the drawn and tired lines grooved into his face. Imperceptibly he nodded in acknowledgment to her, then passed on out of her line of sight. She suppressed the desire to turn and watch his passage along the open road, but instead raised her fist and shook it at Blase.

He rolled his eyes as though he had difficulty focusing, and hiccoughed before declaring, 'Did you hear how this young cockerel insults me!'

He swung out wildly, his fist missing Ruth by several inches even before she ducked aside. Carried onwards by the impetus of his movement, he appeared to overbalance. With the piglet clutched firmly under one arm, frantically circling with the other to recover himself, he earned a chorus of jeers from the troopers. Over his shoulder, Ruth saw the four riders quickening their pace as they left the village and trotted over the stone bridge spanning the River Adur.

'In God's name, what is the meaning of this brawling?' a young fresh-faced officer bellowed at the crowd as he came out of one of the houses further down the street. 'Have that man arrested for drunken behaviour and disturbing the peace!'

Ruth glanced fearfully at Blase, who now slouched only inches from her, his expression implacable. They were surrounded by Roundheads. If he were seized now and then recognised, he would be hanged as a spy. She clenched her hand to check her impulse to reach out and touch him. For a moment she had been so caught up in the excitement of being reunited with Blase, and working with him to dupe the Roundheads, that she had forgotten the threat to their lives. But she could not delude herself: Blase had come to Sussex with the king's party, not to see her. Their meeting had been a chance one, and changed nothing.

Even dishevelled, dirty and in rags, his nearness set her blood afire with yearning. The enraged officer was pushing his way towards them. Her throat dried with foreboding that Blase would be arrested. She could not fail him now and leave him at the mercy of the Roundheads again. Loving him, she would sacrifice everything to save him. 'Go!' she whispered. 'The king needs you. Take my horse from outside the wheelwright's.'

Fleetingly, the shutter blanking his eyes lifted, and what she saw sparking in those midnight depths brought a rush of heat to her cheeks. Suddenly there was no need for words. Within moments their lives would be dragged apart again, each of them thrown into the danger and the consequences of upholding their cause. That stare, once so bold and assured, showed a man in torment, torn apart between loyalty and devotion. Then his eyes were again guarded, his voice sounding as though dragged from the depths of his stout peasant shoes as the officer drew near. 'My horse is hidden in the castle. Take care of him for me.'

At the approach of the officer, the soldiers' laughter and jeering fell silent. Ruth felt an air of tension building around them. Abruptly Blase spun on his heel to face the officer, who had pushed his way through the crowd, beckoning to a couple of troopers to seize Blase. Ruth held her breath. Blase was unarmed. He could not escape so many. Even as she racked her brains to help him, he suddenly thrust the pig he was holding into the arms of the astonished officer, and before any guessed his intent, sprinted down the street towards her mount. Slipping the tether, with the speed and grace of an accomplished cavalry officer, he leapt on the startled animal's back, bringing it instantly under control to set off at a furious pace down the street.

'Get after him, cabbage-heads!' the officer shouted, 'That's no swineherd!'

'Upon my soul, 'tis not the king, is it?' a young village lad piped out. 'He's tall enough and dark.'

'Poltroon! Of course he's not Charles Stuart!' the man gritted out. He could be no more than twenty, and youthful frustration and impatience raised the pitch of his voice. 'Do you think I would not have recognised him, if he was? But he is a damned Royalist trying to flee justice.'

Four soldiers started forward, but checked as Spartan growled menacingly as he barred their way to the horses.

'Get that hell-hound out of the way!' the officer fumed. 'Or I shall have it shot.'

Ordering Spartan to silence, Ruth saw that Blase was already at the edge of the village, but instead of crossing the Adur, he was pushing through a gap in the hedge and across the fields in the opposite direction to the one the king had taken.

The officer glared at her. 'Arrest this man. Take him to Lewes Gaol.'

Ruth went cold, her stomach quailing in alarm, but as a soldier reached for her arm, a middle-aged sergeant stepped forward, signalling for the trooper to stay back.

'With respect, Captain,' he said quietly, 'this gentleman is Adam Melville of Saxfield Manor. He is cousin to Captain Melville. And not to place too fine a point on the matter, sir, you are new to this district, and Captain Melville has been making his own enquiries concerning his cousin's sympathies. Captain Melville is well respected by our commanding officer. It might be taken amiss should you continue with this arrest.'

The officer stiffened, and appeared to hesitate before jerking his head for the men to fall back. Still he appeared uncertain, and beneath the steel faceguard of his metal helmet a flush stained his cheeks as he glowered at Ruth. 'The swineherd—who was he? Are you in league with him?'

'I do not associate with swineherds,' Ruth said freezingly. 'The man was in his cups and a menace to decent people. It is your job to arrest lawbreakers.'

Furious, he turned on his troop, who were now mounted and ready to pursue Blase. 'I want that swineherd taken alive for questioning.'

He mounted his horse and delivered a parting shot to Ruth. 'We will tolerate no lawbreakers, especially those who are suspected of treason. Give me your word, sir, that you will make no attempt to leave the district, and

out of deference to Captain Melville, you shall remain
at liberty to return to your home.'

'Why should I wish to go anywhere, Captain? I have
nothing to fear,' Ruth retorted. 'You have my word.'

The look the officer shot her was a warning she had
not heard the last of the incident. The danger was closing
in. Saxfield was no longer the haven it once had been.
Next time, she might not be able to bluff her way out
of arrest.

CHAPTER FIFTEEN

BLASE CROUCHED low over the horse's mane, the reins held firmly in one hand while the other clamped his battered hat hard down on his head. He had hoped to slip away from the village quietly, not to bring the Roundheads with him. Now he must draw them away from the king. Once off the road, he turned towards the steep slopes of the Downs and sped on, the thunder of hoofs closing behind him. Thank God they were following him and not the king! He gave the horse its head, turning along the ridge towards Cissbury Ring. The grey gelding appeared as tireless as his own black mare, but it did not carry his sword or saddle-holster, and his only weapon, if he were forced to make a stand and fight, was a dagger hidden beneath his jerkin. He had no intention of being taken prisoner. It had been arranged for the king to take shelter this night at the George, a small coastal inn in Brightelmstone a few miles away, and nothing must go wrong again. There had been so many disappointments for his Majesty, who bore them all calmly. This time, Blase vowed, the king would set sail for France even if he had to steal a boat and row him there himself.

Another need drove him on, one that until now he had thought vanquished. During the last month, as he had ridden in close proximity to the king's party, but not a part of it, he had had little time to think of Ruth. By day he lived on his wits, either riding as vanguard or keeping a watchful eye on the houses where his Majesty took shelter, and his few precious hours of sleep were the dreamless oblivion of exhaustion.

At one time, during a narrow escape from capture, the king had been forced to hide in an oak at Boscobel while the Ironsides searched the wood. Blase had lain in hiding in bracken a mile away. After that, it had been six nerve-shattering days before he had found the king again at Bristol, where for three days they tried to secure a passage for him to France. It was his Sovereign's safety that must come first, Blase told himself as he rode away from Bramber and Ruth. He had been unprepared for the shock of seeing her again, or how it would affect him. He had done the right thing, and he should not regret it. He focused his mind upon that, although remorse about Ruth tore at him.

He had no wish to bind himself to any woman, but inexplicably he was tied to Ruth with bonds that were invisible, and the more constraining for that. With her golden beauty burnished in his mind, it was the treachery of her family, which had once gnawed at him so sharply, that now was hard to rekindle. Not all Melvilles were alike! Ruth had proved her loyalty time and again.

The horse began to slow of its own accord, and, realising that Saxfield lay less than a mile away, his hand paused on the bridle. Then sanity returned. The Roundheads were too close. He must lose them in the next wood, and when dusk began to fall, head back to rejoin the king at the George. Even for Ruth he could not forsake his duty. Yet, as he rode on, all he could think of was the memory of her lying in his arms on a moonlit night in Worcester.

As the troop clattered down the narrow street after Blase, Ruth imitated Adam's whistle to bring Spartan to heel, tipped her hat and made a few pleasantries to the women as she moved through the crowd towards the castle. Before climbing the slope to the ruins, she glanced back, relieved that no one was following her. Blase's horse was hidden near the far curtain wall, the doorway to the ruins partially concealed by a curtain of ivy. Leading it into the open, she noted with dismay that the saddle-holster still carried its pistol, and through the blanket-roll at its back stuck the point of Blase's sword. Fresh terror set her body trembling as she pulled herself into the saddle. Let him not be harmed, she prayed. The unspoken message in his eyes had burned brightly. They had been through so much. Fate could not be so cruel to part them now.

She was shaking so violently as she slid from Blase's horse in the stableyard at Saxfield that she leaned her brow against the horse's sweating flank, too shaken to remove the saddle and harness. A form blocked the light from the stable door.

'Mistress, what ails you?' Sam strode forward as she straightened and began to undo the girth. 'That looks like Drummond's horse.' He shot her a fierce look. 'What happened?'

'It is a long story. First tend to the horse, then come to the house and I shall tell both you and Hettie the most amazing tale.'

Some hours later, the servants' questions finally answered and the routine of the house once more taking over, Ruth stood in the kitchen helping Hettie prepare the evening meal. Absently she cut the meat into strips as she fretted about Blase. Had he escaped, or was he a prisoner? And what of her own safety? The questions gave her no peace. To the servants, she had glossed over the threat delivered by the young officer. When Henry learned of the incident at Bramber, he would come to question her. Who could help her now? Blase was with the king, where his first loyalty must always be.

Sam entered the kitchen from the courtyard, his face set and determined. 'You must leave Saxfield, mistress. Once Captain Melville learns of the incident at Bramber, he will come here. It is what he has been waiting for...the proof that you have helped Royalists.'

Ruth clutched the kitchen knife tightly in her trembling hand. 'I gave my word I would not leave.'

'Just leave Saxfield. There is no need to leave the district. Take refuge in one of the safe houses for a day or two. If they arrest you,' he went on brutally, 'they will show no mercy when they discover that you are a woman. You will face further ridicule and humiliation for having tricked them.'

Ruth hesitated. She was no coward, but all her instincts were warning her that if she was to escape with her life, she must go, and quickly.

Sam put his hand upon her shoulder, his thick brows drawn down with concern. 'It is too dangerous to stay here, so I have saddled the black gelding in readiness. It will take but a few minutes for Hettie to pack a change of clothes and what else is necessary.'

'If I leave Saxfield, you and Hettie must leave, too. But if I go, what if Blase returns?' Her voice was choked with distress at the true reason which was keeping her at Saxfield. 'He will not know where to find me.'

'It is not only yourself you must think of, but the child!' Hettie burst out.

Ruth put down the knife and hung her head, her hands gripping the edge of the table as her mind churned.

'Major Drummond will leave no stone unturned to find you,' Sam contended. 'Word will be left with those we can trust of the route you will take and your final destination in France.'

She chewed her lip, reluctantly coming to a decision. 'So be it. I shall leave at once for the safe house at Pulborough until a passage can be arranged for me.' As she spoke, Spartan began to bark from some way off in the grounds.

All three looked at each other, their faces turning deathly pale. 'Someone is on the grounds! And it isn't Blase. Spartan would not bark at him,' Ruth gasped, tearing the apron from her waist and snatching up her doublet and sword-belt. 'It's too late to flee.'

'There's still time,' Sam insisted, pushing her towards the back door. 'The black is saddled. You could just reach the priory ruins.'

A loud banging on the front door echoed through the house. 'Go, mistress! The door is bolted. I shall delay them all I can.'

'No, Sam, you will be in danger,' Ruth cried as he wrenched open the courtyard door. Her hand froze at Hettie's scream. Two Roundheads stormed into the room.

'I trust you were not thinking of leaving, sir,' the sergeant she had seen at Bramber jeered. 'Captain Melville will be expecting you to attend him.'

Ruth hid her fear beneath a haughty glare. 'Saxfield's hospitality is always open to my cousin, but since when has he taken to ordering me in my own home?'

The sergeant's hand rested on his sword-hilt, his expression taut and hostile. 'Known Royalists have no homes in the new commonwealth. You are summoned to answer the charges brought against you.'

It had been dark for some hours as Blase sat in the tap-room of the George at Brighthelmstone, staring grimly into his tankard of ale. A short time earlier he had seen Captain Tattersall, the owner of a coal-barque, ushered into the king's presence in the back parlour. Colonel Gounter appeared in the tap-room and, noting the absence of the landlord, beckoned to Blase. He sauntered over, apprehensive at the Colonel's haggard expression.

'What do you know of Tattersall?' Gounter asked without preamble.

'I believe him honest enough, though I would caution against making his Majesty's identity known to him.'

'There's the rub. He seems to have recognised the king, and is now haggling over a higher price.'

'A plague on the man!' Blase fumed. 'If he's lily-livered, *I* shall sail his miserable barque to France. Where is it moored?'

'Would it were as simple as that!' Gounter dropped his voice, his eyes bloodshot from lack of sleep, and anxiety. 'Tattersall ran it into the mouth of the Adur, just off Southwick, but until the tide turns it's stranded on the mud. Besides, he will not hear of hiring the vessel.'

'Then we shall take it!'

'Nay, his Majesty will have none of it. It must be with Tattersall or no one. It looks as though we shall have to meet his price, but as it will be some hours until we leave here, I would rest easier knowing that you stood watch lest Tattersall makes an attempt to leave, or speaks with anyone but ourselves.'

Blase nodded, and Colonel Gounter returned to the back room. Returning to his stool by the fire, he propped his long legs up on a table, pulled his hat down over his eyes, and folding his arms across his chest appeared to doze, while actually listening and noting each creak of the floorboards and movement of the occupants of the inn. No one could come or go near the king without his being aware of it.

Yet it was not the danger surrounding the king that tensed every muscle of his body, but thoughts of Ruth. How had she fared? Images of her being hunted or arrested tortured him, and it took all his iron will to remain seated and on guard, knowing that she could be in dire peril. Never had duty been such a torment, caging him like a beast. It another hour, two at the most, his Majesty would be safe aboard Tattersall's ship, *Surprise*. Then, and only then, would he be free to go to Ruth.

Ruth, surrounded by a dozen soldiers, stood in the sparsely lit great hall. Sam was held prisoner by four soldiers, his head bleeding profusely from a long gash that had knocked him to his knees and enabled the soldiers to overpower and bind his giant figure. On the dais, one hip arrogantly resting on the table covered in a red and gold carpet, Captain Melville waited, his raised eyebrow and haughty line of his thin lips that of the lord of the manor receiving a lowly vassal. Freezing tentacles of fear clutched at her that had nothing to do with the unheated air in the room. The moment she had dreaded for these last four years had come. Henry had the evidence he needed, and already saw himself as master of Saxfield. Tilting her chin defiantly, she met his triumphant stare.

'What is the meaning of this?' she demanded, refusing to give her cousin the satisfaction of seeing her inner quaking.

Hettie, coming late upon the scene, began to scream, 'Fiends! Satan's apostles! What have you done to my husband?'

'Silence the wench!' Captain Melville bellowed. 'And tie her up in the kitchen out of my sight.'

Ruth rounded on her cousin. 'What right have you to treat my servants so scurvily?'

He stroked his beard, and waited while Hettie was dragged kicking and screaming from the room before replying. 'I have every right when questioning traitors,' he sneered. 'But your servants are not my concern—for now.' He looked pointedly at the sword-belt still in her hand. 'I must ask you to surrender your weapon. You are my prisoner.'

'The devil I will!' She gripped the sword tighter, as two thick-set soldiers advanced, their faces alight with the prospect of a fight. To resist would give Henry the satisfaction of humiliating her further. Seething with impotent rage she handed her sword to her cousin. As he laid it behind him on the dais, her stomach lurched. Unarmed, she was now defenceless.

'You are beginning to show some wisdom!' He fairly gloated. 'Where's Drummond? And don't think to trick me—he was recognised by one of the villagers.' Ruth clamped her lips shut. 'Silence will not serve you, cousin. It was your horse he took at Bramber and his black gelding is in your stable.'

'My horse was stolen at Bramber by some scoundrel posing as a swineherd. That horse was found wandering in the grounds this evening. Sam stabled it, intending to ask in the village for news of its master.'

'Spare me your lies!' Captain Melville growled. 'Neither I nor our new Justice of the Peace is fooled by them.'

A man's figure detached itself from the darkest shadows, and as the light fell upon his face, shock hit her. This was something she was not prepared for! She stared stupidly at the new Justice of the Peace, unable to believe her eyes. Why had she not heeded the signs which had been there? Disillusion was a bitter philtre to swallow—friendship had blinded her.

'You look surprised, Adam,' Daniel Fowkes jeered. 'Yet you have suspected my loyalty for some time.'

Ruth battled to think and act as Adam would have done. She felt drained by this final betrayal. Dazedly, she noted that Spartan's barks had risen to fever pitch at being shut out of the hall. 'You were my friend, and almost like a brother to me. I prayed I was wrong…that at the last you would be too honourable to betray those who trusted you.'

'They were misguided fools! What need have we of a pleasure-loving monarch, the son of a Papist whore? England has been cleansed of such would-be tyrants.'

'To be governed by the military who would rule by the sword!' Ruth flared, her strength returning as anger stung her blood.

'Silence!' Daniel shrieked. 'By your own words you condemn yourself, Melville, and before witnesses. Ere the night is out, I shall learn the whereabouts of Drummond, and why he was acting as he did at Bramber. You are a traitor. Justice must be done!'

Sam started forward, straining against his bonds, and managing to shake off two of his captors as he bellowed, 'This is the devil's work! It is Saxfield you want, not justice!'

A pistol-butt rammed into his stomach doubled him over.

'Leave Sam alone!' Ruth protested, her dash towards him halted by a soldier grabbing her arm and wrenching

it up behind her back. She bit back a cry of pain, droplets
of perspiration forming on her brow as she gritted out,
'Sam has done nothing.'

Ignoring her plea, Captain Melville shot Fowkes a
blistering look, clearly resenting the superior way in
which he had taken over the interview. 'Put the servant
in the cellar. And take care you bind him securely. He
has the strength of an ox.'

'He's as guilty as hell!' Daniel's eyes glittered with
malice as he puffed out his chest. 'He will be publicly
flogged before he's hanged. This household will be an
example to others who would set themselves against the
government.'

Helpless to stop them, Ruth watched the soldiers
roughly manhandle Sam from the hall. The Roundhead
holding her released her with a cruel shove, and as she
resisted the urge to massage her bruised wrist and aching
shoulder, she glared contemptuously at Henry and
Daniel. Distrust and antagonism sparked between the
two men. Each obviously resented the other's presence.
Did each see Saxfield as a rich picking for himself?

'This has gone far enough!' She sought refuge from
her fear in outrage. 'Sam is innocent of any crime. Any
blame attached to this house is mine alone. Take care
of what you accuse me, Fowkes. We worked together in
the past, so if I am guilty, so are you!'

The challenge hung in the air between them and the
soldiers shifted uncomfortably. Only Melville remained
unaffected, a satisfied smile thinning his lips at Fowkes's
discomfort. Ruth pressed the point, her voice scathing.
'You know that I was wounded and could not have
fought at Worcester. As to the rest, your informant was
wrong. Drummond was not at Bramber. The swineherd
was in his cups. The soldiers were amusing themselves
by ridiculing him.' She hoped the bold lies sounded
convincing.

From the corridor came the crash of furniture sent
flying, then sounds of claws slithering on polished boards

and a deep-throated growl echoed round the vastness of the hall as Spartan, hackles raised and fangs bared, sprang into the room. Drawing a pistol from his sash, Daniel put the width of the dais table between him and the mastiff, his voice shaky with fear. 'Call the dog off, unless you want him shot!'

'Down, Spartan!' Ruth commanded sharply, terrified lest the dog should give his life for her. She had no wish to lose yet another friend. 'Down!' she repeated, as Spartan stood quivering, reluctant to obey, and then slowly sat.

'At last you are being sensible!' Daniel crowed. 'Look, there is no need to make this more unpleasant than it is. My evidence alone will condemn you as a Royalist, yet I would spare you if I could. Tell me the names of those who pledged to raise men for the late rebellion, and the law will be lenient with you.'

'I will not barter my life at the expense of those of others!' She could feel Henry's strangely-coloured eyes burning into her, but could not meet his gaze. He would not help her. He could feel Saxfield within his reach. Against that, the ties of kinship would mean nothing to him.

Daniel snatched up a whip from the dais table. 'You are pale and thin, and not fully recovered from your injuries at Tewkesbury. How long do you think you can withstand questioning?'

Ruth clenched her jaw against the wild shrieking terror rising in her breast. This monster could not be the Daniel she had loved and trusted all her life. He was inhuman. He actually meant to torture Adam! She looked across at Henry, expecting him to be gloating at the discomfort she was suffering. Instead, she saw him studying her oddly.

Daniel kicked forward a high-backed chair from behind the table on the dais and snapped, 'Guards, off with Melville's doublet and tie him to the chair.'

Henry moved forward as her arms were grabbed and the doublet jerked from her back. Thank God, beneath the fullness of her linen shirt her breasts were tightly bound, but, even so, she felt naked and exposed to her cousin's piercing stare. As she struggled wildly to prevent her hands from being dragged behind her back and bound, the sleeve of her shirt ripped.

Her body smarted with humiliation as Henry pushed a soldier aside and caught her arm, his grimly-set lips as bloodless as his face. 'That's enough, men. Stand back,' he said hoarsely. Keeping his back to Fowkes, he looked down at her slender wrist, his gaze travelling to the dagger-length scar below her elbow.

Ruth gasped, trying to snatch her arm free, fiery tongues of shame searing her neck to heat her face, as he held her fast. The ruse was over. Henry knew the truth. Expecting no mercy, her eyes flashed with defiance as she waited for his sarcasm to break. Instead, she saw horror in his eyes—not repulsion for her scars, but genuine shock at his discovery. It vanished beneath the hard countenance turned upon his men.

'Sergeant, take the men and search the coast,' he ordered harshly. 'That was indeed Major Drummond in Bramber. He does nothing without reason. I want the coast checked carefully for any longboats putting ashore, and also Broadwater Creek. I have a feeling that we shall flush a nest of fugitives out this night.'

'No!' Daniel cut in. 'The men are needed to escort your cousin to Lewes to stand trial.'

'My cousin will not be going anywhere, tonight.' There was an edge of steel in Henry's voice she had not heard before. 'My men have other duties.'

Daniel started forward, his expression furious at having his orders countermanded. 'As Justice of the Peace, I demand that Adam Melville be placed under arrest.'

The soldiers hesitated. 'You have your orders, Sergeant,' Henry blazed. When the last of his men had filed out of the hall, he turned on Daniel. 'My cousin has as yet not been proved guilty. My men are needed elsewhere, and in the circumstances, house arrest will suffice.'

'Drummond is a valuable fugitive to capture.' Daniel eyed Henry suspiciously. 'There's a reward of one hundred pounds on his head, yet you do not ride with them.'

'Have you really been so blind that you do not know what has been going on here?' Henry scoffed. 'The price on Drummond's head is not the only reason I sent my men away. At any moment they would have spotted the truth. It was to spare us both from committing a grave error before witnesses. Have you not eyes in your head, man? This is not Adam. It is Ruth!'

Ruth breathed deeply. Now that the truth was out, this madness would end. Henry was showing an unexpected concern for the delicacy of the situation. He must be up to something, but what it could be escaped her for the moment. But he had overplayed his hand. Daniel would never imprison her. He loved her. Or did he? A sickly bubble lodged in her throat. Why, then, was the horror that had accompanied Henry's discovery absent from Daniel's face?

'Where's Adam?' The question was hoarsely accusing.

'Safe from your vile scheming,' she retorted. 'He was spared witnessing your treachery.'

'From that, I take it, he died at Worcester.' The callous, unsympathetic statement shocked Ruth beyond reason. To what depths had Daniel sunk? He was looking at her coldly, but talking to Henry. 'It changes nothing. This devil's handmaiden is as deeply embroiled in treachery as ever her brother was. From the way she threw herself at Drummond, it is obvious that she has the morals of a camp-follower. What decent woman dresses in men's clothing and rides about the country-side unescorted? I would be shamed before man and God if my sisters displayed such wanton conduct.'

Realisation broke over her like a landslide. Daniel's protestations of love were all an act. It was *he* who had been betraying the Royalists, and that was how he had staved off his creditors. But he had become greedy. Pieces of gold were not enough for him now. He wanted wealth, land and power. He wanted Saxfield!

'You bigoted jackanapes!' Ruth vented her fury. 'What would you know of honour and decency?'

A vicious slap sent her sprawling across the floor, her tirade ending in a muffled cry. A black shadow sped past towards her attacker.

'No, Spartan!' she screamed, levering herself up with one arm. The valiant mastiff was deaf to her command. He sprang at the white-faced Daniel who, eyes bulging with terror, shakily aimed the pistol.

'For the love of God, Daniel, no!' She scrambled to her knees, her sight of the dog suddenly blocked by Henry looming over her like a marauding Viking.

CHAPTER SIXTEEN

BLASE SCOUTED the shore in the moonlight while the king's party hid in a derelict hovel on the outskirts of Southwick. In the early hours of the morning, the hamlet was silent and sleeping as the tide slithered into the creek from the river. Since a troop had ridden past a quarter-hour earlier and cantered along the shingle beach towards Sompting, the coast and river were now free of patrols.

The night dragged endlessly on, each passing hour gnawing at him as he fretted to rejoin Ruth. In his mind the dread festered that she was in danger. Fortunately the young officer at Bramber was inexperienced, and she had had the wit to talk her way out of trouble there, he thought with a bleak smile. But when Captain Melville learned of the matter, there would be no reprieve! Tortured by fear, he returned to the hovel. His duty to his king was almost at an end. In less than an hour he would be with Ruth... Pray God he got there before Henry Melville!

'Is the way ahead safe?' Colonel Gounter asked from the open doorway as Blase dismounted.

'There's no sign of further patrols.' At his words, the king appeared. 'Sire, *Surprise* is still high on the mud. It will be an hour or two before the tide refloats her.'

'I shall board her while it is still dark.' The king gave a sardonic chuckle as he put his hand on Blase's shoulder. 'You have served us well, Major Drummond. I regret it is not within my power to repay you as you deserve.'

'The only reward I seek, Sire, is that you reach France safely.'

The dark heavy-lidded eyes regarding him sparkled merrily in the moonlight. 'Amid all my adventures these past weeks, I vow there was none so amusing as your ruse at Bramber. I pray that neither you, nor the brave fellow who so cleverly followed your lead, will suffer because of it.'

Blase grinned. 'That "brave fellow" I hope shortly to make my wife. If she will have me.'

The king laughed appreciatively. "Odsblood! A wench! You have chosen a woman of rare spirit and wit. May God bless and preserve you both.'

Blase bent his knee, but before he could kneel, his hands were clasped by the king, staying him. 'God willing, I shall come into my own again. Then, my friend, you will kneel to me and arise Sir Knight.'

Colonel Gounter stood at the king's side. 'Sire, it is time to board.'

Blase watched the king stride across the mud and swing his long legs over the side of the coal-barque. Emotion cramped his throat and he blinked rapidly. Again Charles Stuart was an exile, as must all be who would acknowledge no other as their liege and Sovereign. When his Majesty passed below deck, he turned aside and ran to his horse. By God's grace, his work here was now done. Once the tide was full, the barque would sail towards the Isle of Wight to avoid arousing suspicion that the vessel was not about her normal duties, and then head out to sea. Vaulting into the saddle, Blase turned his horse towards Saxfield. Luck had been with him so far, but he dared not think of the possibilities should it run out.

'Down, Spartan, down!' Ruth's scream scraped her throat raw as the pistol pointed at the mastiff. This time he dropped to the ground just as the great hall rang with the sound of the pistol-shot. Ruth shuddered, staring beyond him at the triangle of plaster dislodged from the wall. The shot embedded at its centre had missed the dog by a hand's-breadth. The mastiff began to bark, his sleek black body quivering as he inched forward on his belly, ready to spring into attack at her command. Daniel swore as he reached for his powder-horn and pouch of shot to reload his weapon.

With him occupied in the lengthy procedure, Ruth scrambled to her knees, ready to make a dash for the door. As she came upright, Henry caught her arm, jerking her up against him. Furious, she twisted round, her free hand raking at his face to gain her freedom. 'Let me go!'

He captured her hand with infuriating ease and wrenched it down to her side. 'Be still, Ruth,' he warned. 'You are making it worse for yourself.'

'So, our steel-hearted maiden has a chink in her armour!' Daniel jeered. 'You may regard your own life cheaply, but clearly not that of the dog—or those of your servants! Give me the information I ask, and you shall all go free.'

'I never betray my friends!' she spat contemptuously. She looked towards the table where her sword lay, her hand throbbing to run this turncoat through, but she could never reach it before Daniel got there. Insultingly her gaze travelled up from his lace-topped boots, over his immaculate crimson velvet breeches and doublet to the unruly light brown curls falling past his shoulders on to a heavy lace collar. 'Nothing I say will spare us. It is wealth and power you want, not justice! You would make fools of us all.'

'As you have made fools of us!' Daniel snarled, spilling gunpowder over his hands as they shook with rage. Careless of the charge already applied, he tipped more into the barrel and, fumbling at his pouch for a shot, he strode towards her.

'Put the pistol away, Daniel,' Henry ordered. 'There will be no shooting.'

Daniel ignored him, and keeping well out of the way of Spartan's jaws, waved the half-loaded pistol at her. The threatening danger set her flesh crawling. 'You will not be so proud once the villagers have had their fun with you! Even those who pitied the scarred beauty

behind the veils will abhor the brazen way you parade
as a man. You will be treated as all whores...stripped
and flogged through the village.' His hand whipped out
to catch at Ruth's hair, and as she twisted aside, Henry
freed her.

'This has gone far enough, by God!' he shouted, capturing Daniel's wrist. 'My fight was with Adam, not
Ruth.'

Spartan came to her side, his growls echoing round
the hall, and she held his collar to restrain him. Even
with him to protect her, she would never get away before
being overpowered. If she were to extricate herself and
her servants from this nightmare, it must be done through
her wits. For reasons of his own, Henry had taken her
side, and there might still be a chance to save the day.
To run would be to admit her guilt.

Daniel flushed, the smattering of pock-marks on his
cheeks indenting sharply as his rage exploded. 'You'll
not renege on our arrangement, Henry. The estate was
to be split between us.' His eyes narrowed savagely. 'Or
do you still think to wed Ruth and have it all? She never
married Drummond, you know.'

'Is that true, Ruth?' Henry asked in strangled tones.

She threw back her head to hurl her contempt in his
face, but the naked pain in his eyes stopped her. Incredulously, she held his gaze as he searched her face,
his expression softening. He was looking at her intently,
only the barest flicker entering his eyes as he glanced at
the tiny scar at the side of her temple. All at once she
realised that it had not been revulsion he had shown when
he had first seen the scar on her arm, but anguish at
what she must have suffered. The knowledge disconcerted her. For all his harsh words and brashness, Henry
was in love with her...his bullying bluster but a shield.
The fury and recriminations he had hurled at her when
finding her alone with Blase had been borne out of
jealousy. The years fell away, and she saw again the sullen
boy, resentful of criticism, hiding his feelings behind a

barrier of silence. He was not as cold-hearted and evil as she had believed.

'I did not marry Major Drummond,' she answered softly.

'Then the knave will die for the shame he brought upon you,' Henry declared. 'He used you to avenge his brother's death.'

'He did not use me—in any way I did not wish to be used.' She looked down at her hands curled over Spartan's collar. She still might not like Henry very much, but understanding him had mellowed her hatred, and he was her only living relative. Whatever Henry had done, the tie of blood was something her heart would not deny.

She went on heavily, 'The war between king and Parliament has left few unscathed, but it is over now. The Battle of Worcester wrung the last drop of blood from the Royalist army. We each have to rebuild our lives as best we may. I lost my heart to Blase Drummond the first time I met him.'

Daniel rammed the shot into the pistol with unwarranted force. 'The Royalist whore is condemned by her own words!'

Henry blenched and stepped back. 'Dear God, have you no shame?'

Ruth tossed back her head defiantly. 'There will be no other man to take his place. Blase was my soul—I love him—why should I feel shame?'

'You would throw your wantonness in my face!' Henry bellowed, recovering from his initial shock. 'I worshipped your innocence and courage. I wanted to save you from the scorn of the villagers. But your virtue...' His colour rose with each accusation he threw at her. 'Your virtue, it seems, is like your mask and veils—just a sham. Fowkes is right: you are no better than a camp-follower.' A glazed look entered his eyes, which she knew and dreaded. Vengeance!

Seeing that Daniel was about to bring up his pistol, she loosed Spartan. 'Seize him, boy,' she ordered. At the same time, anticipating Henry's grab at her, she sidestepped and made a dash towards the door.

'God rot you, Captain!' Daniel shrieked above Spartan's ferocious growls. 'Don't let her get away!'

His shout was cut short by a howl of pain as Spartan's jaw fastened over his arm, and the two of them, the dog on top, fell to the floor. A hand clamped over Ruth's shoulder to drag her back when the door crashed open. Blase, a long dagger his only weapon, stormed into the hall with Sam directly behind him.

'It was careless of you not to post guards,' Blase declared in a murderous tone. 'It was a simple matter for me to release Sam, and you now find yourselves outnumbered, gentlemen.'

'Outnumbered, yes, but at last we fight!' Henry stated, unsheathing his sword.

'Damn your eyes, Captain,' Daniel gasped out through clenched teeth as he squirmed beneath Spartan's savage jaws. 'Get this beast off me!'

Ruth edged towards the dais table, watching Henry and Blase as they circled each other, dagger and swordpoint touching. She bit back a scream as Henry lunged, but with lightning speed Blase parried the blade flashing towards his heart and leapt aside. Although her attention was fastened on Blase's tall, graceful figure fighting for his life, she glimpsed Sam pushing Spartan aside and dragging Daniel to his feet, both men grappling in a wrestling hold. Unobserved by the fighting men, Ruth flung herself at the dais table, and as her hand closed over her sword-hilt and drew it from its scabbard, she saw Blase's lips tighten as Henry's sword pierced his loose-fitting sleeve. 'Blase! Catch!'

He caught her sword with a speed and agility that gave Henry no opportunity to press home an unguarded attack.

Spartan, over-excited, barked furiously, his attention now on seizing Henry's leg. Fearing that the dog would distract Blase, Ruth grabbed his collar and hauled him back. On the far side of the room, Sam knocked Daniel against the wall, and arms outstretched to grip him in a bear-hug, the giant moved towards him.

The hollow ring of clashing metal filled the hall, and Ruth stood paralysed as the wicked silver steel of Henry's sword darted towards Blase's body. The poor candle-light threw distorting shadows over the men, making it difficult for either to foretell the other's feints or passes. Henry, a competent swordsman, fought viciously. Each deadly cut and thrust was parried with practised ease by Blase, and within moments their positions were reversed. Henry was being forced into retreat, his florid face glistening with sweat as he lunged, vaulted, ducked and side-stepped in a macabre death dance. Blase was merciless, his handsome face set into bleak concentration as he pressed home his advantage. His blade flicked to the left and right with the speed of a viper's tongue, then, with a bound and a half-twist, he wrenched Henry's sword from his hand, his own blade pressed against his opponent's throat.

'Stop!' Daniel shouted.

Ruth spun round and froze. Her heart plummeted as she saw the black muzzle of Daniel's cocked pistol pointing at her.

'Put down your sword, Drummond, or the wench dies!' Daniel ordered. 'And if the servant or dog moves, I shall fire.'

Ruth stared at Daniel's dishevelled figure. The exquisite lace collar, savaged by Spartan, hung in tatters about his throat and a streak of blood smeared his chin. Behind him, Sam was staggering to his feet, shaking his head dazedly, a livid gash across his temple where Daniel must have clubbed him with the pistol-butt.

'Surrender your sword, Major,' Daniel persisted.

Defeated, Blase lowered his sword and stepped back from Captain Melville.

'No, Blase!' Ruth screamed. 'He would see us dead anyway.'

Black eyes turned upon her, their depths shimmering with his unspoken love. 'Spare Ruth, and I shall do as you say.'

A cruel smile twisted Daniel's lips. 'Brave words, Drummond, but too late. You shall watch your doxy die.'

Her heart stood still as Daniel's finger tightened over the trigger.

'Ruth!' Her name was an agonised cry upon Blase's lips as he charged across the room to deflect the shot.

She released Spartan and made to duck, but it was too late: nothing was close enough to shield her.

There was a loud retort—a flash of yellow flame— and the smell of gunpowder hung in the smoke-filled hall. Ruth stood rock-still. There was no pain, just the roaring of her blood in her ears. Unable to believe that she had not been hit, she stared down at her shirt and breeches. No blood stained her clothing. Then she saw why. A blackened, bloody void that had once been a man's face swayed before her vision and crumpled to the floor. She turned away, fighting against the horror and nausea rising in her throat. Daniel's carelessly loaded pistol had blown up in his face. He was dead.

'Sam, cover him over!' Blase said, as he gathered Ruth into his arms, pressing her face against his chest. 'My darling, are you all right?'

His peasant coat, smelling faintly of the pig he had been carrying at Bramber, was rough against her cheek, but she scarcely noticed. The powerful beat of his heart beneath her hand stilled the violent trembling of her body, bringing new life to her exhausted limbs. 'Oh, Blase, I have never been so frightened,' she sobbed.

'It's over now.'

His lips brushed her temple as he gently put her behind
him, his sword again threatening Henry. Her cousin,
looking pale and shaken, was staring at the bloody corpse
over which Sam had thrown his jacket. Henry raised his
eyes, dulled with resignation.

'You risked everything to come back for Ruth,' Henry
said heavily. 'I never meant to harm her. My men will
not return until dawn. Take her to France. I cannot stop
you.'

'You have forgotten an old score we have yet to settle,'
Blase returned darkly.

'Blase, no!' Ruth's heart contracted in agony. The road
to France lay open to them. Surely Blase did not mean
to throw that away by avenging his brother? Any inves-
tigation into Daniel Fowkes's death would show it was
an accident, but to kill Henry would be another matter.
Blase would be an exile for life.

'Let it end here, Blase,' she pleaded. 'If you avenge
Lionel's death, you will destroy yourself.'

The black eyes boring into her were cold and implacable. 'Would you have my brother's murderer go
free? He would have killed us both. Do you want this
knave to be master of Saxfield?'

'I do not condone what he did at Marston Moor, but
at Worcester I saw how terrified some of those young
men were—fear and horror made them insane with the
need to survive.'

'You see such things through a woman's soft eyes.
There is no place for cowards in the army.'

'Tonight, Henry saved me from imprisonment when
he knew I was not Adam. Had Daniel got his way, I
would now be rotting in Lewes Gaol with no hope of
reprieve or escape.'

Blase glowered at Henry. 'Ruth pleads eloquently for
your life. What say you to that, Captain?'

'She always did have more heart than sense,' Henry
answered, bowing respectfully to her. 'But I'll not plea

with you. I'm not proud of what happened at Marston Moor, and I do not expect mercy.'

'So, you have learned to face death without flinching.' Blase paused, his expression grim. After a moment he lowered his sword. 'You are a worthless rogue, but kin to Ruth, so I shall spare you. That does not mean I trust you. You will be bound and gagged and left for your men to discover. That should give us time enough to cover our tracks.'

He gestured for Henry to sit on the high-backed chair. Defiance glazed Henry's eyes, then with a resigned shrug, he sat down as Blase ordered Sam to fetch some rope. Once he was bound, Ruth stood before him, staying Blase when he would gag him.

'You have it all now, Henry,' she said. 'It is at least easier to bear, knowing you care for the place.'

He raised his eyes to the roof. 'No, I do not have it all. I just have Saxfield, a shell without its family. But I shall make it great again, I promise.'

Blase positioned the gag, and for a long moment the two men summed each other up. 'You helped Ruth tonight, and for that I would not have you blamed for our escape.'

An ironic light flared in Henry's eyes. 'Do what has to be done.'

Bunching his fist, Blase hit Henry hard on the chin, rendering him unconscious.

'Was that necessary?' Ruth gasped, appalled at Blase's brutality.

Unrepentant, he turned to her. 'What else would prove that he was not a party to our escape?' A grim smile twitched his lips as he pushed back a dark lock which had fallen across his brow. 'It was no more than he deserved... That was for Lionel.'

'Is your honour now appeased?' she said with an uncertain catch in her throat. 'You vowed vengeance upon all Melvilles.'

'So I did.' He raised his brow sardonically. 'We have our own score to settle. But I have a notion that it will take a lifetime to resolve.'

Twelve hours later, Ruth stood gazing back at the land as the fishing-vessel slipped out of the Arun into the sea. She pulled her hood over her ringlets and gathered the edges of her cloak together across the low neck of her gown as the wind freshened. They had escaped the patrols after a night ride to Arundel and spent the day hidden in the woods while Blase found a ship. She had scarcely seen Blase all day, and their departure from Saxfield had been so rushed that there had been no time to talk. She had been so sure of his love at Saxfield—but in his absence her doubts had grown. What if only duty had brought him back to her?

The dark outline of the South Downs against the night sky was fading. Ahead lay exile and uncertainties. She glanced across at Sam and Hettie, who sat side by side in the protection of the cabin. It would be comforting to have old friends with her in the strange country which would in future be her home. Her stare moved to the black form curled up near the fishing-nets—Spartan, too, had not been forsaken. Conquering a sigh, she looked back at the disappearing land.

'Regrets?' Blase said softly, his arm taking her waist and pulling her towards him.

'No, but it is not an easy sight to bear.' She dragged her eyes from the coast to gaze up into his face, pale in the moonlight.

'It's not for ever. England will be there waiting for your return. God willing, the king will come into his own again.' He pulled her close. 'It is not the end, Ruth, but a beginning. Will you marry me?'

Her heart skittered, her eyes searching his taut expression. Was it out of duty he spoke, or did he truly love her? The sail swung round, shadowing his features. She had to be certain. Even for the sake of the child, she would not marry him because convention demanded it. Without his love, it would be an empty gesture.

'If it is because of what happened at Worcester, I told you then it changes nothing. Because, if you are taking pity on a homeless waif, then...' she said hollowly.

'No.' A fervent light danced into his eyes. 'Because of you... Because of us. Because I could not bear exile without you. These last weeks have shown me that. I love you, my darling.'

His lips claimed hers, and through half-closed lids she saw his eyes blazing with his need, his love matching her own hunger. 'I've done with soldiering,' he whispered in her ear. 'It is time I settled down and took the responsibilities of my partnership with my brother seriously. Sam and Hettie will always have a home with us. For a few years you may have to put up with a sea-captain for a husband, but I want you at my side—at sea and on land. Say yes, my love? We shall be married at La Rochelle.'

How she longed to give him the answer he demanded, but stubbornly she held back. She must tell him first of the child. He might not relish the thought of fatherhood.

Breathless, she eased back, her voice husky with yearning. 'I would follow you to the furthest waters of the earth, and beyond. You speak of a life of adventure, but...'

'No buts!' he laughed softly against her ear. 'Together we shall...' He paused, looking intently down at her. He gripped her shoulders firmly as he held her at arm's length, frowning. 'You are troubled!' His stare pierced her. 'Or—dear God!—are you saying you are with child?'

She nodded dumbly, her heart too full to speak at the joy shining in his face, as he went on, 'Why have you said nothing of this before? Of course we shall marry. You could not have believed that I would desert you?'

'I wanted your love—not misplaced duty, or pity. And I had already wronged you grievously. I thought you were the government spy.'

He raised a dark brow sardonically. 'I know, and very unflattering you were, too! You also thought me a seducer of innocent maids. You always belittled your charms, my love. Even masked and veiled, you were all woman, a provocative and fiery challenge to any man. And now you doubt my joy at knowing that my child lies beneath your heart.'

Then his lips captured hers, moving with slow savouring tenderness, his embrace tightening more urgently at her shiver of ecstasy. 'You are my heart's desire—my life. Marry me!'

'Yes!' She rose on tiptoe, her lips seeking his.

'Now you are mine,' he murmured huskily. 'No more pretence, no more false roles. The masque is over, my darling.'

Her fingers locked behind his neck, her silent passion more potent than words, answering the promise of a future rich in the rewards of an abiding love.

STORIES OF PASSION AND ROMANCE SPANNING FIVE CENTURIES.

CLAIM THE CROWN – *Carla Neggers* _____ £2.95
When Ashley Wakefield and her twin brother inherit a trust fund,
they are swept into a whirlwind of intrigue, suspense, danger and
romance. Past events unfold when a photograph appears of Ashley
wearing her magnificent gems.

JASMINE ON THE WIND – *Mallory Dorn Hart* _____ £3.50
The destinies of two young lovers, separated by the tides of war,
merge in this magnificent Saga of romance and high adventure set
against the backdrop of dazzling Medieval Spain.

A TIME TO LOVE – *Jocelyn Haley* _____ £2.50
Jessica Brogan's predictable, staid life is turned upside down when
she rescues a small boy from kidnappers. Should she encourage the
attentions of the child's gorgeous father, or is he simply acting
through a sense of gratitude?

These three new titles will be out in bookshops from January 1989.

W●RLDWIDE

Hello!

As a reader, you may not have thought about writing a book yourself, but if you have, and you have a particular interest in history, then now is your chance.

We are specifically looking for new writers to join our established team of authors who write Masquerade Historical Romances. Guidelines are available for this list, and we would be happy to send a copy to you.

Please mark the outside of your envelope 'Masquerade' to help speed our response, and we would be most grateful if you could include a stamped self-addressed envelope, size approximately $9\frac{1}{4}'' \times 4\frac{3}{4}''$, sent to the address below.

We look forward to hearing from you.

Editorial Department,
Mills & Boon Limited,
Eton House,
18-24 Paradise Road,
Richmond, Surrey,
TW9 1SR.